Readers adore

LOVE ON A BOOKSHELF

'Such a cute romance especially for bookish readers. I highly enjoyed the chemistry. Five stars'

'An exceptional book; I laughed, cried and rooted for Clarrie and Declan the entire way through'

'One of the cutest romance books I've ever read'

'I loved reading how Clarrie & Declan fell for each other over the book tour'

'Any book that makes you cry is a winner!'

"The perfect read if you're looking for something fun and carefree'

'A sweet premise and some charming moments'

'A beautiful, clean romance'

'Author comes at you with both barrels and knocks you out of your shoes!'

Kiah Thomas started telling stories as a child, re-imagining the endings in books she read. She rediscovered her love of storytelling when she had children of her own, and started writing beginnings as well as endings. She is now the author of ten children's books, and she lives in Melbourne, Victoria, with her husband and three children. *Love on a Bookshelf* is Kiah's debut adult novel.

LOVE ON A BOOK SHELF

Kiah Thomas

First published in 2025 by Headline Accent
An imprint of Headline Publishing Group Limited

1

Cataloguing in Publication Data is available from the British Library

Paperback ISBN 978 1 0354 2756 7

Typeset in 11.04/16.56pt Adobe Garamond Pro Std by Jouve (UK), Milton Keynes

Printed and bound in Great Britain by Clays Ltd, Elcograf S.p.A.

Headline's policy is to use papers that are natural, renewable and recyclable
products and made from wood grown in well-managed forests and other
controlled sources. The logging and manufacturing processes are expected
to conform to the environmental regulations of the country of origin.

Headline Publishing Group Limited
An Hachette UK Company
Carmelite House
50 Victoria Embankment
London EC4Y 0DZ

The authorised representative in the EEA is Hachette Ireland,
8 Castlecourt Centre, Dublin 15, D15 XTP3, Ireland (email: info@hbgi.ie)

www.headline.co.uk
www.hachette.co.uk

For Luke

Prologue

Do you ever have days where you wake up and everything is great?

The sun shines through your bedroom window to gently caress your face and you can practically feel it in your soul. Warmth spreads from your cheeks to your toes; you're smiling before your eyes even open. Your first-thing-in-the-morning stretch hits all the right muscles and you can almost hear somebody whisper: *Today is going to be a good day.* Hell, you feel so good that it might even be you who whispers it. You spring out of bed, ready to embrace not only the morning, but life itself.

As you enter your kitchen, the smell of freshly brewed coffee and warm bread filling the air, you make eye contact through the open window with your stupidly attractive neighbour. He winks, but in a nice, natural, not-at-all-sleazy way, and says: *I invented another new pastry for you.* And you say, *Another one, Jean-Luc?* but you totally manage to pull it off. Then he says: *What can I say? You inspire me.* And then there's probably some birds singing at your window. At the very least, there's a rainbow or something.

Today, however, is not one of those days.

It's the rain that wakes me. It hammers in sheets against the glass, loud and persistent, and then drips down my wall through the crack in the seal that I haven't got around to fixing.

I keep my eyes resolutely closed.

The past few months have been some of the worst of my life, and Jamie leaving last night feels like the straw that broke the camel's back. I have given myself permission to stay in bed as long as I need.

Apparently, the rain didn't get the memo.

Splat. A drop on my forehead.

Splat. One on my nose.

Splat, splat, splat. Because, seriously, we would hate for my hair to miss out.

I roll over and pull the pillow over my head. *It's 5 a.m.*, I want to scream into it. But the rain doesn't give even the smallest of craps, and it keeps pounding until the side of my pillow is wet too.

I lie still for a few minutes, trying to decide whether it's better to be wet, angry and vaguely rested, or tired and marginally less drenched.

In the end, I can't get back to sleep anyway.

I flip onto my back and stretch my hands above my head. A muscle in my groin screams in protest. My groin. In an *arm* stretch.

I limp my way over to the mirror. A wet, cranky version of myself peers back at me through eyes that are rimmed with dark circles. My nose is red and puffy, which should nicely match my new down jacket, and my short brown hair is already frizzing out at the sides in rebellion against the unprovoked rain attack. As well as bedraggled, I look like I spent half the night crying. Which is, sadly, accurate.

I hobble into the kitchen, treading carefully in case my groin decides to just completely give up. The tiles are icy cold under my bare feet and the sink is filled with last night's dishes: a single plate and a butter knife. On the plus side, there are no saucepans, frying pans or any other cutlery, which is one of the many benefits of having toast for dinner. That, and my fancy Wolf toaster is pretty close to perfect even when nothing else is. Still, my breath catches at the starkness of it. *Dinner for one, please.*

It's still early enough that it's dark outside, darker still because of the rain, but the light is on at Mrs Potts' house next door. I can see her, bustling around her kitchen, making breakfast for her husband of twenty years. Fried tomatoes with scrambled eggs, bacon and freshly baked bread. Same as every morning. Her kitchen is somehow both beige and happy, and the scene is so domestic that for a second it makes my heart hurt, imagining the two of them falling in love and moving into what has become their home. They probably danced around that same kitchen, kissed against that exact fridge. Told each other stories of their lives at their big wooden dining-room table that looks worn with love and time.

Then Mrs Potts catches me watching her. She opens her window, motioning for me to do the same. The rain spits at me as soon as I do, finding the gap with an immediate vengeance that is both impressive and affronting.

'You left your light on again last night,' Mrs Potts calls out her window.

After everything that happened, I did stay up late. Reading. And crying. Then reading and crying some more. One of the perks – and pitfalls – of being a bookseller is the joy of discovering new books and the necessity of doing so even when you feel like total rubbish.

'Just reading,' I call back, miming the action with my hands.

'Tell someone who cares,' yells Mrs Potts. 'It shines directly into our bedroom, so either read in the dark or shut your effing blinds!'

Believe me, Mrs Potts, I would love to, but they are very much broken, like at least thirty per cent of the things in my apartment. And good morning to you too.

I don't get to call this back though, because Mrs Potts has already slammed her window shut.

'I hope your bacon is cold,' I mutter instead, having apparently already stooped to talking to myself.

I pull my own window shut and a moment later a pigeon lands on the windowsill. It ruffles its feathers, seemingly unbothered by the fact that they're slick from the rain. For a second, I forget about the pain in my groin and my angry neighbour and even my damp head. That pigeon has braved the elements. It has made a home and a life for itself, despite the hardships, and it still has the tenacity to fix its hair when it finds a moment of shelter. My heart lifts. Maybe today won't completely suck.

Then the pigeon flies away, leaving a pile of crap on my windowsill. *Excellent.*

It's five past nine by the time I finally make it to Brooks' Books, the bookshop that my grandparents started with blood, sweat and tears fifty years ago. I've held the keys for over a month now, but I still can't think of it as anything but theirs.

There's a random bike sitting in front of the stoop and I'm about to shift it out of the way when there's movement in the doorway of the antique shop next door and a moment later Ruth appears. She's smiling with her usual perpetual warmth, and just the sight of her makes my throat burn.

'Clarrie!' she cries with genuine delight. My gut twists. I don't think I can do this today.

'Morning, Ruth.'

'Knit, Stitch and Yarn is on tomorrow night,' she says. She doesn't even blink at my lack of enthusiasm and another stab of guilt rushes through me at all the things I'm not doing. But Knit, Stitch and Yarn was Gran's thing, not mine, and the idea of being there without her makes me want to be sick.

'Thanks, Ruth. I'll keep it in mind,' I say, even though we both know that I won't be there.

Ruth watches me for a moment, then reaches out and briefly squeezes my hand. Her skin is soft and wrinkled, but her grip is surprisingly strong. 'You have a good day, Clarrie,' she says.

I blink back the tears that have suddenly sprung to the corner of my eyes. 'You too, Ruth.'

She ducks inside and it takes me a minute to catch my breath before I can make myself move again. I shift the bike from in front of the shop and shove the key in the bookshop's temperamental lock. Obviously, it doesn't twist, and I reach up to jiggle the top of the door loose. But then: my groin.

I look down, like that might be able to somehow, I don't know – will it better with my eyes? – and that's when I notice the ladder in my stockings.

'Of course,' I whisper, just as someone makes a noise behind me.

My heart leaps momentarily, stupidly thinking it might be Jamie, come to win me back. Or, at the very least, a customer.

But it is, in fact, just a very irate-looking man who proceeds to yell at me for daring to touch his bike. And as I'm standing there, trying to find the right words to tell him that a pigeon crapped on my windowsill, all I can think about is how Gran would've convinced him to come inside for a cup of tea by now. She would have had him laughing in no time, joining in herself, with that bright cackle of hers – the one you could hear from down the street when the door was open. And, it goes without saying, she would have *definitely* sold him a book.

But I'm not Gran. I'm not even close.

Instead, I finally manage to mumble that I'd appreciate it if he could park his bike elsewhere. He shakes his head as he wheels it away, and a wave of directionless anger swells in my gut. She was meant to be here. She was meant to do this with me. And instead she's in a nursing home that she will hate until she forgets that she hates it, and her memories of this dream that she built slowly slip through my fingers.

I shove the key in the lock like my hand isn't trembling, daring it to fight me this time. But it doesn't. The lock twists, and I slip inside, leaning back against the door for just a second as the smell of books hits me.

Home.

And occasional prison.

I stand there until I realise it's so cold that I can see my breath in the air. I sigh, then reach over to turn on the old, sad air-conditioner that will pant and puff out heat for at least two hours before the shop is a vaguely comfortable temperature. Like most buildings in Australia, Brooks' is not well insulated.

I make a cup of coffee and spend the next few hours unstacking the new boxes of books that almost definitely don't fit on the shelves, figuring that the physical activity at least will keep me warm. There are no customers, and by 11 a.m. I'm already wondering if it's too early to go home. I put the kettle on again instead, closing my eyes and listening to the steady, rising shriek. But, just before it hits a crescendo, it cuts out.

So do the lights.

And the air-conditioning.

Because of course it does.

The power does this, occasionally.

It's delicate, my gran was fond of saying whenever it happened. *Like a flower.*

It's one of the shop's quirks – one I used to love. She'd turn the dark into an adventure. We'd go searching for treasure, we'd gaze at stars. Sail a ship in the dark and fight pirates. Become pirates, ourselves. Like something straight out of one of the books on her crooked shelves, but somehow better.

Today, sailing alone in a pirate ship in the dark feels cold and wet and difficult. So, instead, I slump down onto the floor.

The bookshop is silent, and I can almost imagine the books are asking me questions.

Why are we still here? Why are you *here? Do you really think you can make this bookshop work?*

The stories sound suspiciously like my mother. Or Jamie, just before he left. And, in the dark, I can't help adding my own question:

What on earth am I doing?

It's then that the bell above the door rings its jaunty, happy jingle.

I consider pretending I'm not there. I mean, really, even if whoever it is wants to steal something, how many books can someone feasibly carry out with their bare hands in the almost-dark?

'Hello?' calls a man's voice, and I sink silently into one of the beat-up chairs. *Stuff the stock.*

But then I look up and even in the low light I can see the scratches in the wonky table my grandpa built when they first opened the bookshop fifty years ago. The table I've sat at more times than I can count. And I know that in this terrible, horrible, no good, very bad day, letting a customer go is only going to make me feel worse.

Also, it's pretty dark in the bookshop and that feels very much like a lawsuit waiting to happen. So I press my hand against the wall and I pull myself to my feet. But – almost like my thoughts have somehow made it happen – I trip on the step on the way out of the kitchenette. I bang my knee against the corner of the display shelf and shuffle over to try to – unsuccessfully – half hide behind the counter.

There is silence for a moment. Blessed, very strange silence. Maybe the man has gone. Maybe he has padded feet like a cat, and he somehow managed to find his way out without ringing the bell.

But then he clears his throat. 'Are you . . . okay?' His voice is low and a little gravelly, and I feel it in the base of my spine.

Not a cat.

I hunch behind the counter, rubbing my knee with much more ferocity than is entirely necessary. I don't know how this stranger's voice has somehow taken up residence in my abdomen, but I'm so distracted that my fingers catch the ladder in my stockings and in the heavy silence I hear it rip further.

Damn it.

I wait for another beat. Logically, I know that I can't stay down here for ever, but I can't seem to make myself stand up either. I don't have it in me to face a mysterious, gravelly voiced man today. Yet, short of dropping to the floor and commando-crawling my way back to the kitchenette, I don't have a whole lot of options. *The spine-tingling is probably just a by-product of whatever muscle I pulled in my groin,* I tell myself. I'm not in any way convincing, but it's enough to motivate me to push to my feet, a tight smile forming on my lips.

It drops as I take him in.

He has a cap pulled low over his face, like he's a famous person trying to hide. *Is* he a celebrity? What kind of person wears a cap on a day like today? His eyes glint in the dim light, and dark hair covers the lower half of his face in what might have been a five-o'clock shadow a month ago. He's wearing a half-smile that even in the dark I can tell invites people to smile back.

Mostly, though, he's far too attractive, and he's a man, so I'm immune to any charms he may have. It was, after all, a man who dumped me last night and told me that trying to save my grandparents' legacy was a waste of time.

I stand up straighter and the man glances down. He can almost definitely see the ladder in my stockings. He looks back up and his eyes catch mine and hold. In the dim light I can't quite make out the colour, and it makes me irrationally irritated.

'Welcome to Brooks' Books,' I say, stumbling slightly over the words.

The man coughs, like he's trying to cover a laugh. At me. He's laughing at me. 'Do you need another minute?' he asks, and the words themselves are fine, but his voice is so patronising that a wave of fresh mortification washes over me.

'I'm fine. Thank you.'

'It's just, you were down there a while.'

An expectant silence follows his words. And is he *smirking*?

I clear my throat. 'I'm fine,' I repeat. 'How can I help you?' I turn towards the computer screen and click the mouse, ready to search for whatever it is he's looking for and get him out as soon as possible. Nothing happens, so I click it again. The screen stays determinedly black. *Wonderful.*

'I'm an author,' says the man finally. 'I was hoping to sign some copies of my book.'

I've been staring at the screen for long enough now that I don't think I can tell him my computer isn't working without making it really weird – that is, if he hasn't already noticed that it's not emitting any light in the dim store. Now would be a great time for that pirate ship to appear to sail me anywhere but here.

'Oh. What's the book?' I might know it off the top of my head, but it's unlikely.

'It's called *Flight Risk*,' says the man, and in fact it's worse than not knowing the book.

Because I do know it.

It was well written, worthy – and very boring. And I know that I sent the twenty copies of it we had back to the publisher yesterday.

'Unfortunately, the power has just gone out. My computer isn't working,' I tell him, because, hell, at this point it feels better than the alternative.

'Right,' says the man, like he's raising an eyebrow under his ridiculous cap. 'Is that a recent development?'

'Sorry?'

'Your computer,' says the man. 'You've been staring at the screen for almost a minute. Did it just suddenly stop working when I asked about my book?' There's a thread of amusement in his voice again.

'I . . .' I blink back at him. 'No.'

'So you were just pretending your computer was working?' His tone is mocking now.

'I was . . . thinking about how to fix it.' My voice is significantly more defensive than I'd like it to be. 'Not that I need to explain myself to you.'

'Sorry,' says the man, sounding anything but. I swear his eyes are twinkling in the dark. 'Should I come back another time, or are you expecting your computer to be down indefinitely?'

'You know what?' I tell him. 'I can just have a quick look on the shelf for you now, save you having to come back again.' I'll try and fail to find the book, and then he'll leave. There is no way I want this man and his dry amusement in Gran's shop again.

I realise I've made a mistake as soon as I step out from behind the register. Without the solidness of the counter between us, the space somehow tightens. In the cold of the bookshop I can *feel* the warmth of his body as I move past. He shifts slightly on his feet, and I fix my eyes on the bookshelves ahead.

I stride over to where the book would be, running my

finger along familiar spines. 'Unfortunately, it looks like we're all out of copies of *Flight Risk*,' I say. It's vague enough that he might think the book has just sold out.

'I guess that's either good news or bad news,' he replies, his gravelly voice even, with a calculated amount of self-deprecation.

I smile tightly at him, then go the long way back round the counter, trying to make it look like that's my preferred route even when his too-big, too-warm body isn't blocking the path. 'Is there anything else I can do for you?'

He glances at the computer. 'It seems unlikely.' The corner of his mouth twitches and he touches the edge of his cap. I grip my hands together behind my back to stop myself reaching out to pull it down over his smug face.

Then finally, *finally*, he turns round and starts walking back out of the door. I close my eyes and exhale briefly in relief, then turn to make my way back to take refuge in the kitchenette.

Only to trip on the same freaking step.

I don't fall but it's loud and the ladder in my stocking rips all the way to my thigh.

The man pauses in the doorway.

'Maybe you *should* fix a few things around here,' he says.

'Maybe you should write a better book,' I mutter before I can swallow the retort.

For a second, I freeze, and I hear him still too. The words that I very definitely said out loud – the words that he very obviously heard – shuffle in the space between us.

Crap. Crap, crap, crap, crap, crap.

But before I can apologise or laugh it off, or even turn round, he speaks again.

'I guess it was bad news, then,' he says mildly.

Then the bell laughs merrily, and he is gone.

Chapter One

Eighteen months later

'I've been waiting five minutes, Clarence,' says a voice behind me. A foot taps along with the words, punctuating each one of them.

I put the last few boxes I've been carting around out the back, then paste a smile on my face and turn around to Annabel Stone, who has been standing at the front counter for four and a half minutes at most.

Yumi's eyes glitter with amusement over Annabel's shoulder, like she's just waiting for me to look pointedly at a clock. Unfortunately, despite only having been working here twelve months, Yumi can read me . . . well, like a book.

I resolutely ignore her and focus my entire attention on the stern and rather intimidating regular in front of me.

'I'm so sorry, Annabel, we've got a children's event in less than half an hour so we've been flat out this morning.'

Annabel sniffs as though the idea of having children around books is abhorrent.

'I understand, Clarence,' she says. It doesn't matter how

many times I've told her to call me Clarrie, she still insists that full names are a sign of respect. 'Perhaps you could personally assist me, so I can be out before the event begins.'

'Of course, Annabel,' I say, like I didn't know that was coming.

'There's a book that's too high for me to reach,' she adds.

'I'll grab the stepladder,' I say, already on my way to do just that. Yumi is straight-up laughing now, though she turns it into a cough after I glare at her.

I'm at the top of the ladder, freeing the book – whose spine I couldn't even *see* from the ground – when Annabel asks her next question.

'Tell me, Clarence, do you have the new Francis Coates?' she asks imperiously.

'Sorry, the . . . who?'

It's only the start. This is what Annabel does. She follows me around, pointing to books I can't reach and naming authors I've never heard of until one of us cracks. Spoiler alert: it's pretty much always me.

It's twenty-five minutes before I manage to find one that she wants to buy. She nods the Annabel Stone seal of approval, and I breathe a discreet sigh of relief.

'Excellent choice,' I tell her, even though I honestly had no idea that the book in my hand even existed, let alone that it was in stock in our shop. I'm just about to ring up the purchase when she taps a finger on the counter.

'Declan Archer,' she announces.

I almost drop the book I'm in the process of scanning.

Annabel barely notices, though. She's busy running her eyes over the bursting shelves and bright displays that have always been one of Brooks' Books trademarks. They pause on the stand that showcases new releases.

'I'm surprised you don't have Declan Archer's book on display,' she says. 'He has a new one.'

I'm surprised that Annabel Stone knows who Declan Archer is, let alone that he has a new book. Not that anyone who's been in a bookshop in the past two weeks would have been able to miss him. His latest book, *Talking to Trees*, has gathered something of a cult following; so much so that the media coverage that was initially just local has begun to spread internationally. People do actual pilgrimages to the places mentioned in the book. It's on the brink of becoming something seriously big. The man himself is apparently reclusive, and has given a total of *one* interview. It was written, not even in person. Which, of course, only seems to add to his mystery and appeal.

Yumi glances up from where she's just finished setting up an under-the-sea display, her eyes twinkling. She's heard the same question from more than one customer in the past few days – has asked me the same question herself.

I give Annabel the same answer I gave all of them.

'There's a display of Mr Archer's books down the back,' I say with a smile that doesn't even hurt a little bit. A display that I fought tooth and nail to avoid putting up, until the pile of overdue reminders got so big that they no longer fitted in the drawer into which I'd been shoving them. Until the cash register that's been in the shop at least half my life finally began to die at the same time Yumi was pointing out the paint peeling in the break room. There is no avoiding that we desperately, urgently need sales. And Declan's book sells. 'He seems to be doing very well on his own,' I tell Annabel, 'with or without a front-counter display.'

It comes out more pointedly than I intend it to, and I cringe inwardly. There's a look of pure delight on Yumi's face, and I know I'm not going to be able to get out of answering questions about this later.

'Yumi, don't you have to get changed soon?' I say to her over Annabel's shoulder. I am perversely glad Yumi drew the short straw and is the one dressing up today. She sticks her tongue out at me, like an employee most definitely shouldn't, but then dutifully tramps out to the back room.

'Right,' says Annabel, looking at the new-release stand again. 'He's a local, you know. Declan Archer.'

'Is he?' I say, pretending I don't know. 'That's so lovely.'

The bell above the shop door rings, and I have honestly never been so glad in my life to see a horde of rampaging children dressed up as crabs.

The floor is covered in beanbags, crêpe paper and pipe cleaners, and there are at least five misshapen sea creatures hanging from the shelves in the children's book section – all signs that Read Under the Sea was a raging success.

Yumi picks up a one-eyed seahorse from where it's dangling upside down next to *Lord of the Rings*. She holds it up to her face and looks it in its one eye, which is accompanied by an angry slash that I think is its eyebrow.

'I love kids,' she says with a sigh.

I pick up a crab with six pincers from the story-time chair.

'Me too,' I say. The words come out more softly than I mean them to, and Yumi looks up at me and rolls her eyes.

'Sap,' she says.

'You said the same thing!' I say, as though it might actually be worth protesting.

She really is the worst employee in the world. But she's the best, too. During her job interview she announced that we were going to be best friends. There are a lot of things when it comes to the bookshop that I'm unsure about – like whether the power problems that were once a sweet quirk have become an actual fire issue – but hiring Yumi is not one of those things. Despite my every intention to maintain a professional distance, in the twelve months since she started, she's become – well, one of my closest friends.

Her hair is currently purple, because she made a bet with one of our elderly customers that she could finish a book before they did, and lost. They adore her, and so do the kids and angry teenagers.

'It was a good idea, the story time,' I tell her.

'I know,' says Yumi, flopping down onto one of the bean-bags. 'I am a low-key genius. Maybe even a high-key genius.' There is an almost imperceptible pause. 'Which we'd know if you tried any of my other ideas.'

Familiar guilt rolls in my stomach. When I first took over

the bookshop and everything happened with Gran, I was doing everything I could just to keep my head above water. Yumi was a godsend, but the idea of changing anything – of shifting Brooks' in any direction that Gran wouldn't recognise – made me feel physically sick. Then council rates and electricity prices went up, and the number of people buying books went down, and *everything* started to feel like a risk.

'Yumi—' I begin.

'I know.' She holds up a hand. 'It's okay, Clarrie.' She studies me for a second, and when she speaks again her voice is so unexpectedly gentle that it brings a lump to my throat. 'Tell me – how bad is it?'

I hate that she knows the state of the shop's finances. I tried to keep the worry from her – I've done my best to keep it from *myself* – but it's difficult to hide the broken tap out the back that hasn't been fixed; or the fact that half the bills that arrive have bright red lettering stamped on them. I don't pretend not to know what she's talking about.

'If sales don't pick up, we have six months,' I tell her, the truth stark in the air. 'Maybe less.' Then I make myself say what I've selfishly been avoiding saying for a month now: 'If you want to start looking for another job, I understand.'

Yumi rolls her eyes, then leans back in the beanbag. '*If* the day comes, I've got a few offers,' she says, waving her hand in the general direction of the street. 'But let's face it, you'd be lost without me.' She winks and pushes a beanbag out towards me.

I don't deny it. I sigh and flop down next to her.

'Ruth popped in when you were at the till towards the

end,' says Yumi, changing the subject. 'She asked me to tell you that Knit, Stitch and Yarn is on again this Thursday.'

I used to go sometimes with Gran, but I haven't been since she went into the nursing home just over eighteen months ago. Ruth invites me every month anyway. She was – *is* – Gran's closest friend, and has been for the last forty years.

'Thanks,' I say. Yumi doesn't push on it like she normally does, and I realise too late it's because she has another agenda.

'So,' she says after she's been quiet for four whole seconds. 'Declan Archer.'

I shake my head and lean back into the beanbag again.

'What about him?' I say in my best disinterested voice.

'Come on, Clarrie, every time you point to the display down the back, I can basically see you gritting your teeth. And it's our highest selling book – by a long way – I'd have thought you'd be dancing naked in front of the stand to draw attention there.'

'I'm fairly confident that would drive people out of the shop,' I say, even though she's right. About the sales, not about the naked dancing. At this point, Declan Archer is literally almost paying for Gran's shop to stay open.

'Have you read it?' says Yumi.

'I started it,' I tell her truthfully. 'But, to be honest, I just didn't find it that engaging.'

'How many pages?' she asks. She knows one of my mottos is that every author deserves to have you try for at least a hundred pages.

'Enough,' I tell her. 'There's really nothing of value in there.'

'You're the one always telling me that every book has a reader,' she says, waving a finger in the air. 'Annabel mentioned he was a local . . .'

'If the shop goes bust, you should really consider a career as a detective,' I tell her, but Yumi's not even listening any more.

'. . . so maybe your problem is more personal. Is he an ex-boyfriend or something?'

I scoff. 'Hardly. I've only met him once.'

Yumi grins. *Crap.*

'You've met him!' She wiggles her eyebrows and lowers her voice. 'The plot thickens!'

'You really need to work on your book jokes,' I tell her. 'And I tell you that as your boss, not your friend.'

But Yumi won't be put off. She pushes herself off the beanbag with purpose and starts striding towards the *Talking to Trees* display.

'Yumi, don't!' I try to roll out of my own beanbag, cursing the beans shifting under me and wondering how Yumi managed to get out so nimbly.

But I'm too late: she's already plucking a copy off the shelf.

'If you open that book, I'm going to fire you.' I narrow my eyes at her.

Yumi raises an eyebrow at me, then clears her throat and opens the first page.

She doesn't need to go any further than that.

I curse myself a thousand times over, because honestly, if I hadn't been so weird about it, she never would've known. She would have just one day opened the book, maybe laughed a little at the dedication, then carried on reading.

Instead, she pauses. Her eyes light up and she looks up to grin at me, then back down at the page again.

A nicer employee might let it go, or sympathetically pat me on the shoulder. They'd listen to the story and tell me that Declan Archer probably had another encounter, that it definitely wasn't me he was referring to.

But Yumi is not a nicer employee.

'Clarence Brooks,' she says. 'Is this dedication talking about who I think it's talking about?'

'I have no idea what you mean,' I tell her, but it's too late. She clears her throat and, in what I think is meant to be her Declan Archer voice, she reads the dedication out loud. But I'm not listening, because I already know what it says.

For the bookseller who told me to write a better book.

I hope you managed to fix your lights.

Yumi looks up at me again, and her eyes are bright with amusement.

'You told Declan Archer to write a better book!' she whispers, her tone full of the kind of scandalised delight she usually reserves for her breakdowns of *The Bachelor*.

'In my defence, his first book was boring,' I tell her.

'Did you – Clarence Brooks, a bookseller whose sacred

duty it is to defend authors and their precious works – just call a book *boring*?'

I rub my forehead, trying to pretend the sight of *Talking to Trees* doesn't make me feel physically ill. I can still remember the moment I first opened it, looking to give an author I'd offended another chance. Then the hot and cold embarrassment when I read the dedication and his dig about fixing the lights. All nicely rounded out by bone-deep mortification when I – against my own protests – read the one interview that Declan Archer gave with a hot new book blog.

'He came in the same week Gran went into Glenhaven,' I admit to Yumi, trying to ignore the twisting in my stomach. 'Jamie had just broken up with me and it was . . . not a great day. I was in a bad mood.'

Yumi gasps theatrically. '*What? You?*'

'Do you want me to tell you this story, or not?' The urge to be done talking about it is strong.

Yumi mimes zipping her lips shut, her eyes laughing.

'Declan came in and he was all attractive and arrogant and sure of himself.' I rub my forehead. 'And I maybe happened to tell him that his book skills could use some work. I mean, allegedly.'

And there are my four semesters of law really paying off.

'How attractive are we talking?' asks Yumi.

I look up. 'Seriously? That's your takeaway?'

'I don't understand how that's *not* your takeaway,' says Yumi. 'Also: you're an idiot. I mean, not for saying what you did – even though, knowing you, you probably beat yourself up over it – I mean you're an idiot for not telling *everyone* about it.'

'What?' I lean back in my beanbag to study her, but the angle is worse because now I can see Declan's smug face on the back cover.

'Clarrie – people are *obsessed* with this book.' She pulls out her phone. 'Siri, search *talking to trees bookseller dedication*.'

There's a beat of taut silence, and part of me is almost waiting for the bell above the door to ring and break it. Yumi scans the phone, and when she holds the screen up to me, her eyes are almost as smug as Declan's.

'Look.' She jabs her other finger at it. 'There are literally forums dedicated to working out who the dedication is about. Declan even referenced it in the one interview he did. You are *famous*. To, you know, the smallish but passionate group of people following everything about this book.'

I'm shaking my head before she's even finished talking.

'You know what Declan said in that interview with Read, Repeat, right?' I make myself say like it doesn't matter, swallowing down the bile in my throat.

Yumi waves a hand, still looking at her phone. 'It's irrelevant,' she tells me.

'Tessa Dalton asked him how the bookseller had responded to the dedication, and Declan said he thought she was "probably still stumbling around in the dark".' My voice almost catches on the last word, and I curse myself for letting it get to me *again*. It's stupid. So stupid. But, somehow, his words managed to pierce their way to the centre of my insecurities, rip the heart out of them and display them for the world to see. And no matter how much I tell myself that it's not a big deal, every time I see the cover of his book, all I can see is him laughing at me.

Yumi looks up, searching my eyes with hers. She holds up her phone. 'Even so, half these weirdos on the internet argue that you are the bookseller who inspired Declan Archer. You're this handsome and mostly reclusive author's *muse.* According to Treesaremyjam66, Declan made that comment in the interview because of "pent up sexual tension".' She frowns at her phone, her eyes scanning the text. 'Actually, some of this is kind of gross.'

I just keep shaking my head. Then Yumi's eyes soften and I know that no matter how invested she is in Declan Archer chat, she hasn't for a second forgotten the earlier part of the conversation.

'I know your parents are pressuring you to sell,' she says.

My throat feels thick. Mum and Dad have always been so disparaging about me taking over the bookshop that I usually try not to talk to them about it. But then a couple of weeks ago at my brother Ben's birthday dinner I accidentally let it slip that the lights had been shorting more frequently, and they haven't let me forget.

'I'm not saying you have to want to be famous,' she continues. 'But this could give us a publicity boost. It could keep your dream alive.'

I don't correct her. Don't tell her that what sticks in my gut more than anything is that maybe Declan Archer was right about me stumbling in the dark. When Gran first suggested that I run Brooks', it was like a lifeline. I'd just left a law degree I hated, I had no way to pay rent and I had no idea what I wanted to do next. Brooks' had always felt safe and warm, and the idea of building Gran's dream alongside her felt like the first meaningful thing I'd done in years. I didn't know if it was permanent, but Gran told me that was okay, that it was all going to be okay. And, like an idiot, I believed her.

But I can't afford to dream. It's taking everything I have just to stop hers from falling apart.

'Just think about it?' says Yumi.

'Call the electrician you know for me tomorrow?' I counter, out of pride more than anything. Yumi just grins.

Chapter Two

Thanks to a terrible night's sleep that may or may not have been plagued by dreams of Declan Archer, I'm not feeling great on my walk into work the next morning.

There are a few people waiting outside, which is unusual but not unheard of. They're all watching me as I walk up to the front step and search my too-big bag for my keys. One of them has a cap pulled low over his eyes. He looks up and my heart stops in my chest.

Declan Archer?

I freeze for half a second, my gaze locked on his. Stupidly, all I can think is that his eyes are green. I force myself to take a step forward – to do what, I don't know – but then someone walks between us, and by the time they've passed he's gone.

Or he was never there in the first place.

Someone coughs beside me, jolting me back to myself. *I'm imagining things.* A lack of sleep and the stress of talking about the dedication with Yumi yesterday are making my brain insert Declan Archer into a scene where he doesn't belong.

I shove my hand into my bag to hide the fact that it's shaking, and in the first good news of the morning I find my keys almost immediately. I mentally beg them to be kind to me today, exhaling in relief when the right key slides smoothly into the lock. I'm about to push the door open in a way that is both triumphant and nonchalant, when someone behind me speaks.

'Are you Clarence Brooks?'

There are only three people who call me Clarence: Annabel Stone, the man from the gym who calls once a month to politely ask if I'd like to reinstate my membership and my mother.

I turn round to see a woman about my age looking back at me. Her skin is smooth and glowing, like she actually knows which skincare products she should use, her hair is in the kind of chic messy bun that I aspire to but can never achieve and she has a pen tucked through the top.

She is not my mother, or Annabel Stone, or Mark from Fitness First. And there's something about her smile that makes me uneasy.

'Yes?' I say, hoping that my lack of confidence in whether or not I'm Clarence Brooks might make her give up and leave.

She doesn't.

'Excellent. I'm Elizabeth.' That's it. That's all she says.

Who introduces themselves with just their first name?

I mean, most people, probably. But it's not very helpful for rapidly getting basic and possibly unreliable information on the internet about someone.

There's silence as I open the door to the bookshop.

I walk in slowly, my key-related success all but forgotten.

I'm ready to close the door behind me to indicate that we're not open yet, but Elizabeth somehow slips through the gap.

'Sorry, I'll be with you in just a few minutes,' I tell her as the other customers filter in behind her, and I'm hoping a meteor hits the earth before the time is up.

She nods. 'That's no problem,' she says. 'I'm just browsing for now.'

It's the 'for now' that worries me.

I drop my things out in the kitchenette and rapidly google 'Elizabeth' on my phone, just in case. But, despite her smooth skin and great bun, unfortunately this Elizabeth is not in the world's top ten. I splash my face with water and stop short of giving myself a pep talk, because I learned the hard way that sound travels from here to the shelves. The last thing I need is for the entire bookshop to hear me talking to myself again.

I take a breath, square my pointy shoulders and walk back out into the bookshop.

Elizabeth is studying the shelves by the door, but she turns to smile when I come back in.

'Wonderful bookshop you've got here,' she says.

I think she might genuinely mean the words. But then she follows them up with these: 'I'm just not sure why you don't have Declan Archer's book displayed up front. He's a local, you know.'

It's the same question so many people have asked in the last few days, but there's something about the way she says the words that makes cold trickle down my spine. I have a sudden awful premonition that something is about to happen. And, like a freight train hurtling its way along the tracks, there is not a single damn thing I can do to stop it.

Still, I can damned well try. I look absentmindedly at the shelves. 'There's a large display down the back,' I say, cool and calm like a cucumber. 'And Declan's book is doing very well for itself already.' Elizabeth raises her eyebrows at me and I know my cheeks start to flush. *Some cucumber.* 'We have many talented local authors,' I add. 'I think it's important to give all of them shelf space.'

'I understand,' she replies smoothly. I look away, busying myself in the hope she might leave, but I can sense her gaze fixed on me.

'Is there something else I can do for you?' I ask her, adopting a polite but firm voice I'm pretty sure I've borrowed from my mother. 'I'm rather busy this morning.'

Elizabeth looks around the shop, empty but for one of the men who was waiting outside earlier. Her eyes are gleaming more than her beautiful skin, and she leans forward in a conspiratorial manner.

'Have you read it?' she asks, her brown eyes never leaving mine. 'The book?'

She's asking the same questions that Annabel and Yumi did yesterday. *Why? Why now?* The book has been out almost a month already.

You're being paranoid, Clarrie, I try to tell myself, but Declan's words feel like they are clawing their way up from my gut: *She's just stumbling around in the dark.*

I follow Elizabeth's lead and look around the shop as well, like that might buy me some time to get my crap together.

And then I see it: the camera the other man in the shop is holding. He's taking pictures of the books, and the shelves, and . . . hang on, is he pointing it at *me*?

'Sorry,' I say to Elizabeth, glancing at her and then back over her shoulder. 'Excuse me, sir?' I say in a louder voice. 'Can I help you?'

The man looks up. His eyes flick to Elizabeth and then back to me.

'You can help him by answering my questions,' says Elizabeth, smiling and pulling all my attention back to her. 'We'd love a comment from you.'

'Sorry?' I say again. I'm a bit dizzy now. Like the cold at the base of my spine has numbed something in my head. I'm hoping a little desperately for Yumi to come in, to save me from whatever this situation is.

I told Yumi about the dedication yesterday . . .

But before I have time to see the thought to its conclusion, Elizabeth is speaking again.

'The book has a dedication in the front,' she says. 'To a bookseller. Who told Declan to write a better book.'

'Does it?' I ask innocently. The words sound thin, even to my own ears.

Elizabeth smiles again, and with her lips curved to reveal shiny white teeth she looks a little like a shark. A shark with really good skin and hair.

'You wouldn't happen to be that bookseller, would you?'

I'm shaking my head before she's even finished. 'I'm sorry, I don't know what you're talking about,' I tell her. 'You must have me confused with someone else. I don't know anything about any dedication.'

Is lying bad if it's to save yourself from scrutiny and unwanted questions?

Probably, yes. *But why are they here?* I don't ask them, though. I just keep shaking my head like whatever is happening might just stop.

'Would you mind if I have a look at your lights?' asks Elizabeth, and it throws me enough that I finally stop shaking my head. Then it dawns on me that she's asking because of the second half of the dedication. The part about the bad lighting.

But this – this I can work with. The lights might be an unreliable fire hazard, but when they work the lighting is *excellent*. If they'll just hold up for a few minutes, maybe Elizabeth and her cameraman will leave with nothing more than a few shots of me looking confused.

'Not a problem,' I say, hoping that's true.

I gesture awkwardly to the light switch on the wall beside the counter and Elizabeth saunters over to it. She looks back over at the camera person and raises her eyebrows, and he obediently takes a step closer to capture whatever magic it is they're expecting to witness.

Two flicks, I silently beg the lights. *Behave yourselves for two flicks, and I will never turn the kettle on again.*

Elizabeth glances at me and I try for a look that says I am

bemused and faintly amused, and also that I'm a bookseller who has known the difference between the two for longer than six months.

Then with a great flourish, she flicks the light switch.

The lights go on, illuminating the bookshop in a warm, friendly glow.

Then she flicks them off again.

And you know what? They turn off, and nothing shorts out.

Elizabeth narrows her eyes, and flicks the switch again. On. Then off. Then on again.

And the lights behave *perfectly.*

Elizabeth frowns, then turns to the cameraman.

'Everything okay?' I ask her, only a little smugly. My chest expands, like I can finally breathe again.

'Fine,' she says tightly. 'Thanks so much for your time this morning, Ms Br—'

The bell above the door rings. I turn, expecting to see Yumi walking through the door. Instead, a spritely old man wearing overalls and carrying a toolbox walks in, whistling.

'Hiya, I'm Mike,' he says, plonking down his toolbox and reaching out a hand. 'Yumi phoned yesterday, said you were having trouble with your lights?'

Chapter Three

The article appears overnight.

It's online, on the homepage of one of the local news sites, and I wake the next morning to find out via no less than eight text messages.

The last thing I feel like doing is reading exactly what Elizabeth has to say about me after our interaction yesterday, but it's either that or go into the whole thing blind. And while the crap lights in the shop mean I'm used to occasionally sitting – or stumbling – in the dark . . . today that just doesn't seem like a good idea.

So I close my eyes and I click on the link.

Bookseller who inspired *Talking to Trees* dedication still has bad lighting . . . and a mysterious attitude towards its author.

BY ELIZABETH MACKIE

It's about what you might expect. Elizabeth (Mackie!) has leaned heavily on my lighting and the fact that Declan Archer is a local author – probably because I didn't give her much else to work with. But, despite her obvious feeling that I should walk around with a poster of Declan Archer pinned to my clothes, she also . . . isn't horrible.

> When asked about the book, bookshop owner Clarence Brooks simply says that she is interested in supporting all local artists.

The anticipation and dread that has been knotting in my chest since yesterday morning starts to ease. Elizabeth really hasn't been as cutting as I thought she might've been after our interaction. She even describes Brooks' Books as a 'sweet, warm, family bookshop', before going into more detail about Declan and the book itself. Apart from a brief twinge of mortification in my chest when Elizabeth mentions she approached Declan and he declined to speak with her, I'm okay. And then I get to the last lines.

> And yet it would be remiss of me, dear reader, not to mention that despite refusing to comment, Declan Archer himself paused when the bookshop was mentioned, and Clarence blushed when I spoke his name. One can't help but wonder what the history between the two might be, and what spark lit the fire of such a dedication.

And then it ends.

Seriously? *Seriously?*

Who does Elizabeth Mackie think she is? Jane Austen? And what is she, an entertainment writer or a romance sleuth?

A romance sleuth probably isn't a thing, but my face is hot and I can't think, my mind and my body both apparently stuck on the fact that she asked Declan about me. An image flits through my mind: a low cap and amusement dancing in eyes that I strongly suspect are green.

There are a couple of comments at the bottom of the article, but I can't bring myself to read them. Instead, I chuck my phone back on the bench and open the window, hoping for a blast of icy wind to knock me in the face. Unsurprisingly, though, the day is stupidly mild, and I'm forced to resort to fanning myself with the closest book I can find.

Someone has written about me blushing in an actual article, and the fact that they have is making me blush *again*. I shove a piece of bread into my cheap toaster, staring at myself in the dull metal.

Just the thought of walking into the bookshop makes me want to hide under my bed.

I pick up my phone, ignoring the thirteen messages now sitting there staring at me, and just open the one from Yumi. When she finally arrived at the bookshop yesterday, she swore that she hadn't told anyone about the dedication. Being Yumi, she also told me that she'd drafted three anonymous posts to different sites advertising the fact, but that she hadn't actually posted any of them – she even checked while I was standing there to make sure she hadn't done it accidentally.

I know that she's telling the truth – it's really not in her nature to lie – but it does leave the question of how the hell the press found out and why they even care.

She's sent me a link to the article, and a comment that she's drafted in response to it – something about me being a young, single, sexy bookseller.

U ok if I post this? 😉.

No. Please be on time today?

It sounds a little earnest, so I send another.

Or I will probably dock your pay.

Yumi just sends back another winky face, but I know she'll be there.

I change my top while the bread is toasting and my phone starts vibrating just as the toaster pops. I look down, half expecting that Yumi's posted the comment and someone is calling about it – only to see that it's my mother. I don't have the fortitude to answer right now, so I stand and watch it ring, shovelling toast into my mouth until it seems like I've eaten enough to survive the next few hours.

The vibrating finally stops. There's a pause, then the phone beeps once more as though it's making sure it's definitely had the last word. I stare at it for another moment, swallow down the last of the dry toast, then brace myself, snatch it up and dial my voicemail, praying that she hasn't seen the article.

'Good morning, Clarence. I hope this didn't wake you.'

Her tone is brisk. I close my eyes, trying to tell myself that she's just being kind, that she's not being passive-aggressive and that I don't need to read anything into the fact that she thinks I'm still in bed.

'I was looking at my calendar and it looks like I'm free at midday tomorrow. It's been a few weeks since we've seen you so I'm going to book us a table for lunch. Let me know if you have any problems with that.'

The dial tone clicks, and then the kind man on voicemail tells me I have no new messages.

I swallow again to try to clear the lump in my throat, thankful that at least she doesn't seem to know about the article. It's not a bad message. There's nothing overtly mean about it; in fact, she actually wants to have lunch with me. But, just once, I wish that she would ask instead of telling. Instead of making it my fault if I can't come.

It's always been like that between us, but things have been worse in the last few years. Since I've taken over the bookshop it's as though she thinks she has to organise everything because I can't be trusted to make decisions for myself.

But I can't think about any of that right now. I throw my phone into my bag, then shove my feet into my boots, trying to focus on what lies ahead instead of behind . . . until I remember that the fallout from the article is what lies ahead. My chest tightens and, despite knowing how much Yumi will tease me for doing so, I brush my hair and put on the lipstick she got me for Christmas. I need all the confidence I can get today.

I only half recognise the girl staring back at me in the bathroom mirror. She looks flustered and worried, but she also looks something I haven't seen her look in a little while – she looks like she's *anticipating* something. Stupid, stupid.

Before I can talk myself out of it, I pick up my keys and walk out of the front door. I run down the steps from my apartment, and out into the unseasonably mild day at the exact same time as my neighbour Mrs Potts.

I haven't spoken to Mrs Potts since the day my ex-boyfriend took and sold my Wolf toaster. In her defence, I did yell at her through the window and then sob for fifteen minutes into a piece of untoasted bread.

Since then, apart from the occasional glare through the window, we've largely ignored each other.

But not this morning.

Mrs Potts stops – fully stops in the street – and runs her eyes over me. Then she raises her eyebrows and sniffs.

Hot and cold shame washes over me. She's read the article. Everyone has probably read the article by now. Everyone knows, and all the lipstick and neat hair in the world isn't enough for me to hide.

'Bold choice! I salute you!'

The words almost make me jump out of my skin, and a second later a woman on a bike cycles past and sticks her hand out in an unmistakable thumbs up.

Bold choice? Did she see the article? Is it code? What does that have to do with dedications?

I look down, to gather myself and to work out what to do.

Only to realise that I'm still wearing my pyjama shorts.

Idiot.

The crowd out the front of the bookshop is bigger than I've seen in the eighteen months that I've been in charge at Brooks'. The sight of all the people makes me want to turn and scurry home, but just as I'm contemplating how to do just that Yumi swoops in from nowhere and hooks her arm through mine. Her grip is solid and surprisingly firm, and she marches a path through the crowd, holding up her hand to fend off the bustle of sound that swallows us up.

'She isn't taking anyone's questions right now,' says Yumi loudly, pulling me forward. 'But if you come inside and buy a book in just a few moments when we're open, you can ask her one each while she rings up the purchase.'

'Yumi,' I hiss, but my rogue employee isn't even listening.

She eyeballs every last person on her way to the door. Then she pulls out her key – which is still the same very shiny silver it was when I got it cut for her six months ago – and dramatically inserts it into the door. It sticks, and for the first time today I feel a laugh bubble in my chest. A slightly hysterical laugh, sure, but a laugh nonetheless.

'Wiggle it a little to the left,' I manage to breath out of the corner of my mouth.

Yumi sniffs, but she does what I say and it slides into place. She pushes the door open then turns back to the crowd.

'We open in five minutes,' she announces. 'Remember: no purchase, no question.'

Then she sweeps into the bookshop, her purple hair bouncing behind her.

I slip inside too and Yumi pushes the door shut behind us, dulling the noise of the crowd to a muffled buzz.

'Have you ever used that key before today?' I ask her, in part to distract myself from the spinning in my head.

Yumi scoffs. 'You know I haven't,' she said.

I walk to the counter and rest my head against it. The wood is cool against my skin.

'Are you okay?' Yumi asks.

'I've been better,' I tell her, without looking up. I close my eyes and take a deep breath, trying to steady myself. *Five minutes.* We've got five minutes. 'Did you really tell the people outside that to ask a question they had to buy a book?'

'I really did,' confirms Yumi, patting me on the head.

I half groan, but as much as I would like to keep the door locked and my head on this blissfully cool counter there's a crowd outside the bookshop. If I can steel myself, if I can ignore all the awful things people are undoubtedly saying on the internet, and can fumble my way through questions about Declan Archer's book, we might manage to hit our targets this month. I might even be able to pay some of the bills in the drawer out the back, and the relief at the thought makes me feel like weeping.

'You should probably start thinking about your answers,' says Yumi.

She squeezes my hand, then strides to the kitchenette and flicks on the kettle. We both look up at the lights – Mike the electrician did some temporary fixes, but he said he's going to put together a quote for rewiring. I've mostly managed to push that worry to the back of my brain for the moment, but I can feel it lurking. Yumi grins.

And even over the dread in my gut, as I push myself up and straighten my hair, I can't help but think – *Gran would have loved this.*

I've been asked everything from *What does Declan Archer eat for breakfast?* (granola is what I finally burst out after the first three people who asked weren't satisfied with me telling them I didn't know) to *Is it true that he threatened to burn down the bookshop?* (No. Emphatically no, despite Yumi nodding and giving me a thumbs up in the background, then pretending to light a match.)

The crowd of people in the bookshop is crushing, and we've almost sold out of our copies of *Talking to Trees*, including the three boxes we had in the storeroom out the back.

Still, the line of customers waiting to get in stretches down the block. We have a *queue.* And after half an hour we have a security guard – also known as Dave the delivery guy, who Yumi dives on and somehow manages to talk into working at the shop for the rest of the day. My first instinct is to tell her its unnecessary, but three people have tried to grab at me across the counter, and one woman yelled abuse about hurting Declan until another customer managed to get her to calm down. Mentally, I'm shaken, but there's enough adrenaline coursing through my system that I just keep moving.

I have honestly never seen so much fuss over a book.

By lunchtime, the article has – unbelievably – been picked up nationally.

It's not the lead article – it's not even the lead puff piece, thanks to a new, and very sweet, giraffe romance at Sydney Zoo – but it's enough to send more people down to check out the shop.

My phone has thirty-four messages and counting. That's more than I get on my birthday . . . by a lot. And everyone in the neighbourhood has come down to see what's happening.

'But, seriously, are you selling drugs or something out of our back room?' I ask Yumi in one of our brief respites out the back. 'Because there's no way people are actually this curious about a dedication.' My head feels like it's on fire. With Dave looking menacing by the front door and vetting anyone wearing T-shirts with Declan Archer's face on them, the day hasn't been as bad as I know it could have been, but I am exhausted. I'm not sure how long I can stomach questions about Declan Archer.

'Have you seriously missed how obsessed people are with this book?' asks Yumi. 'I've never seen anything like it. People are really, really into Declan Archer's descriptions of trees. Or his face. Or both.' She pauses. 'We should really think about making a tree with Declan Archer's face on it for our window display.'

'But . . . all of that has nothing to do with the dedication,' I tell her.

'Declan Archer is *mysterious*, Clarrie,' says Yumi, lifting her hands in what I think might be exasperation. 'The dedication is one of the few crumbs about his life that we have. Bloodhounds will follow anything that even vaguely smells like the right track.'

'Is that true?' I ask her.

'I have no idea,' says Yumi. 'But it sounded good.'

The bell above the doorway rings, and we both look towards the door.

Yumi shoves a bagel into my hand. 'Eat,' she says. 'Take a drink of water, and five minutes. I'll handle the counter until you're done. I can pretend I'm you for a bit.'

'That's definitely fraud,' I call as she jumps down the step and back out into the shop. I take a bite of the bagel, listening as she greets the newest customer.

'Hi, I'm Clarence Brooks from Brooks' Books, which is the bookshop you just entered. My bookshop.' Yumi's voice trickles back. 'How can I help you?'

'I have a question.'

A low, gravelly voice responds, and the sound sends a jolt straight through my stomach. A voice I've only heard once, more than a year ago, but that seems to be etched in my nervous system.

Crap.

I'm on my feet before he's even finished speaking. Yumi is typing something into the computer, only half her attention on the customer at the counter. 'About Declan?' she says. 'No problem, you'll just need to buy a book first,' I vaguely hear her say over the ringing in my ears.

My cheeks are tingling, and there is nothing I want more than to burrow deeper into the back room, but I can't bear for Yumi to keep talking, to reveal any more about what's been happening in the bookshop before she realises who is standing in front of her.

I take a breath, readying myself to come face to face with Declan Archer for the first time in eighteen months.

But when I step down it's to see that his stupid baseball cap-covered head is already fixed in the direction of the kitchenette.

Staring at me.

Chapter Four

'What's your question?' I ask, swallowing to try to clear the lump of bagel that's lodged in my throat.

Yumi's head spins towards me and I'm pretty sure she's glaring at me for not taking an actual five minutes, but I can't think about that right now. Then her attention turns fully to Declan, and I hear her gasp quietly as she realises who exactly has just stepped into the store and what exactly is happening.

I'd be lying if I said that I haven't imagined seeing Declan again. Looking down my nose at him and telling him that I don't know whether his book is better because I've been too busy to read it, but that it's nice that he tried. In most imaginings I am full of poise and class; sometimes I ride a silver stallion off into the sunset. In none of my fantasies am I choking on a bagel.

Up close, he looks unfairly put-together, even with the ridiculous cap. His shoulders fill out his black T-shirt and his blue jeans hang casually from his lean frame. He looks exactly the kind of relaxed handsome that wouldn't be out of place on a magazine cover.

'My question is fairly simple, really,' he says, his eyes

sharpening as he watches me take him in. His tone is mild, but there's a current running beneath it and his face is still when I step up to the counter. 'What the hell are you doing?'

Green eyes catch mine and I hear my heartbeat thudding in my ears.

It *was* him, yesterday morning. It was him, and he didn't say anything – why? And why is he here again now?

The person standing in front of me is not quite the measured, slightly mocking man I remember from eighteen months ago. And all I can think about is the stupid line from Elizabeth Mackie's stupid article: *Declan paused when the bookshop was mentioned.*

'I'm running a bookshop,' I tell him, hating the feeling of guilt that creeps up my throat, hating that I'm the one who is on the back foot here.

'Running a bookshop?' says Declan, raising one eyebrow. At least, I think he raises an eyebrow. It's difficult to tell. Until he leans in closer. And now I can not only see his eyebrow but I can smell his skin – a mix of soap and something else, something that I suspect is just *him*. It's more information than I want to have about this man, and my cheeks heat again. 'Selling information about me is how you run a bookshop?'

'We're selling books,' I say, as glibly as I can. Like I can't feel the warmth of his body, inches from mine. 'You just happen to come up in conversation.'

Declan's jaw pulses. 'Who gave you permission to talk about my personal life?'

And that's when I snap. Because, honestly, *he is the one who started this.*

'You did,' I hiss. 'When you dedicated your *freaking book* to me.'

Declan's gaze is hot on mine, and there's a part of me that wants to spit fire at him and another part of me that wants to check my hair and I *hate* the fact that he makes me feel so unbalanced.

'I didn't—' he begins, but before he can finish whatever weak retort he's cooking up, Yumi clears her throat.

'Uhhh . . . guys,' she says. 'I don't mean to break up . . . whatever this is . . .' She gestures between the two of us. 'But you might consider keeping your voices down. Or, you know, taking this elsewhere.'

I look up to see a fresh wave of people in the bookshop. Some are pretending to browse, but one has their phone out and is very clearly trying to get a picture of the encounter. Even Dave the delivery-turned-security guy is leaning in closer to listen.

Declan's whole body seems to tense and, for a second, I think he's going to yell whatever he was going to anyway, consequences be damned. But then he straightens, the anger melting out of him from one second to the next. And, somehow, I'm even madder at him for that.

'Of course,' he says, his voice soft and – dare I say – *charming.* He turns to me. 'Clarence, would you like to go for a cup of coffee with me?'

There's something about his tone and the sight of him that

makes me want to scream *No, never, I will never go anywhere with you, you butt brain*, because apparently, my insults get worse when I'm mad.

But I am a grown-up. And despite my personal feelings about this man, he is an author and I am a bookshop owner. Maybe we can both be professional enough to put this behind us. But . . . that's not what I say.

'I don't drink coffee.'

Declan watches me for a moment, as though he knows I'm lying through my teeth.

'Tea, then?' he clips.

'Tea is fine,' I say, and I feel stupidly proud, like I have somehow won.

'Excellent,' says Declan. A curl has come loose from under his cap, but he doesn't seem to be aware of it. His eyes are steady and reasonable on mine, and I want to tuck the curl back in and even the thought of doing it makes me mad again.

'Are you okay on your own for a bit?' I ask Yumi.

She grins unnervingly widely back at me.

'Take your time,' she says. 'I've got plenty to do here. And if things slow down too much, I've always got some good reading material.' She plucks a copy of *Talking to Trees* from under the counter and waves it at me and *when did she even get that?*

Declan coughs, but I refuse to look at him.

'Bring me back a brownie!' calls Yumi as the bell above the door jingles.

*

Declan's legs are longer than mine, so I'm doing a step and a half for every one of his. By unspoken agreement we're walking about a metre away from each other.

'There's a deli called the Garden on the next block,' I say in a professional, polite tone, my voice slightly raised to cover the distance between us.

'I know,' says Declan. He tucks his hands into his pockets, and the silence between us gets bigger.

'They do really good brownies,' I add, like I need to explain Yumi's comment. It also feels important to be more local than him somehow.

'Okay,' says Declan, infuriatingly calm. I'm desperate to ask whether he's had the brownies or not before, but I refuse to give him the satisfaction.

Thankfully, the deli is less than a two-minute walk away. I breathe out a small sigh of relief when we arrive.

The Garden is cosy and relaxed. It's a place that's always buzzing with warmth, and it's one of my favourite cafés in the city and now I have to sit at a table and make conversation with/be yelled at by Declan Archer and *this is a really bad idea*.

The thought makes me stop in the middle of the doorway, which turns out to be a bad idea, because Declan's chest bumps into my back and he automatically reaches out to steady me. His fingers are hot against my shoulders, and a spike of heat rushes to my chest.

'Are you okay?' he asks, his voice warm and too close. I jump away like I've been stung, and when I look back it's to see him watching me from under his cap, his eyebrow definitely raised this time.

'Fine,' I say, even though I am absolutely not. 'I'm fine.'

I can feel the weight of his presence behind me as I wind my way through the happy, bustling deli to a four-seater table in the back corner. I sit in the first seat I come to, slipping my shop keys out of my pocket and putting them on the table so I don't end up with a key-shaped indent in my bottom. Declan looks fleetingly at the seat next to me, but then sighs and sits down on the opposite side, facing the room.

He hesitates for a second before sliding his cap off. As though he doesn't want to, but can't bear the bad manners of wearing a hat indoors.

He runs a hand through his messy black curls, and when his eyes meet mine the green is so piercing that it feels sharp in my stomach. I clear my throat and focus instead on the faint mark on his head from his cap.

I've met this man once. I can literally count on two hands the number of sentences we've spoken to each other – or, at least, that I've spoken to him – and while the dedication burns through normal etiquette, it also puts me off balance. I've never had a book dedicated to me before.

I can still feel his eyes on me when a waitress arrives beside the table with a friendly smile and a notepad.

'What can I get you both?' she asks.

'A brownie, please. And a coff— tea,' I say, realising my error when Declan's gaze cuts to me. 'I would really love a tea.'

The words are like dirt in my mouth, and I am cursing the petty version of myself that thought it was a good idea to tell Declan Archer that I don't drink coffee.

Declan glances down at the menu, and for a moment he's not the outraged Declan, or the stiff, formal Declan. He's the man who first came to the bookshop – the too-handsome, too-bright author who I may have been too rude to. *The man who chose to write that dedication*, I remind myself.

His gaze flicks to me for a moment, and the corner of his mouth hitches almost imperceptibly. 'I'd kill for a coffee,' he says, turning to smile at the waitress. A full, proper smile that feels a little like lightning. 'The coffee here is amazing,' he tells me, his eyes laughing, and he one hundred per cent knows that I know it's amazing.

'That's lovely,' I say, like I'm not gritting my teeth.

'Isn't it?' says Declan.

The waitress leaves, and Declan runs a hand through his hair again. He meets my eyes and the smile falls from his face. As though he'd briefly forgotten why we were here.

'Look, I don't know what your intention was, alerting the media—' he finally begins.

'I didn't alert the media,' I say, before he can finish his sentence.

Declan sighs and rubs his head like he's already exhausted with the whole thing. 'There's no point in lying to me,' he says. 'It's done now.'

I clench my jaw at how dismissive he is. He's clearly already decided on his version of what happened.

'Why would I invite a crowd of people into my shop?' I ask.

Declan raises an eyebrow. 'Seriously?'

'Fine, but then why would I wait this long to do it?' I ask.

'Momentum for the book has been building,' says Declan, and it's an arrogant thing to say but there's something off about the way he says it – almost like he doesn't really want to be mentioning it. 'Maybe it's only just now that it's become worth your while.'

The waitress reappears and slides our order onto the table, and I manage to murmur a thank you.

Declan lifts his coffee cup and takes a sip, his green eyes sharp on mine.

I want to reach across the table and snatch it from him, to wipe the smug look off his face.

I didn't ask for any of this. I can't pretend I wasn't rude, but the dedication and anything that came after it? That's on him.

'I don't care what you believe,' I tell him. 'If you came here to yell at me, go ahead, get it over with and let me get back to my life.' I don't take a sip of my tea.

Declan huffs out a laugh. He closes his eyes.

'It's a little more complicated than that.'

Chapter Five

Despite everything, I seriously consider stealing a sip of his coffee while his eyes are closed and *what is wrong with me?*

I take a bite of brownie instead, to distract myself. It's satisfying and sweet, and gives me a very real burst of elation. So much so that I might actually moan a little.

Declan's eyes snap open. He swallows and I see the muscles in his neck tighten. The moment stretches for way too long, and the chocolate goes dry in my mouth.

I have got to get out of here.

'You have one minute to simplify it for me,' I manage to get out.

Declan's expression is shuttered. He rubs his forehead, then looks somewhere over my shoulder and clears his throat.

'My publicist has been hassling me for months about who the bookseller in the dedication is,' he says, his voice low.

'That's unfortunate for you,' I say, because, damn it, he makes me unbalanced. I have to get away from this man and his intense green eyes.

'You have thirty seconds now,' I tell him.

'Isn't that a little childish?' says Declan, his eyes returning to mine.

'Twenty,' I say, and the annoyance in his eyes is perversely satisfying.

'Have you read the book?' he asks suddenly.

'No,' I say. I don't tell him that I tried. That after what I'd said to him, I was determined to read it without judging it. 'I didn't get past the dedication. Probably I was too busy stumbling around in the dark.'

Even I can hear that the words are bitter, and they freeze in the air between us.

An unreadable expression flickers across Declan's face, and he opens his mouth as though to say something, but then closes it again and leans back in his chair. His shirt tightens over his arm muscles.

'It involves trees,' he says.

'I might've guessed,' I say, annoyed at him, annoyed at myself. 'From, you know, the title.'

'More specifically, it's about a man's search for himself through the wilderness,' says Declan.

'Of course it is.'

'Given the content, my publisher decided that it would be a good idea to do a series of book events in remote locations,' he says, ignoring me.

'Excellent. I hope you have fun with that,' I tell him, trying to push down the part of me that is curious. It may be petty and small-minded, but I don't want him to know I'm interested. I wrap the rest of the brownie in a napkin. Me and my brownie are leaving. 'That's a minute,' I tell him. 'Your time is up.'

'They want you to come.'

Declan doesn't yell, but the words are still too big for the space.

And, like an idiot, I hesitate.

'I'm sorry, what?'

'They want you to come,' Declan repeats. 'On the tour. My publisher wants you to come. The bookseller who they'd lined up had to pull out. My publicist thinks that having the bookseller from the dedication will give the book a boost. A "personal interest" angle.' He says the last part like it's choking him.

I laugh, and he watches me until it catches at the back of my throat and we're left staring at each other in silence.

He's not joking.

I shake my head. 'No.' Then, because I'd hate to add impoliteness to his list of grievances about me on top of everything else, I add, 'Thank you.'

Declan studies me. 'Why not?'

'Are you kidding me? Why the hell would I come?'

'They want you to sell books,' he says quietly. 'Hopefully, a lot of books. I'd have thought you'd jump at the chance. Isn't this why you leaked the dedication?'

His hand is still resting against the side of the coffee cup and he's looking up at me and I should leave, but I haven't. I should correct him, but I don't.

Instead, I stand there like a fool holding a brownie.

'I told my publisher I wanted to support independent booksellers where possible,' says Declan. 'Most of the places we're visiting don't have local bookshops, so I asked Fully Booked if they'd supply and sell the books.' He names my favourite bookshop in the city, and it makes me irrationally angry that he likes them too. He smiles, but there's no humour in it, no lightning. 'They had to pull out due to a family emergency, which just happened to be when you told the media that you were the bookseller in the dedication, and apparently managed to kill all my birds with one stone.'

I feel a fresh wave of fury in my gut.

'I didn't kill any birds,' I tell him, because I don't think he needs to know about the pigeon that flew into my windscreen six months ago.

'I assure you, you definitely killed some birds,' he says.

'What do you want, Declan?' I don't mean to say his name, and for a second he stills.

'I'm not sure how much clearer I can make it,' he says finally, looking away. 'My publisher will email you as well, but they want you to be the bookseller on tour. You bring the books, you sell the books. My publicist has a field day, and your bookshop makes some money. Everyone wins,' he adds, but in a way that leaves an unspoken 'except me' at the end of his sentence. Even though me being there sells more books for *him* too.

I pause.

'So you're saying that you need me?'

Something flares in Declan's eyes. 'You can frame it

however helps you sleep at night,' he says. Our eyes meet again, and there's a hint of mockery on his face. He pauses, then adds carefully, 'I should warn you that some of the tour would involve camping. I'll understand if that's not your thing.'

In this moment, I would rather drink a whole cup of tea than admit that I don't love camping. Which is just the sort of thinking that got me stuck with a cup of tea in the first place.

'Maybe the wilderness is where I go to find myself too,' I say, which is another straight-up lie.

'Is that a yes, then?' Declan asks. And there is such a stupid, inscrutable, superior look on his face that all my logic and reasoning and care goes out of the window.

I blame him entirely for everything that happens next. Including the madness that overtakes me and makes me reach across the table and pluck his still too-full coffee cup from in front of him. The smell steadies me for a heartbeat before I drain the rest. It's warm and rich and I wish the moment could last for at least thirty seconds longer.

Then I meet Declan's eyes and put the cup back on his saucer. Despite the buzz of sound in the deli, the clink it makes is sharp. I pull some cash from my pocket to cover the bill.

'It's a hell no,' I tell him, slapping it down on the table.

It's maybe my best exit ever, and I'm feeling prouder of myself than I'd like to admit, consequences be damned. I spin on my heel and I swear my hair *flicks* over my shoulder. And then I run into the chair behind me. *Crap.*

'Sorry,' I murmur to the woman very much sitting in it.

She frowns, tucks her handbag in closer to her chest, then shuffles her chair towards her table.

I can sense Declan's eyes on my back, and then he stands. I feel the air shift, compressing and tightening in the space between us.

'No problem,' he says, and there's just a hint of smugness in his voice, like maybe provoking me into saying no was actually exactly what he wanted. 'I'll let my publicist know, but if you could just confirm that via email when they contact you that would be great. Nice to see you again, Clarence,' he says. He slides too much money onto the table on top of mine, tugging his cap on his head as he walks past.

Then he's weaving his way back through the tables, and now there's no way I can leave without it looking like I'm following him.

'Your cap is silly,' I say loudly. The woman at the table shifts a little further away from me, and damn Declan Archer for stealing my exit.

Chapter Six

The email from Declan's publicist comes in the next morning. I barely notice it, though, because the quote from Mike the electrician comes in at the same time.

For five minutes I can't do anything more than lie in bed and stare at the crack in the windowsill that I haven't fixed.

It's bad.

So bad, that if I do rewire the shop – which I *have* to – I won't be able to pay any of the other bills in the drawer. We won't survive past the end of next month.

I try to focus on my breathing, but it keeps catching in my throat.

I want to go back three years. To curl up in the beanbag in the corner of Brooks' and watch Gran bustling around the shop, filling it with life and energy and hope. To remember when it was a place that felt safe and happy, instead of a place whose survival depends solely on me. To hear Gran tell me that everything is going to be okay.

I rub my chest and reach for my phone. I have no idea what to do, but I know I need to see her today.

Can you open up this morning?

Yumi replies almost immediately.

No problem, boss. Take all the time you need.

It's so sincere that I know she's hacked my email again and seen the quote from Mike and I can't even bring myself to care. Then, as though realising that she's given herself away, Yumi sends a follow-up message.

Locking up yesterday and opening today
will mean I've used my key three times now.
You should definitely consider buying me a gift.

A calendar alert comes through a second later: a reminder from Mum about our lunch today.

I close my eyes and then push myself out of bed.

I always have mixed feelings about coming to Glenhaven.

The building itself is beautiful – an old, Queen Anne revival-style house that has been renovated just enough so that it's not freezing in the winter, but not so much that it's lost its heart. It also has gardens everywhere, pockets of space where residents can be outdoors without having to talk to anyone else if they don't want to.

But it's also a reminder that Gran doesn't live in her town house any more. The one that had barely any garden but was also somehow bursting with plants. She never had enough space, but she never cared, because the park was only a short walk away. And if the park was full of people? Well, that was just an added bonus.

Someone buzzes me in, and I head straight to Gran's room. She isn't there, and it makes my heart trip with hope. Maybe she's having a good day today.

Mary, the nurse on duty at reception, greets me with a warm smile. 'How's tricks today, sweetheart?'

'I'm okay. How's your new grandson?'

Mary's eyes light up with a joy so bright that my chest aches again and the edges of my smile slip. 'He's the cleverest baby in all of Australia,' she confides. 'And the most handsome. Not that I am in any way biased. I'll bring him into your bookshop one day soon to show him off.'

I breathe through my nose. 'I'd like that.' I don't tell her it will have to be in the next few weeks.

Mary winks, then nods down the corridor. 'Last I saw your Gran she was in the relaxing room.'

I hesitate for a second. 'Is she . . .'

'She's doing pretty well today,' Mary says, her eyes softening along with her smile. 'Though knowing Margaret, I'm sure she's telling everyone what's what down there.'

'Thanks, Mary.'

The relaxing room is just a classier name for the TV room. Sure enough, that's where I find Gran, arguing with one of the other residents about changing the channel on the communal television.

'No one wants to watch a show about cooking.' The man is towering over Gran but she stares him down from her place on the couch. 'Give us the handsome doctors!' she chants. She glances at me when I walk in. 'Tell him, Peggy, no one wants to watch a cooking show.'

A wave of guilt washes over me even as a too-familiar punch of devastation hits me in the gut. Peggy is my mum's name. But Gran is up and alert. It's a good day, no matter that she doesn't recognise me. That she might never recognise me again.

'Sometimes there are handsome chefs on the cooking shows as well,' I tell her and the man she's arguing with crows in delight. He takes advantage of Gran's momentary distraction to snatch the remote from her hand and turn the volume up. Then he pushes his walker triumphantly back to his seat in the front row, waving the remote control around like a freaking sceptre.

Gran glares at me. 'What did you do that for?' she asks.

'I wanted you all to myself,' I tell her. It's not even a lie. 'If there were too many good-looking men and women on the screen, I wouldn't get a word out of you.'

Gran looks away, and I allow myself to swallow before I gently steer her out of the relaxing room and into the living area, away from the man and his remote control.

It's quieter in the living area, and I carefully help Gran into an armchair at one of the coffee tables on the edges. She leans back in the fading green chair and looks around, the dispute over the cooking show seemingly forgotten.

There's a couple playing chess two tables away from us, their speed probably averaging about a move every five minutes. On the opposite side of the room, there's a man reading a book and a woman just staring out of the window at the trees.

For a moment we sit in silence. When Gran was in the bookshop, she was perpetually in motion or in conversation with someone. She knew everyone in the neighbourhood by name, and some days it seemed like she had more regulars than books in the store. Some people who came in didn't even pretend to look at the shelves. They just came for a chat.

Everyone has stories, Clarrie, she would whisper to me. *They might not all have a shiny cover.*

I clear my throat, trying not to let the memories choke me. 'I brought you something,' I tell her. I reach down into my bag and pull out a new jumper and a thriller by a debut author I read last week that I know she would love, and I put them on the table. Gran looks at the book, but doesn't pick it up.

'What's that for?' she asks.

'I thought maybe I could read you some,' I tell her past the lump that perpetually lodges itself in my throat when I visit. I shouldn't be mourning – Gran is right here; she's sitting right in front of me. But every time I see her it's like a little piece of the grandmother I remember has faded. Like the memories I have are being rewritten into a new story that I don't quite understand. And every time I have that thought it's followed by a wave of guilt because it's so *selfish*, but I still haven't found a way to stop it creeping in.

'I have a bookshop,' Gran tells me. 'It has the best window

displays in the city, you know. We made one for *Charlotte's Web* once. Arthur will tell you.' She looks around. 'Where is he?'

'He's not here at the moment,' I tell her softly.

She shakes her head. 'Arthur is hopeless with crafts. I do all the displays in our bookshop. It has the best window displays in the city, you know.'

'I can imagine.'

She looks at the table, her eyes drifting to the book again. 'I should go. I have to pick up Clarrie from school and take her to the shop. She loves it there almost as much as I love having her there. Like two peas in a pod, we are.' She tries to push herself up, and I should help her, should find a way to distract her, but for a second I'm frozen in place.

She loves it there almost as much as I love having her there.

She mutters in frustration when she can't easily get up and it yanks me back to myself. I reach out a hand to steady her back into the chair, then open the first page of the book. My voice only shakes a little as I start reading and she gradually relaxes back into her seat.

I try to imagine what she would say about the shop's wiring.

She'd probably have found six solutions already, and would want to hear about Declan Archer and the book tour instead. She'd have already read his book, laughed for hours at the dedication, then taken my hands and told me that I deserved to be the subject of a thousand dedications.

She and Yumi probably would have made a stack of posters weeks ago announcing that I was the bookseller in the dedication and conned every local business within five miles to display them in their windows.

Or maybe none of that would have happened, because I wouldn't have been alone the day Declan Archer came in. She would have still been there with me, the way she was always meant to be.

But being here with her reminds me of one thing: she'd have fought for the bookshop with everything she had to give.

For a second, I think about the money that guaranteed extra sales on a book tour would bring in. A fleeting image of Declan Archer's green eyes, of him arching a smug eyebrow flits through my mind, and I push it away. A loan from my parents is preferable to that.

Even if the thought is like lead in my stomach.

Chapter Seven

Bernard's is a restaurant halfway between my parents' house and the bookshop, and it's one of those places that always makes me feel like I've got the dress code wrong.

My mum is already waiting at her usual table. She stands when she sees me, a frown lightly puckering the skin on her forehead.

'Clarence.' She leans forward and presses her cheek briefly against mine in one of those moves I'm never quite sure is a hug or a kiss. We both sit. I tug the cloth napkin from the table onto my lap, trying not to fiddle with the edges as Mum opens the menu. 'How are you?' she asks. She barely pauses her scanning to glance over the top at me. 'Are you well?'

Not really, no. At the moment, I feel like every part of me is braced for impact, and the idea of asking if I can borrow money to fix the electricals in the shop makes me want to break out in a cold sweat. I'll do it. Just . . . not yet.

'I'm good, thanks,' I say just as a waiter arrives at the table. He fills our water glasses, then picks up Mum's napkin and shakes it with a flourish. She leans back slightly, still looking at the menus while he places it on her lap, and the two of them somehow do it so smoothly that it looks like the whole thing was choreographed. The waiter turns to me, and I see the panic in his eyes as his gaze flicks between the table and the napkin already thrown haphazardly onto my lap. But unlike me he is not an amateur, and it takes less than a second for him to nod discreetly and back away gracefully like it never happened.

'How are you?' I ask Mum.

'Fine,' says Mum. 'It's been a busy week as usual, but Ben came for dinner last night with the kids. He's up for a promotion,' she tells me.

'That's great,' I say. I genuinely mean it. Ben always wanted to be a lawyer, and I know how hard he works. But there's something about the pride in Mum's voice that makes me feel like a ten-year-old trying to get her attention again. I take a sip of water.

The conversation stalls, and the waiter rematerialises at my elbow to top up my water. *Is he watching us? It feels like he's watching us.*

'Sorry I couldn't answer your call yesterday,' I tell Mum, instead of asking her if she thinks the waiter is watching us. Or, you know, for the money I need to stop Gran's dream dying. 'We had a busy day at the bookshop.'

I don't miss the slight purse of her lips at the mention of the bookshop.

'I heard,' she says, stacking her menu on top of mine. 'Heather Bradley phoned. She told me that there was an article about it on the internet.'

My mother's group of friends could honestly run the

country if they wanted to. They know everything – often two hours before everyone else does. I used to love hearing their take on the world. Until I heard one of them telling Mum what a shame it was that I'd dropped out of law school – before I'd actually worked up the courage to tell her.

'It was something to do with Declan Archer, wasn't it?' she continues. 'I've heard his new book is very good. Beth is friends with his mother.'

I try not to grit my teeth. Mum has never been a big reader. Gran always used to joke that it was the ultimate case of teenage rebellion – to have parents who owned a bookshop and not like reading. This is the first time Mum's mentioned anything even vaguely related to books in the last six months – and of course it's a book that I haven't read, by a man I can't stand.

'It's done very well,' I say, twisting my glass and wishing for a heartbeat that we had the kind of relationship where I could talk to her about everything that's happening. Not just to ask her for help with the loan . . . but to really talk to her. To tell her about Declan, and about the dedication, and about how worried I am about the drawer full of bills.

Mum signals to the waiter and he appears seconds later with a pen and notepad in hand. She orders a steak, which she always does, and I pick the one vegetarian option before the waiter glides away again.

I clear my throat, readying myself to ask about the loan, when Mum speaks again. 'I ran into Mitchell Harper a few days ago – you remember, the dean of your law school?'

My chest tightens. 'I remember,' I say, instead of reminding her that I don't have a law school.

'He mentioned that if you wanted to go back, you could get credit for the subjects that you've already done,' says Mum.

'Did he?' I say, my heart twisting as familiar disappointment washes over me. I don't know why I thought it would be different, this time.

'You know, it's not too late for you to build whatever career you want to have, Clarrie,' she continues.

'I'm pretty busy running Gran's bookshop right now.' It comes out sharp, and Mum's hands still.

'There is no need for that tone.'

'Sorry,' I say. I rub my head and meet her eyes. 'I'm sorry.'

'You look tired, Clarence,' she tells me, and I immediately want to take back my apology. 'You're spending too much time at that shop.'

'It's my job. I have to be there. I want to be there. And I don't *want* to go back to law school.'

Mum ignores the tone this time. 'I told you weeks ago that we would help you sell,' she says. 'I've already arranged to speak with an estate agent this week and Ben told me last night he's spoken to someone about drawing up the paperwork.'

The words hook themselves into my stomach and tug hard, taking me by surprise, even though they shouldn't. For a whisper of a second, I actually let myself imagine the possibility and I hate myself for it.

I'm shaking my head before I can finish the thought. It's always the same thing.

'It's Gran's legacy, Mum – the thing she literally spent her life building. Does that not matter to you?'

Mum is silent, and my stomach drops. There's no way I'm going to be able to ask her for a loan now. 'Clarence, don't overreact,' she says finally in her best measured voice. 'We're just thinking about your future.'

I close my eyes, wondering why I thought there might even be a chance that Mum and I could have a conversation that didn't inevitably go this way.

'I saw Gran today,' I tell her.

'Lovely,' says Mum, but I can hear in her voice that she doesn't mean it. Gran has been in Glenhaven for over two years and, as far as I know, Mum has visited her a grand total of six times, on holidays and special occasions – because she's a dutiful daughter like that. *She's your mother*, I want to scream, but yelling never works.

'Right,' I say, and the silence between us feels like it could swallow me.

The waiter arrives with our food, but he's so damn graceful that even him putting the plates on the table doesn't manage to break the silence.

Then Mum makes a comment about the weather, and from there we move on to food and Dad's new fishing rod and Ben's new house. We don't talk about the bookshop, or Gran, and by the end of lunch all I want to do is curl up in a ball and weep.

Brooks' is half full when I finally make it back, and Yumi throws herself at me when I walk through the door.

'Are you okay?' I ask, mildly alarmed.

'Grand,' says Yumi. She studies me, and I try to keep the emotion of the day, of another failure with my mother, from my face. 'Do you want to talk about it?' she asks.

'No.' I might, at some point, but everything feels too raw right now.

'Okay,' says Yumi, but she doesn't move, and after much too long of her staring into my eyes she sighs dramatically. 'This means I can't ask you about Declan Archer today as well, doesn't it?'

Even in this state his name sends a bolt of panic through my stomach, and I swear at least two customers look up.

'It does,' I confirm.

She points a finger at my face. 'When we do finally cover your date, the detail had better be excellent.'

'It wasn't a—' but Yumi just steps back, closes her eyes and holds out her hand.

'I'm ready for my gift now.'

Her message this morning feels like a year ago. I've honestly got nothing, but I fish around in my bag just in case and my hand closes around the cloth napkin from the restaurant. *Whoops*. Still, I place it in her outstretched palm.

'I don't even need to open my eyes to know that this is a very disappointing gift,' Yumi says disapprovingly.

'You can go home early instead if you want,' I tell her, rubbing my forehead. There's a part of me that knows it's money the shop can't really afford, but Yumi is incredible, and I want to be able to give her this. To feel like today hasn't been crap for everyone.

'Now?' says Yumi, her eyes still closed.

'Now,' I confirm. At least the people milling around the shop mean I won't be completely alone with my thoughts.

'Deal. But I am also keeping this very fancy napkin.' She tucks it into the front of her dress – somehow managing to make it look cool – then slides her bag over her shoulder. 'Don't think I don't know you're partly sending me home because you want privacy to think about a certain very handsome and clearly-hot-for-you author.'

The idea that Declan Archer is hot for me almost makes me laugh out loud, but the way I'm feeling today it's entirely possible that if I start laughing it will quickly lead to hysterical sobbing. I look over Yumi's shoulder and sort of vaguely smile like there's a customer there, and Yumi rolls her eyes.

'I see right through you, Brooks,' she says.

She hugs me tight, and I blink back the tears that spring to my eyes.

Thankfully, I manage to pull myself together and, by the time I do, there actually *is* a customer at the counter.

The afternoon is steady, but not nearly as hectic as it was yesterday, and it goes by quickly. At least half of the sales are *Talking to Trees,* and every time I sell a copy I'm honestly too exhausted by the whole thing to even feel like grinding my teeth. By the time the end of the day rolls round, I can see the cover on the back of my eyelids. The only thing I'm thankful for is that Declan's arrogant face isn't on it.

The bell finally jangles for the last time, and I flip the

sign to *closed*. The books stare silently back at me, as though they're waiting for something, but I don't know what to offer them.

I pull Mike's quote up on the computer, and, because I apparently am a sucker for punishment, I open the drawer full of bills too. I stare at them all until my eyes blur.

What the hell am I going to do?

I could approach Dad about the loan, but that would just end with him talking to Mum, and then me arguing about the bookshop with her anyway. Asking Ben won't be any better. And I know that it's stupidly, desperately urgent, but, after seeing Gran and after everything that happened with Mum, I feel too wrung out to think about it today. Maybe I'll win the lottery overnight. It's a mark of how desperate I feel that I actually, seriously think about going via the newsagent to buy a lottery ticket on the way home.

We're in trouble. Trouble that can't be fixed by shoving my problems in a drawer.

I sit at the front counter until the light begins to dim outside, flick on the fairy lights in the display window because Yumi will kill me if I don't, then I pull the door closed behind me and lock it.

The night nips at my bare skin and it's a few minutes before I realise that I left my jacket inside. My shop keys aren't in my bag though, and I don't remember where I put them – I haven't used them since I opened up yesterday morning. On top of everything, it just feels like too much.

I lean back against the side of the shop, the bricks already cold from the chill that has hold of the air, and I realise that I am stupidly, desperately close to tears. Over a jacket.

Three breaths, Clarrie.

Three breaths and then I'll find the energy to hunt for the keys again, or to start walking.

I'm only up to the second breath when I hear someone coming down the street. I wipe my eyes with my sleeve, wondering why it is that I even care so much what a stranger on the street thinks of me.

But as they get closer I realise it's not a stranger.

It's Declan freaking Archer.

Chapter Eight

My breath tightens in my chest. I've got maybe twenty seconds before he recognises me – if he hasn't already. But there are no good options: it's not dark enough for me to hide against the wall of the bookshop, but there's also no way I can run to the end of the street without him seeing me.

Then I see that the light is on in Ruth's antique shop. It's not ideal, but it's better than the alternative. Maybe she hasn't left yet. Maybe, if I ask really nicely, she'll let me take refuge in her shop for five minutes. I dart to her bright red door before I can talk myself out of it, lifting my hand to knock softly, if a little desperately.

Less than a second later, the door swings open.

'Clarrie?' Ruth's eyes are wide through her blue-rimmed glasses. She has a massive pink scarf wrapped round her neck, and she looks like a hug. It always hurts seeing her, because she reminds me of Gran, but today my overwhelming feeling is relief that on top of everything I'm not going to have to try to spar with Declan Archer. 'You came!' The delight in her voice squeezes at my heart, but also: *we don't have time for this.*

'Hi, Ruth.' I try to smile and my cheek muscles hurt almost

immediately. 'Is it okay if I come in?' I resist the urge to look back over my shoulder.

'Of course, of course!' she says, opening the door wider.

I pretty much dive inside the light, warm shop, relief coursing through me when the door clicks closed behind me.

Ruth stares at me for a moment, shaking her head. And there are . . . *are they tears in her eyes?* Just the sight of them has me blinking back my own again. *Please don't let her ask me how I am.* But she doesn't. Instead, she reaches forward and takes one of my hands.

'I'm so pleased you're here, Clarrie. We've missed your grandmother so much. Not that that's why I asked you . . . Oh, I'm rambling. I'm sorry, dear – do come on in.'

I'm about to ask what she's talking about when it finally sinks in. The pink scarf. The reference to Gran. *Crap.* It's Knit, Stitch and Yarn night. I can't believe I forgot it was Knit, Stitch and Yarn night. I don't want to see anyone right now, let alone a gang of Gran's friends. I want to be at home on my couch with a blanket at least three times the size of me and a tub of ice cream.

But then Ruth is leading me to the back of the shop and she's chattering about how wonderful it is and how thrilled everyone will be to see me. There's no way I can leave now without it being horribly rude. *Half an hour*, I tell myself. *I can last half an hour.* At least then Declan Archer will have well and truly disappeared from the street.

Hopefully, no one will notice that the glue holding my smile in place is not really sticking.

Ruth's shop is a collection of wonders. It's filled to the brim with *stuff*: display cabinets, old sewing machines and enough crockery to cater for a wedding of about 6,000 people. Somehow, though, there doesn't seem to be a speck of dust in the entire shop. As though Ruth personally threatened every last one while wearing a kind smile and a home-knitted sweater. The familiarity is both warm and crippling. Before Gran went to Glenhaven, I came here with her sometimes. I loved listening to the conversations and watching her and her friends bicker and knit. But it's been eighteen months since I've seen most of them.

As we near the back of the shop, deeper into the collection of furniture, soft voices and the click of needles filter towards us. I follow Ruth round a massive bookshelf to a long table covered with fabric, baskets of wool and half a dozen different projects. There are six people sitting around it – four women and two men. I recognise all but one of the women – an older lady with bright pink hair who is furiously knitting. Then there's Sofia from the bakery, plus Diane and Min, who used to play bridge with Gran. There's gruff Frank from the butcher, and then there's Alistair, who I only met once, but who Gran sometimes told stories about. The conversation halts when they see us, and Ruth wraps an arm around my shoulders.

'Everyone, you remember Clarrie – Margaret's granddaughter. Clarrie, this is everyone.'

'Hi, Clarrie,' the group all chorus, and Sofia gives me a little wave.

'Hi,' I say, waving back at Sofia like I'm on autopilot.

Ruth eyeballs Alistair. 'I'm trusting you to remember the rules and make Clarence feel welcome. We want her to come back again.'

Alistair – spry, mischievous-looking, with light grey hair and sparkling eyes – winks at me. 'Always,' he says. 'I'm so focused on this blanket that I couldn't possibly find time to cause any trouble.'

'That same blanket you've been working on for the past two and a half years?' says Ruth, raising an eyebrow.

'Masterpieces take time,' says Alistair.

Sofia pats the seat between her and Alistair, a warmth on her face that threatens to make me crumble.

I mutter hellos to everyone as I make my way round the table. Halfway down, the woman with the short pink hair glances up at me. I'm smiling politely at her when she shoots out a hand to grab my arm. Before I can ask her what on earth she's doing, she tugs on my sleeve and pulls me down towards her. Then she studies my forehead, her deep wrinkles sucking in even more of her skin as she frowns. I'm so shocked that I don't move a muscle, and I'm still standing there five seconds later when she starts shaking her head and sighing like I've disappointed her.

'Your head is too small,' she announces. Then she lets go of my sleeve and picks up her knitting again, as though the encounter never happened. I blink, and then I've somehow been ushered down the table and am sitting on a chair that's at least as old as I am, staring at blankets, scarves and what must be ten baskets full of wool.

What the hell just happened?

'Don't mind Susan,' says Alistair, leaning in and watching the woman with the pink hair who is knitting and muttering. 'She's making a beanie for her grandson and apparently all of us have the wrong sized head.'

I'm not sure whether to laugh or to cry.

'Clarrie, it's so good to see you,' says Diane, and I look up to meet her eyes between blankets across the table. 'We've missed Margaret so much.' Her eyes fill with tears and I feel mine threaten to do the same. *She's still there,* I remind myself, the way I always do. *Gran is still around.*

Diane reaches across the table to take one of my hands, and I'm just about to pull away and excuse myself – I was wrong; there's no way I can even get through half an hour – when she knocks over one of the baskets, and the short gruff man next to her furrows his thick, grey eyebrows.

'Steady on, Diane,' he says.

'Oh, shut it, Frank,' she says, looking at me with a smile even as she snaps at him. 'I just want to check in and see how Clarrie is.'

'I'm fine, thanks, Diane,' I say, hoping the short answer will prevent too many follow-on questions.

'And how is Margaret? Have you seen her recently? We all just think it's so lovely that you're running the bookshop.'

It's well meaning, but it still makes my stomach twist. I think of the light in Gran's eyes earlier today and of the quote burning a hole in my email.

I'm just working out how to breathe and answer when

I'm saved by the most unlikely source: a loud knock at the front door.

Everyone from the table looks up, and Frank's eyebrows jump up his forehead.

'Another newcomer?' he mutters under his breath. 'No, thank you.'

Ruth hasn't sat down yet, and she's already making her way back towards the front door to see who it is.

Diane hushes Frank and then smiles worriedly at me, like I might take it personally that he doesn't really want me here. Although, if anything, his attitude is actually making it easier not to break down. All of which I register out of a small corner of my brain. Because, after the initial rush of relief, my stomach has been flooded with something else: trepidation.

Declan Archer was the last person I saw on the street.

I tell myself that I'm being stupid. There's no way Declan would be knocking on the door of a random antique shop. *He didn't see me.*

But then I hear a low voice that rushes down my spine, and I don't know whether to hide under the table or to grab an armful of wool, throw it into the air in an attempt to distract everyone and run out as fast as I can. The point is moot, anyway, because I can't move.

I can't move.

'Come inside!' I hear Ruth's muffled exclamation. *No, please stay the hell outside, thank you.* I cannot see Declan Archer on top of everything else today.

'I really must get going,' says the voice, and there's no

denying that it's him. *How has it taken him this long to walk the twenty steps to Ruth's door? Did he stop for a coffee on the way?*

'I insist,' says Ruth. 'Just for a few minutes, until you warm up!' I can't believe that five minutes ago I thought her voice was kind. *Stop being so damn pushy, Ruth!*

Declan's protests are clearly in vain against Ruth's aggressive friendliness. It's a small comfort that he doesn't actually want to come inside.

So why the hell is he here?

Chapter Nine

I sink lower into my seat, briefly meeting Alistair's gaze as I do. He doesn't say anything, but his eyes glitter with curiosity and warmth.

I stare resolutely at the table. Maybe if I don't actually *see* Declan, I can pretend that the voice doesn't belong to him. Never mind that my whole body feels like it's on alert.

'Clarrie!' calls Ruth, her voice clearer as she emerges from behind the bookshelf. I can feel everyone's eyes on me, and my breath is tight in my lungs. I wish there were another six tables' worth of wool between us. But if I keep my head down he's going to think I'm *scared* of him.

So I look up.

Ruth is grinning at me, her smile wide and conspiratorial. And beside her, his curls sticking up in a way that looks unfairly good and his green eyes bright, is Declan. He holds my gaze, and I feel my stupid breath catch in my throat. Dimly, I realise that he's not wearing his cap. Because of what I said yesterday? Or more likely, you know, because it's dark outside. *Get it together, Clarrie.*

'Clarrie, you won't believe it, but Declan here found your

keys.' Ruth waves a set in her hand and I tear my eyes away from him to look at what she's holding.

My keys to the shop.

They were on the freaking table in the deli yesterday.

And, just like that, anger flares in the pit of my stomach. 'Did you steal them?' I blurt out. He did – very memorably – leave before me.

'If I stole them,' says Declan with infuriating patience, like me leading with an accusation isn't surprising, 'why would I bring them back here?'

'Oh!' gasps Diane in a voice I'm pretty sure is meant to be a whisper but is very much not. 'Maybe he wanted an excuse to see you again!'

Declan doesn't look at her, but his eyes flash, and does he *flinch*? An answering flush rises to my cheeks and *damn it.*

'I had to go back to the deli for something,' clips Declan. 'They gave them to me.'

'Why would they do that?'

'I don't know,' says Declan. 'Maybe they thought we were friends.'

I'm suddenly aware that *everyone* in Knit, Stitch and Yarn is following our conversation like we're in a tennis match. Declan doesn't even look at them, his gaze fixed firmly on mine. My face feels like it's on fire.

'Thank you,' I manage to choke out. 'That's so kind of you to bring them here. How did you know where I was?'

'I was on my way to the bookshop and I saw you come in here,' says Declan curtly. 'I tried this morning, but there was a crowd. The shop was already open, so I thought you'd manage until tonight.' His gaze flicks around at the group of people, as though just remembering they're there, then down at the floor.

'Right,' I say.

This group of people who were very talkative a few minutes ago is completely silent. Waiting.

Declan clears his throat.

'Well, thanks for your assistance,' he says to Ruth, like he's about to leave.

'No.'

The word is short, firm and decisively uttered.

The silence – if possible – becomes even more stark, and everyone turns to look at pink-haired Susan.

She rests her knitting on the table, then narrows her eyes until they almost disappear.

'I need your head.'

Declan frowns at me as though it's me insisting that he can't leave because of his head. For the first time since my conversation with Mum, I almost feel like laughing. Though in a desperate, hysterical kind of way.

When he hesitates, Ruth smiles at him kindly – I'm not sure she knows another way to smile.

'You don't have to stay, Declan,' she says. 'Though you are, of course, most welcome to.'

'He does have to stay,' says Susan. Then, in a move I definitely didn't see coming, her whole posture softens. When she speaks, it's with a totally different tone to what I've heard come out of her mouth since I've been here. 'My grandson lives in

London,' she explains to Declan with tears in her eyes. 'He can't afford to come back home for holidays, and I can't afford to visit. I'm making him this beanie to connect us. Your head is the same size as his.'

Everyone looks at Declan again. There's no way he can possibly refuse without looking totally heartless.

For a second, he looks like he's on the brink of leaving anyway, but then he exhales sharply and with a glance at me so quick I might've imagined it, he starts moving around the table to where Susan is sitting.

Her tears dry up almost instantly, and she points to the seat next to her.

'Sit there,' she says.

Declan sits and I keep my gaze carefully fixed forward. Out of the corner of my eye, I see Susan wrapping a piece of wool round his head to measure it. Declan moves slightly, and Susan smacks him on the arm. A laugh hums unexpectedly in my stomach, and I meet Alistair's eyes to see him grinning.

The silence that's overtaken the table begins to thaw, and gradually chatter starts up again. It feels as though Declan and I have always been part of whatever this madness is.

Then Sofia rests her hand against my arm. 'He's very handsome,' she says. 'Did you say you aren't friends?'

'No,' I say. 'I mean *yes*. I mean we aren't friends.'

I stumble over the words and before I can stop myself my eyes flick to Declan again. His gaze is on Susan in front of him. He doesn't move, but there's something about the way he's holding himself that leaves me in little doubt that he can hear every word. Although the tension could just be from the fact that she's waving her knitting needles in his face.

'Oh, look at that,' breathes Diane, looking between the two of us. My cheeks heat immediately and, not for the first time in the past forty-eight hours, I curse both Declan Archer and whatever genetics made me so prone to blushing.

'Maybe you're not friends because you're destined to be *lovers*,' says Min before I can recover, and *holy crap*.

'Hush up, all of you,' says Alistair, leaning forward in his chair and banging on the table.

This time Declan does look over. Unreadable eyes meet mine before I can look away, and heat spreads through my chest. *Seriously, is there no way to stop a blush before it makes it the whole way across your face?* If Alistair notices, he doesn't say anything. Just points a finger at Diane.

'You're just trying to take the attention off the sparks flying between you and Mr Grumpypants over there.'

Diane's eyes go wide and Frank's disappear under his eyebrows while Sofia crows with delight beside me.

'This old fart?' says Diane, recovering more swiftly and with infinitely more class than I managed to. 'Like I'd have him.'

Frank guffaws. 'Think very highly of yourself, don't you?'

'As I rightly should,' says Diane.

Their bickering carries the conversation forward, the others joining in with their own opinions, and then Ruth brings a pot of tea over which seems to calm the whole situation down. Whatever the case, it has the very relieving effect of taking the focus off me.

When I manage to pull myself under control, I turn to face Alistair in the seat beside me.

'Thank you,' I whisper to him.

'We're a nosy lot,' says Alistair. 'I would have hidden you with my blanket, but I'm afraid it's only just big enough to cover your forehead so far,' he adds with a wink, holding up what must be six rows of stitching.

He notices my scrutiny of whatever it is he's making.

'Two and a half years,' he says proudly. 'It's the least anyone has managed to accomplish in the history of the group, not that your gran didn't try to beat me at being the worst.' His voice softens. 'She was up to row seven, last time we compared.'

My eyes meet his, but he doesn't say anything. He just covers one of my cold hands with his warm one and before I can start crying, he begins talking loudly about how superior knitting is to crocheting, setting off another argument across the table between Frank and Diane.

I end up staying for almost an hour, and I don't talk to Declan the entire time. Still, his presence is like an annoying magnet, tugging at my senses. I must get used to it eventually, though, because as time passes I begin to feel . . . not comfortable, exactly, but not like crying any more either. Alistair helps. He acts as my buffer, chatting to me between dropping bombshells in the conversations around us.

But when, towards the end of the evening, I overhear Diane enquire about Declan's relationship status with what is most assuredly a furtive look at me, I freeze. *What the hell, Diane?*

'I'm not dating,' says Declan. His voice is slightly husky – he hasn't spoken in the hour he's been here – but there's a firmness in it that I haven't heard before. He doesn't offer anything further, and the entire group falls silent, like his words are still echoing in the air. And *oh my goodness is Min looking at me with sympathy?* I want to announce that I don't even want to date him, but that will undoubtedly make them think I do.

'Hear, hear,' says Frank. Diane glares at him.

'What is it that you do for work, Declan?' asks Ruth tentatively, and a twinge of defensiveness and something else trickles through me.

'I write,' is all Declan says, but his voice is cautious now rather than curt.

'A writer!' says Ruth. 'Would I know anything you've written?'

'Maybe,' says Declan. He doesn't announce that he's becoming the hottest thing since sliced bread – which, okay, fine, would be a weird thing to announce, given that bread is not hot unless you put it in a toaster. And, even then, it's either mildly warm or burnt, depending on how crappy your crap toaster is.

Then Ruth turns to me.

'Clarrie, do you have any of Declan's books in the bookshop?' she asks. She's so lovely and earnest and I want to shove her question back in her mouth.

'We've got a few copies,' I manage to mumble. I think about lying and telling her I sent most of them back to the publisher because it just wasn't selling, rather than that we've all but sold out. But Declan will know I'm lying anyway, and it would probably just make him more arrogant.

'Very good,' she says. 'Hopefully it won't be as busy as it was yesterday – you had quite a crowd outside. Is there another Lord of the Rings book out?'

I don't know how to answer. Declan's mouth twitches, the side curving up ever so slightly.

'If you do decide to buy a copy of my book, I'd be happy to sign it for you,' he says to Ruth, and then he unleashes the smile – the real one – and it stuns at least half the room.

For the first time in an hour, the desperate urge to leave sweeps over me again. This time, though, it's to get as far away from that smile, from his smugness, as I can. I manage a few more minutes before I push my chair back with a calm I don't quite feel.

'I should be off,' I say to Ruth. 'Thank you for tonight.'

'It was so good to see you, darling,' says Ruth, leaning in for a hug. 'Maybe we'll see you next month?'

She smells like lavender and warmth, and I nod noncommittally against her shoulder. I don't look back, but I can feel Declan's gaze like prickles against my skin. And, even though I'm leaving first, even though he still has a piece of Susan's yarn wrapped around his head, I'm not entirely sure I won this round, either.

Chapter Ten

'Your mum said *what*?' says Yumi, staring at me across the table. The lights flicker above as the kettle coos beside us, all reminders of the quote that is slowly beginning to choke me.

It's midday and after another flat-out morning we've just closed the bookshop to have lunch. I've barely stopped to breathe, and it's the first chance Yumi and I have had to talk. Despite her trying to insist that we start with Declan Archer, so far we haven't made it past my mum explaining to me that she was in the process of arranging to sell the shop.

'It's not the first time,' I tell Yumi, breaking apart the cookie on the plate between us and taking a bite. Thinking about lunch yesterday gives me sharp pains in the chest, but the chocolate is helping.

'Not the first time?' Yumi exclaims. 'I knew she was pressuring you to sell, but I didn't know she was actually trying to make it happen. Why have you never mentioned it?'

I surprise us both by saying the words aloud. 'Because it's easier to pretend it's not happening.' Yumi meets my eyes, then nods and takes a piece of the cookie.

'Can she do that?' she asks, popping it in her mouth.

I shake my head. 'The bookshop is mine,' I tell her, thankful for confidence in this at least. 'Gran signed it all over to me.'

It was just after I'd left my degree. I was working out what on earth I was going to do next, and Gran had sat me down at the table Yumi and I are sitting at now, and she'd offered me a lifeline. There was such a light in her eyes, such a hope for the future – hers, mine and the bookshop's. She had enough passion for all of us.

'We can do it together, Clarrie. I'll be right here with you.'

Then a month later she got lost in the supermarket, and a month after that she accidentally set her kitchen on fire. Two months after that she was in Glenhaven, and a year later she'd stopped recognising me.

Yumi and I both stare at the remaining piece of cookie on the table for a while. After what I'm guessing she thinks is an appropriate amount of time to wait following a serious discussion, she picks it up. Then she pauses.

'So,' she says. 'Can we talk about a certain dark-haired, bright-eyed hunk of handsome now?'

'Hunk of handsome?' It's times like this that I wish I could raise one eyebrow.

'I panicked at the last minute,' says Yumi. 'But I stand by it.'

'I don't know who you're talking about,' I tell her. 'As I don't know any hunks of hand—You know what, I can't even do it. I can't call anyone that.'

Yumi wiggles her eyebrows at me.

'Clarrie and Declan, sitting in a tree, K-I-S-S—'

'Are you seven?' I interrupt her.

'It might just seem that way to you because you're old,' says Yumi. She wiggles her eyebrows again, and I rest my head against the table. 'Go back to work,' I tell her.

I hear her slide the plate out of the way and then I feel rather than see her rest her head on the table opposite me.

'But, really, how was it? It was two days ago and I know it's been busy, but it's weird that we haven't even talked about it,' she says quietly. 'The coffee, not the kissing.' She pauses. 'Although, if that did happen, you should definitely lead with that.'

'It was nothing,' I tell her. 'He's just going on tour. Mostly remote places and camping – it's all to do with the book. The bookseller they'd lined up pulled out at the last minute so they need someone to come and sell stock. His publisher wanted me to do it – I'm surprised you didn't see the email.' I give her a pointed look, which she ignores.

'Declan Archer asked you on a date?' she shrieks, and, honestly, I'm regretting telling her already. 'Why the hell did you lead with your mum and the sale paperwork? What did you say?'

'What do you think I said?' I say.

'I think you said, "Yes, Declan, but only if you kiss me until I can't think straight,"' says Yumi.

'What is with you and the kissing?'

Yumi shrugs. 'I haven't had a date in a while.' Then she narrows her eyes at me. 'And it was preferable to my other guess, which was that you're stupid enough to have said no.'

'Have I fired you yet today?' I ask her.

'Twice,' says Yumi without batting an eyelid. 'Seriously, Clarrie, you didn't actually say no, did you?'

I stand and turn to make a coffee. For all that Yumi teases me, there's a note in her voice that is serious and I need a second to work out how to deal with it.

'I've seen the quote for rewiring, Clarrie,' says Yumi casually. My hands freeze on the mug. 'And I know that we're very busy ignoring it, but I know what it means.'

My stomach sinks. I slowly lower myself back into the chair opposite her.

'I'm sorry, Yumi. I was going to talk to you about it, but . . .' I hesitate, but she doesn't rush me and when I look up to meet her eyes her gaze is steady and supportive. 'I was planning to ask Mum for a loan,' I admit quietly. 'Before all the sale stuff.'

'Oh, man,' says Yumi. 'That sucks.'

I close my eyes. 'It's so unprofessional for me to be burdening you with any of this.'

'No, Clarrie,' she says, her voice surprisingly fierce, 'you are my *friend*. And, even though you are occasionally neurotic, often sarcastic and terrible at cutting your friends' hair, you show up for me in a hundred different ways. You didn't have to bring me pistachio ice cream when Lachie broke up with me, or come to Franklin's funeral – God rest his beautiful turtle-soul – but you showed up, because that's what friends do.'

She pokes me in the arm, then waits until I open one eye. 'And I would not be showing up for you if I didn't tell you that this tour is a really good option.' Her voice is more serious than I've ever heard it. 'It would help the financial situation, but maybe . . . you know, maybe it would also be good for you to get away from all of this. From your mum, from Annabel Stone and her list of obscure authors. Maybe it's a chance for you to discover yourself in the wilderness.' It's eerily similar to what I sniped at Declan the other day, but I suspect Yumi is not joking.

'You actually read the book, didn't you?' I say.

Yumi shrugs. 'It's really good,' she says. Then, 'Seriously, Clarrie, you should do this. You know you should.'

I swallow. I can't believe I'm actually even considering it. But, also . . .

'I can't leave Gran for two weeks,' I tell her.

'I'll visit her,' says Yumi immediately, and a lump forms in my throat.

'You'd be at the bookshop,' I remind her.

Yumi rolls her eyes. 'I can do both. Besides, didn't you say Ruth visits once a week? I'm sure she'd be happy to go more if you asked her. She can send updates.'

I sigh and Yumi hands me the last piece of cookie, as though she knows I'm close to capitulating. 'Declan's phone number is in the system,' she says. 'He must have shopped here before.'

Despite myself, a shiver goes through me. Somewhere along the way, my grandmother might've met Declan Archer.

'You looked it up?'

'You didn't?'

I sigh again, then rest my head back on the table. I don't

want to do this. But the bald truth is that, right now, it's the only solution in front of me.

'I've got his publicist's email,' I tell Yumi. 'I'll email her.'

I procrastinate for another two days. In that time, my mother calls and asks for a copy of the shop's finances (I ignore her), I order more stock of Declan's book and the kitchenette sink starts leaking.

Yumi gets Declan's phone number from the computer and starts writing it on Post-it notes, which she sticks out the back and around the front counter.

'You know this is a breach of privacy, right?' I say when I find one stuck beside the cash register. 'What happens if a customer finds any of these?'

Yumi shrugs. 'Then they'll get a pleasant surprise when they call the number. Tell me that any one of these people wouldn't love to have a chat with the man himself.' She clears her throat. 'Quick survey!' she announces, and everyone in the store turns to look. 'Who here would like to have a chance to speak with . . .'

'Fine,' I hiss at her and she trails off with a grin. 'Fine, I'll send the email now.'

'. . . me!' Yumi finishes awkwardly to the confused-looking customers. 'You can speak with me if you buy a book. Come up to the counter when you're ready!' She winks at me and it's a struggle not to roll my eyes as I make my way out the back.

I pull up the email that Bri, Declan's publicist, sent. She

seems friendly and efficient, and she has included both an itinerary and an estimate of the number of books I'll need to order. It's a lot. Still, my skin feels clammy as I write back to tell her I'll do it.

I reread the email three times. I can almost imagine Gran, crowing over my shoulder with delight. *'Camping, Clarrie! Make sure you take a few good books!'*

I close my eyes and hit send, then ignore my email for the rest of the afternoon.

I'm in the kitchen making coffee the next morning when my phone rings with an unfamiliar number. My skin goes hot and then cold as I stare at the screen. It could be anyone, but when I emailed Bri yesterday I included my phone number. This has to be her.

I swallow, then slide my finger across the screen.

'Hello?'

'Clarence?' A deep, husky voice speaks in my ear and I almost drop the phone.

I grip it until my palm hurts, my heart racing so fast that it feels like it's tripping over itself. Somewhere in my brain I register absently that I was wrong. It's not Bri.

It's so much worse.

I've never thought about phone calls as being intimate. The point is literally that you're too far from the person you're speaking with to say whatever it is to their face. Phone calls are for organising things and for driving.

But with one word I am suddenly and awfully aware of the

man speaking into my ear. I'm the only one who can hear him, and every part of me is conscious of that fact.

'Clarence?' Declan says, a hint of wry amusement in his tone.

Get it together, Clarrie.

'Yep,' I finally manage. I clear my throat and wrap my hand round my coffee mug for warmth. 'Yep. That's what I said.'

There's a beat of silence.

'It's Declan Archer. I'm just calling about the email you sent Bri.'

Unease settles in the pit of my stomach. *What is this about?* 'Okay.'

'Bri told me you changed your mind about the tour,' he says, and there's something so condescending about the way he phrases it that I immediately feel defensive.

'I take it back,' I blurt out stupidly, just as he adds, 'Everyone is thrilled,' in a voice that indicates that 'everyone' doesn't include him.

There's another pause, longer this time.

'Did you just . . . take it back?' says Declan.

I shake my head, even though he can't see me. *What is wrong with me?* I can't take it back. And, even if I could, defensively yelling it at Declan Archer is *not* the way to do it.

'No,' I lie.

'You know that you won't be able to take it back when we're in the middle of the bush with no phone reception.'

His voice sounds so damn smug that I want to hang up,

and I hate that he holds the future of the bookshop in his hands.

'I was joking,' I tell him, wondering whether he'll hear if I bang my head against the bench.

'Bri thought it might be good for me to call before we leave,' says Declan. 'To clear the air.'

'Fine,' I say.

'Fine?'

'You've called,' I say. 'The air is clear.'

'Just like that?'

'Just like that. Nothing in the air around here.' I wave my hand in the air in front of me even though he very much can't see me, and somehow manage to knock my coffee cup off the bench. It drenches the bottom of my shirt and I stifle a yelp as pain lances through my skin and the mug cracks on the floor.

'Was that . . . something in the air?' says Declan.

'No,' I choke out, grabbing a cloth from the bench and ineffectually dabbing at my stomach.

'Are you okay?' says Declan, his voice stilted.

'I'm fine,' I tell him. I tug the bottom of my shirt. The pain has lessened to a dull burn now, but there's no way the stain is coming out of my favourite shirt. 'I'm looking forward to coming on the tour. All that camping and whatnot.' *What is even coming out of my mouth?*

Stuff it, I'm taking it off. I've got my bra on – my fancy, lacy black bra, in fact, that I decided to wear this morning because after agreeing to go on tour I was feeling pretty rubbish. We're on the phone – it's not like he can see me. I hold the handset with one hand and manoeuvre my top off with the other, then flick on the kitchen tap to rinse out the stain.

'Right,' says Declan doubtfully. Then I hear a small intake of breath, like he's about to wrap the conversation up, and suddenly it's desperately important that I do it – that I'm the one who hangs up first.

'Well, I appreciate your—' I begin, glancing up from my shirt to the window – to see Mrs Potts staring at me through her kitchen window, her face a mask of frozen horror.

For a second we both stand there, suspended in a strange tableau, Mrs Potts in a nice blue top, holding her kettle, and me in my lacy black bra. Before I very calmly and not at all frantically throw my shirt in the sink. I duck down behind the kitchen counter and drop my phone, my heart racing as I watch it clatter across the floor along with the coffee and the broken mug.

'Clarence?' I can only just hear Declan's voice, tinny down the line, as I scramble to rescue my phone.

I press it back to my ear just in time to catch him say '. . . okay?'

'Fine,' I say again, trying to sound like I'm not out of breath. 'Yep, I'm fine.'

Declan sighs, and I can hear the frustration in his voice when he speaks again. 'Look, you don't have to do this. I can just tell Bri that you made a mistake. I know this is more than you bargained for when you told the press.'

It feels a lot like he's being condescending, but mostly I just can't stop thinking about the look of horror on Mrs Potts' face. 'I didn't tell . . . No, it's not . . . My neighbour just saw me without a top on.'

Declan pauses. I pause.

Idiot.

'You . . .' Declan starts, clearing his throat again, and I feel the blush all the way from my toes to my face.

'Not like that,' I blurt out, before he can continue. 'I have a bra on.' *You're making it worse, Clarrie. Stop making it worse.* 'I spilled coffee,' I tell him. 'And my neighbour hates me. She saw me the other day in my pyjama shorts.'

'Okay,' says Declan.

'I mean, she doesn't hate me because of that,' I say. 'She hates me because . . . Actually I think she's just a bit of a jerk. Sort of like you.' *Not that.* 'Last week she saw me in my pyjama shorts. They feel a lot like my other shorts, but they're pyjamas.'

Thankfully, Declan doesn't mention anything about the fact that I've said the word pyjamas three times in five seconds, or that I've just called him a jerk.

'Shame about the coffee,' is all he says.

Damn it.

My entire body flushes hot again.

Stupid phone intimacy.

I lean back against the kitchen cupboards, the wood hard against my bare shoulders.

'I'll direct any questions I have to Bri,' I say, like I have any semblance of professionalism left.

Chapter Eleven

Two weeks later

Thankfully, Bri is as lovely on the phone as she is via email, and over the next two weeks she manages to make me feel less like I've committed myself to two weeks of Declan Archer glaring at me and more like this tour might actually be okay. If nothing else, at least she will bring enough cheer for all of us.

All in all, there are going to be eight events on the tour – all in national parks along the coast, and varying in size depending on restrictions. We'll be driving rather than flying, partly because of the large amount of stock we're transporting and partly because it's better for the environment. Bri has even arranged for a National Parks ranger to travel with us. I manage to quell the nerves that periodically surge in my stomach at the possibility of sharing a car with Declan Archer for eight-hour stretches with the knowledge that at least he will want that as little as I do. There's no way he'll let it happen.

Yumi was right in saying that the book is gathering momentum, and I get the impression that it's important for everyone that the tour goes well. In one of our conversations Bri confided that *Behind the Books* are thinking of doing a profile on Declan, which would be huge for publicity. They're sending someone out to interview him during the tour.

Not having a bookseller wouldn't have been a deal-breaker, but logistically it would've made things more difficult.

It gives me a small measure of satisfaction that Declan Archer *does* need me, at least a little. It's also a bit of a relief to learn that while we will be camping it's only for one of the nights. The other nights will be spread between cabins and motels, and, while Bri was very quick to tell me that it will all be fairly basic, it's not quite the total wilderness that Declan led me to believe it would be.

I haven't spoken to him since the disastrous phone call, but it feels like everywhere I go there are traces of him. Some of them are obvious – like Yumi dramatically reading her favourite internet comments about him aloud, and the eye-watering amount of stock I order of his book – but the spectre of him is in unexpected places too. I find myself walking a whole block further to buy a second-rate brownie so I can avoid the Garden, and it's an effort not to imagine him sitting in Ruth's antique shop when I check two days before I leave whether she's still okay to send me updates on Gran.

'I'll go every second day,' says Ruth, pressing a tea towel full of home-made muffins into my chest.

I feel sick whenever I think about leaving Gran. It will be the longest I've gone without seeing her in almost two years, and I'm still not convinced it's the right thing to do.

'But what about your shop?' I ask Ruth. 'If it's too much, I don't have to go.'

Ruth tuts. She wraps a scarf round my neck and pats my cheek. 'It will give me a chance to knit a sweater for Mary's new grandbaby while I natter away with your gran. You go and enjoy yourself, Clarrie. We'll be fine.'

I text my parents to let them know I'll be out of town for a few weeks with limited reception, pack and then repack, and run through everything in the shop with Yumi. She rolls her eyes at me more than once.

Then the day before I'm due to leave, Yumi comes in with a gift.

'It's not a napkin,' she announces before I open it. 'Because napkins are terrible gifts.'

I don't point out that she's managed to find a way to incorporate it into her outfit *twice* since I gave it to her. I slide my finger along the back of the wrapping paper as she pulls out her phone.

'If I was in the wilderness with Declan Archer,' she reads loudly, 'I would push him up against a tree and—'

It's happened enough times in the last two weeks that I manage to get my hand over her mouth before she finishes the sentence, but I hear the rest of it anyway and *oh my goodness.* It's not the worst comment she's read aloud, but I have to go away with this man *tomorrow.*

'There's no way someone wrote that,' I tell her, removing my hand slowly in case she's not finished, and then returning to unwrapping the gift when I'm sure my ears are safe.

'It's honestly like you've never even been on the internet,' says Yumi, leaning back against the table as I unfold the paper.

It's a head torch, and when I look up at Yumi she clears her throat.

'For the record, I quite like you the way you are,' she says. 'But if you find yourself overcome with the sudden desire to do a Declan Archer and find yourself in the wilderness, I thought . . . it might be nice to have a light while you're looking.'

Emotion clogs my chest and I swallow it down.

'Thanks, Yumi,' I say. She just rolls her eyes at me again.

'You can thank me by pushing Declan Archer up against a tree,' she says. *Great.*

At eight o'clock the next morning, a van arrives in front of the bookshop. There's a bearded, fit, capable-looking man behind the wheel that I assume is Jed, the park ranger Bri lined up.

Even so, my heart sinks. I can see before I even walk out the front that the van – while lovely and sturdy-looking – is not going to fit all the stock I've got waiting in the shop to load into it.

My phone starts vibrating the second I step outside, and I slip it out of my pocket to see Bri's name on screen.

'Clarrie!' says Bri, her voice sunny, the way I've come to discover it always is.

'Hi, Bri,' I say, my voice . . . marginally less bright and sunny. 'Where are you? I think we might have a problem.'

Bri laughs, a musical, tinkling sound that's somehow

reminiscent of windchimes in the breeze. Nice quality windchimes, mind you, not the annoying ones.

'Is this about the van?' she asks.

'This is about the van,' I tell her, eyeing the tall, long-haired ranger climbing out. He's wearing cargo pants, a broad-brimmed hat and a National Parks polo and he pats the top of the van like you might a horse to tell it it's done a good job. Then he starts striding over. I'm trying to indicate that I'm on the phone – to little avail – when Yumi bounds from inside the bookshop to intercept him.

Despite having never arrived on time for work in her life, she actually beat me to the shop this morning. She said it was because she wanted to make sure everything was in order before she was managing things alone, but I suspect in part it is also because she knows the last time that I spoke to Declan Archer I told him I'd taken my top off and she wants to see how awkward our interaction is.

Still, watching her coax a confused-looking Jed the park ranger inside, I'm glad she's here.

Books? Yumi mouths over her shoulder, and I nod.

'Not so much a problem,' says Bri in my ear, her voice as cheerful as ever, 'as an *opportunity*.'

'You know the problem is that the books won't fit in the van?' I tell her as a 4WD pulls up. 'How is that an opportunity?'

'Almost all of them will. At least, enough for the first two events,' says Bri brightly. 'Especially now that the passenger seat is free. And the rest you can keep in store to sell. We're just about to do a reprint, so there aren't many first editions in stock, you lucky ducks. You'll run through that in no time.'

The most annoying thing is that she's not wrong. We have a waitlist of people to call when the new books come in. So many, in fact, that Yumi managed to convince me that we already need to put in a new order.

'Re-order whatever doesn't fit, and I'll drive it out when I meet you,' Bri adds, just as the door to the 4WD opens. A brown boot, black jeans, white-T-shirt-clad Declan Archer steps out and my mouth goes dry. He looks good, damn it, and suddenly my jeans shorts feel too short and my top feels too tight. *This is definitely a mistake.*

He's wearing sunglasses, but I still feel it in my gut the moment his eyes find me. My whole body flushes, from my toes to my face, and all I can think is: *Thank goodness Yumi isn't watching this.*

Declan doesn't pat the car like a horse, just glances into the bookshop then slowly makes his way over to where I'm standing.

And that's when what Bri said sinks in.

'Which passenger seat is free?' I ask. 'And what do you mean "when you meet us"?'

Jed emerges from the shop again, carrying the first of the many, many boxes of books, while Yumi directs him. I watch them out of the corner of my eye, but most of my focus is on Declan, walking towards me.

He studies me for about five seconds. I can't see the direction of his gaze because of his stupid sunglasses, but my chest heats again under the scrutiny. I am painfully aware of our last conversation, suspended in the space between us, and very thankful that Yumi is at least ten metres away.

'Is that Bri?' Declan asks, totally skipping past pleasantries as his focus sharpens on the phone to my ear. 'Where is she?'

'Oh, is that Declan?' asks Bri when she hears his voice. 'Put me on loudspeaker.'

I do as she asks, my eyes on Declan.

'You're on loudspeaker now,' I tell Bri.

'Declan?' says Bri, and her voice sounds a long way away.

'Hi, Bri,' says Declan, leaning closer to the phone. His arm brushes against mine and I swear every hair stands to attention. I move my arm away as subtly as I can, resisting the urge to rub it.

'I'm so pleased that the gang is all together,' says Bri. 'Is Jed there yet?'

'He's here,' I tell her. At least, I assume it's Jed. 'But . . . where are you?'

My eyes meet Declan's sunglasses, and he's standing so close that I can almost feel his breath.

'Funny story,' says Bri. 'Did I tell you that my sister is pregnant? She just had the baby!'

She pauses, like she's waiting for something, and I realise a beat too late it's for some sort of congratulations.

I manage to mumble something vaguely coherent, even as my mind is whirring. *Where is this going?*

Declan doesn't say anything.

'Anyway, the baby is healthy, but she's also three weeks

early, and my sister's husband is still on a business trip. She asked me if I can wait with her until he gets back.' Bri lowers her voice. 'She's so tired after the labour, and my goodness but babies seem to need a lot. I told her that I could help.' Her voice animates again. 'The tour schedule is all organised. Between the two of you and Jed, I'm almost in the way! I was thinking I can do my part remotely for the first few nights – even the introduction and the initial warm-up questions. You'd just need to pop me on the computer.'

The first two events are in the one place – a basic cabin at the edge of a forest.

'Will there be enough reception to do that?'

'Sure!' says Bri. 'There's internet everywhere these days. Satellite.'

Declan's forehead creases. I'm half expecting him to say something snarky, but he surprises me. 'Is there no one else they can send?' he asks, his voice unreadable.

'Not without replacing me for the whole tour,' says Bri, and I think I hear a waver in her voice. A note of uncertainty.

For a second, I think that Declan will insist anyway – I know from experience that he's not the kind of person to hold back on the biting comments. But then he lets out a slow, steady exhale.

'We'll be fine,' he says, moving his sunglasses and rubbing his eyes. He doesn't look at me.

'Thanks, Declan,' says Bri, her voice soft.

Then she claps her hands, and the sound echoes down the phone.

'So, the two of you will travel together, and Jed will take the van.'

'*What?*' Declan and I both look up at the same time. Our eyes catch and my stomach tumbles before I manage to look away.

Down the street, Yumi and Jed pause their movements to look at us.

'It makes the most sense,' says Bri, like she hasn't heard the horror in Declan or my voice. 'That way we can fit as many boxes as possible in the van.'

'I'm happy to have a few boxes on the seat beside me,' says Declan. His tone is even, but there's a hint of desperation at the edges.

'You were . . . I mean, we talked about you practising your speech and trying to get some rest on the way there,' says Bri almost cautiously. 'You won't be able to do that if you're driving the whole time. And Jed actually requested he drive by himself, so he'll be fine.'

Declan falls silent beside me, and the phone goes silent too. Like Bri is holding her breath. Or maybe she just knows Declan well enough to give him space.

He glances up at me, and for a second I hate his stupid sunglasses, I hate the idea that my future rests in his hands. I am so damn sick of feeling like I don't have control over what's happening; of Declan being right about me stumbling. Which is the only way I can explain what happens next.

'I'm fine with it,' I say, and the words taste sour, but my heart skips in a little victory, because I'm fairly sure now I'm winning at being the grown-up in this situation. I might have to travel with Declan Archer, but at least I'm not the one who chickened out.

I could swear that Declan narrows his eyes behind his frames.

'That's fine,' he says slowly, his voice tight. 'Thanks, Bri.'

Bri claps again. 'Perfect! You two are the best. You are going to have the best trip. And who knows what sort of best-seller might come out of this? I, for one, am looking forward to the dedication. Speaking of which, Declan, have you thought any more about—'

'No,' says Declan, cutting her off, his voice sharp for the first time this conversation. I look up at him, but he doesn't meet my eyes.

'No problem,' says Bri brightly, and now I want so desperately to know what she was going to say, but there's no way in hell I'm going to stoop to asking. 'Speak soon!'

I slowly press the red button to end the call, and for a few seconds Declan and I just stand there, not looking at each other.

Which of course is when Yumi skips over.

'Jed's just finishing up,' she says. Then she beams at Declan. 'Great to see you again, Declan. I loved the book.'

'Thanks,' says Declan, lifting his gaze to smile briefly at her.

'And did I overhear that the two of you are going to be travelling together?' she asks. Her eyes slide to mine, and there's a wicked smile at the edges of her mouth.

'We are,' says Declan curtly.

Before Declan can say more or I can kick Yumi in the shins to stop her from saying whatever terrifying thing is on her lips – probably one of her freaking internet comments – Jed marches over.

'All packed,' he says. 'She's a great little van, that one.' He turns towards Declan, hand outstretched. 'I'm Jed.'

'Declan,' says Declan. 'Nice to meet you.'

Jed nods, then turns to me. 'Still Jed,' he says.

'Clarrie,' I tell him, ignoring Yumi, who is stifling a laugh.

Jed's eyebrows draw together, and he studies me and Declan.

'You two planning to behave yourselves?' he says, and I have no idea what is happening, but I murmur some sort of agreement without looking at Declan.

Jed nods again. 'Excellent. Let's go meet the forest, then, shall we?'

Declan is driving first. I'd like to think it's because he's trying to be civil, but I did also overhear Yumi telling him that I was rubbish at driving in the city when I was thanking Jed for loading the boxes.

I leave him to get settled in the car while I run into the bookshop to get my bags. It looks different somehow, and for the first time in a really long while I can't hear the echo of my grandmother's laughter. My breath catches in my chest, and for a moment I just stand there, staring at the shop I know so well that it hurts.

What am I doing?

The question thrums through me, tugs at me as I make myself collect my things and then pick a book that I've been wanting to read from the shelf. After a beat of hesitation, I slide the copy of *Talking to Trees* out from under the counter as well.

'Have you read it yet?' Yumi says from the door, watching me with a grin on her face.

'I haven't had time,' I tell her, shoving it to the bottom of my bag. 'You didn't have to tell him I was rubbish at driving in the city,' I say, but without any real heat.

'You *are* terrible at driving in the city,' says Yumi. 'I thought you might want to avoid it, especially with Mr Eyes sitting next to you, making you more nervous.'

'Yeah, but you could've made up something cool,' I say. 'Like that I refuse to be seen driving anything but a Lamborghini around town.'

'I'll remember for next time,' she says.

I take a breath, and Yumi walks closer, then wraps her arms round me. I rest my head against her shoulder.

'Is this a terrible idea?'

I feel, rather than see her shake her head. 'It's going to be great,' she says. '*You're* going to be great. You're making online shippers' dreams come true.'

'Shippers?'

'People who *ship* your relation*ship*,' said Yumi. 'It's a thing. You might be too old for the reference.'

I've generally avoided reading what people say online, though Yumi assures me that there are still quite a few active reddit threads about Declan and me, especially since it was announced that I'm going to be the bookseller on the tour. I'm not entirely convinced they weren't started by Bri, who seems more determined than anyone to make sure it's a success.

'What if I accidentally murder him?' I ask, my voice muffled.

'Isn't your brother a lawyer?' says Yumi.

'Property law,' I tell her. 'It's pretty different.'

'Then stay away from sharp objects,' says Yumi practically.

'Take good care of the shop?' I ask her.

'I will take as good a care of the shop as you take of Declan Archer,' she says solemnly.

It's enough to squeeze a laugh out of me. I step back and pick up my bags, one of which contains a very large quantity of snacks. I can do this. I have to do this. 'I'll be back in two weeks,' I tell her.

'They will be the longest two weeks of my life,' promises Yumi. 'I'll message you pictures whenever I get a brownie so you don't feel like you're missing out.'

She links an arm through mine and we walk to the door of the car together. Then she waits while I take another breath and climb in with my snack bag, peering over me to look at Declan.

'Keep her away from sharp objects,' she says.

Then she shuts the door, sealing Declan and I inside what now feels like a very small cab together.

Chapter Twelve

Declan doesn't say anything as I click my seat belt, or as I rearrange my feet around the snack bag. It's the same as the day we walked to the Garden together, except now it's a thousand times worse because we're in a confined space. And I don't know about him, but I can't stop thinking about how last time we spoke I told him I was topless. I swear the air in the car is *vibrating.*

There's no trace of the charming, calm Declan from Knit, Stitch and Yarn. He's focused, his eyes fixed on Jed getting into the car in front of us, his forearm flexed on the wheel. The white T-shirt he's wearing leaves the corded muscles way too exposed, and there is a very large part of me that would like to ask him to put a jumper on. His black curls are damp, like he showered recently, and he smells stupidly *fresh.* Which I know, because I am about thirty centimetres away from him.

I angle my body towards the window to get a bit more space. Declan glances over at me, but mercifully he doesn't speak.

Jed pulls into the street, and Declan flicks on the indicator. The soft, steady tick feels impossibly loud as we peel out from the kerb, leaving Brooks' behind. Six hours. We're going to be in the car together for *six hours* today.

I don't want to talk to him, but I'm not entirely sure that I can stand *not* talking for six hours either.

The familiar trees that line our pocket of the city flick past, then begin to thin as we near the entrance to the freeway. It feels a little like they're screaming, *You're about to be on a really long road! For a really long time!*

I know! I want to scream back at them, before I realise that I am a second away from – quite literally – talking to trees.

We've been sitting in silence for ten full minutes when our exit appears in front of us.

'Have you driven this way before?' I ask, because it's the first thing that comes into my head. My voice is a little raspy, and I swallow.

Declan's hand tightens on the wheel.

'Yep,' he says, before silence comes to reclaim its space.

I seriously can't do this for six hours.

I lean forward and press buttons on the dashboard until the radio comes on, hoping maybe some music can drown out the deafening silence between us. A man's jolly voice fills the car, telling us about some great deal. But I don't get to find out what I could be saving big on, because Declan immediately switches it off.

I stare at him.

'It was annoying,' he says without even glancing at me.

Seriously?

My fingers itch to turn the radio back on again, to fiddle

with the button until I find music, but I don't. Even though I don't hate the idea of annoying Declan, I'm a big believer that the driver has the right of radio-veto.

'You didn't have to drive with me,' I say after a few more moments of silence.

'You didn't have to tell Bri that you were okay for us to drive together,' he snaps.

'You know I did.'

'Why, because you're scared of driving in the city?' He changes lanes with a decisive flick of the indicator and I want to scream.

'Is there anything I should know about the book?' I ask instead, because I am determined to turn my frustration into professionalism.

'It's about trees,' says Declan. He glances over his shoulder, then moves left into the lane that will take us onto the freeway.

'You could give me a little more to go on,' I say, watching his profile. His gaze is fixed on the road but there's a small tic in his jaw, like his lips either want to smile or grimace.

'You could read the book,' he says.

'The last few weeks have been a little busy,' I tell him. 'As I was asked last-minute to go on a book tour.'

I don't tell him that they've also been peppered by the occasional outraged Declan Archer fan or by talking to my accountant and, in my very worst moments, by me looking at realestate.com for recent sales. I don't tell him that I've tried opening his book, but every time I do it makes me feel like I can't breathe.

'A tour for what book was it again?' says Declan, and I can see him arch his eyebrow behind his arrogant glasses.

Fine. Silence it is.

If this was a movie, I'd drift into an easy, beautiful slumber. We might stop somewhere, and I'd wake gracefully. Possibly a handsome stranger would brush my hair aside and whisper, 'Clarrie, it's time to wake up.'

I'd blink, looking somehow both dazed and beautiful.

I *do* fall asleep, but it's a crooked, uncomfortable sleep that hurts my neck and makes my hair stick out on one side. And I *am* woken – but it's because I snort so loudly in my sleep that I jerk myself awake, banging my knee on the glovebox and almost punching Declan in the groin.

He catches my wrist before it connects with anything, his fingers light and warm against my skin. And then he drops it like it's on fire.

'Sorry,' I manage to stutter, wiping sleep from my eyes and drool from the corner of my mouth with a hand that's only tingling a tiny bit. 'Must have fallen asleep.'

'You definitely did,' says Declan mildly, but there's something about the tone of his voice that makes me look in his direction.

'I normally sleep very gracefully,' I blurt out, and, in my defence, I still haven't quite woken up yet.

'I'm sure you do,' says Declan, his eyes fixed ahead.

'Everyone snores a little bit sometimes,' I say, my voice ever so slightly defensive.

'I've read that,' says Declan with a nod, and I almost stick my tongue out at him.

Rather than doing it and cementing that I am, in fact, a five-year-old, I push myself up and look out of the window.

We're still on the highway, but it's one-lane traffic now rather than the four it was heading out of the city. When I look out of the back window, I can see Jed's van behind us; Declan must have overtaken him at some point.

Houses and powerlines have given way to trees, and it all looks familiar in a vague kind of way. I really should know more about what's just beyond the city.

'Where are we?' I ask Declan, before I can remember that he doesn't like me and might judge me for not knowing. With running the bookshop and Gran being in Glenhaven, I haven't travelled much in the last few years.

Although, even when I was younger, we didn't really drive anywhere further than an hour south of the city. After a childhood spent feeling stuck in the bookshop, Mum always wanted to go as far afield as we could. Holidays were either in Europe with them, or spent with Gran and Grandpa at Brooks'.

'We just passed Welhope,' says Declan. Then, as though he's taking pity on me, he adds, 'About two hours north-east of where we started.'

'Do you want me to drive?' I ask him, straightening in my seat.

Declan turns his head towards me. 'Are you sure you're up to it?' he asks, raising an eyebrow.

And, just like that, I feel frustration race to the surface again.

'Would you like to see my licence?' I ask him.

Declan sighs. 'I only asked because you've just woken up.' But because he's Declan Archer and, apparently, he can't help himself, he says, 'From what looked and sounded like a *very* deep sleep.'

'Hilarious.'

The thing is, I'm not actually even sure I want to drive. I don't particularly like driving. But Declan's been at the wheel for a long time, and I think my concentration is likely to be better than his, dislike of driving or no.

'Bri said you need to practise your speech,' I tell him, 'and you've been driving for two hours.'

Declan hesitates, and it looks like I won't need sharp implements after all because I think it might kill him to admit that he needs help.

'Okay,' he says finally, and I only just manage to stop myself adding, 'Thank you, Clarrie,' for him.

Gravel crunches beneath the tyres as he pulls off to the side of the road. He unclicks his seat belt and opens the door. A crisp breeze sweeps into the car as though to announce proudly the temperature and air quality outside, and pebbles the skin across my arm. I can hear a car pull in behind us, and turn round to wave to Jed, who is looking very happy alone in his van. I mean, anyone would be happy in a van full of books. If you could maybe imagine that they were different books.

I slide across from my seat to the driver's side while Declan walks round the car. The seat is still warm from the heat of his body, and it *smells* like him. I'm shifting around, trying to get comfortable, when he stops by the passenger window and stretches, sunglasses in hand. His white T-shirt rides up above the line of his jeans.

I realise I'm staring when a jolt of heat that has nothing – but maybe a little – to do with the warm seat rushes through me, so I do what any rational person would do: I honk the crap out of the horn.

Declan jumps, banging his elbow on the roof of the car. Then he pulls the door open. The action is calm, and measured, but frustration is written across his face.

He swings into the car and glares at me, slamming his door shut. 'What the hell was that?'

To be honest, I'm not even sure. All I know is that I didn't need to spend any more time watching him stretch. That's not what I say to him though.

'Just checking out the equipment,' I say.

And maybe it's because of the arms or the abs, or because I still haven't woken up properly, but it ends up sounding much saucier when I say it out loud.

Declan raises a confused eyebrow at me and heat flames up my cheeks. 'I'm not sure if you realised, but this is a six-hour drive,' I tell him loftily, pretending my face isn't on fire and taking way too much satisfaction out of the fact that he is having trouble arranging his feet around my snack bag.

Declan stills, his long legs pausing their rearrangement. He looks up to meet my eyes and his expression shifts to something similar to the day in the deli, when I'd lied about drinking coffee. And, all of a sudden, I want to go back to the nice, stiff silence from earlier.

'I'm aware,' he says, searching my face like he's trying to solve a puzzle.

Before I can think of a stunning retort, there's a knock at my window. Declan doesn't even try to hide his amusement when I jerk at the sound, and he points behind me out of the window.

'Jed's here,' he says helpfully.

'Thanks.'

I turn round to see Jed motioning with his hand to wind the window down, as though we're still in the nineties and windows have actual cranks. Although I suppose just miming pushing down a button is much less effective.

Turning my back on Declan, I twist the key in the ignition and press the button to wind the window down.

Jed peers through the gap.

'I know your horn might get some use in the city, but we're on our way to the country now, and it disrupts the wildlife,' he says, his voice on the stern side of friendly. 'I'd advise leaving off the toot-tooting unless it's an emergency situation.'

'Sorry, Jed,' I tell him, trying to stop the fresh flush that I'm pretty sure is seconds from blooming across my face.

Jed nods. 'No harm done. Let's be off now, though.' He winds up his imaginary window again then strides back to the van.

Declan coughs softly, like he might be trying to cover a

laugh. I resolutely ignore him until he shifts his legs again, looking down. 'What on earth is in this bag?' he asks.

'Snacks,' I tell him, grateful for the distraction. 'Did you not pack snacks?'

'I don't eat snacks,' says Declan.

That's about the most ridiculous thing I've ever heard.

'On a six-hour car drive, everyone eats snacks.'

'Not me,' says Declan. He tries to push the bag to one side, but it determinedly bounces back again. 'Seriously, you have enough for about twenty people here,' he says. He tries to move it one more time before he gives up, sighing and shifting his legs to one side.

'Sorry,' I say. 'If you want, I could ask Jed to pull over. Maybe you can ride with him.'

Declan doesn't even dignify that with a response. He leans forward to pull a sheaf of paper out of a slim bag I barely even noticed he was carrying. He settles into his seat and begins sorting through them, occasionally muttering to himself. My gaze flicks to him more than I'd like, and after a while he frowns.

'I can feel you watching me,' he says.

'You're being really loud,' I say, before realising that I'm driving now. I press the radio button with a flourish, then fiddle until it starts playing something bright. Declan raises his eyebrows at me, but doesn't say anything, just goes back to his sorting and muttering.

My love of pop music was always a bone of contention with Jamie (the ex who sold my toaster). He was of the opinion that music should be weighty and meaningful, and could never understand why I picked what to listen to based solely on what made me feel like singing or dancing.

But, even here, the happy notes begin to worm their way under my skin. The countryside is bright and colourful, and as we pass trees and farms I start to think that maybe I should've been a long-distance truck driver. I stop thinking about the bookshop and the tour and I even manage to almost forget about Declan Archer beside me and I just drive.

Out of the window, the bush gradually thickens, and the small townships we pass through – if they can even be called that – get smaller and smaller, until even the sight of more than two small buildings in a row is rare.

The happy music on the radio begins to clip in and out, lyrics chopped in half by bumps and bad reception. Declan clicks it off, plunging the car into silence again. This time I do stick my tongue out at him.

'So mature,' he says, going back to his notes.

I try not to listen to him, but without the music it's difficult not to. Every now and then he sighs softly in what sounds like frustration and, not that I'm counting, but he rubs his head about five times.

After maybe half an hour of Declan's sighs and an increasingly bumpy road, I can't help glancing at him. His brow is furrowed as he looks at the paper, every line of his body tense.

'Are you okay?'

'I'd be better if you focused on the road,' says Declan without looking up.

I'm surprised by the sharp sting of hurt I feel at the words. But what did I expect? Declan Archer and I are just doing a job together. We're not friends.

We lapse into silence again.

Chapter Thirteen

By the time we trade again, my whole body is tense from bracing – against both the road and the atmosphere in the car.

I pull in behind Jed, who stops, revives and survives by running round the car twice and then drinking an entire bottle of kombucha.

Declan slides his papers back into his bag while I unclick my seat belt. The air outside is even crisper than before, and in the loud silence of the empty road I'm hyper aware of the crunch of my footsteps along loose dirt and gravel, of the moment Declan and I pass each other, and of the thud of both our doors as we seal ourselves back in again.

After stepping outside, the air in the car feels thicker, and I pull out my phone to avoid having to think about it. There's a message from Bri, one from my mother, and about ten from Yumi.

I open the message from Bri first – it's to both me and Declan.

YOU GUYS ARE THE BEST! it says. E-SEE YOU THIS AFTERNOON! Then there's a love heart, a party popper and a tree emoji. I send back a thumbs up.

The message from Mum is less effusive. Just a simple: Can you please tell me the address of the bookshop? I don't have the headspace right now to write back.

The first of Yumi's messages is a picture of her behind the counter at Brooks'.

Shop hasn't burnt down yet!

The next nine messages are pictures and links: a series of fake moustaches, glasses and noses. There's even a site that sells stick-on beauty spots.

In case anything happens and you need to go into hiding after the tour.

I half snort, and I feel rather than see Declan glance at me. I don't look at him.

You don't think the police would be suspicious of the fake nose/moustache combo?

She writes back almost immediately.

Did you not read the description on the website? They are *Very High Quality.*

Ah. I can't believe I missed that.

That's why you've got me. I've got your back, boss. You all ready for the event tonight?

My fingers hover for way too long over my response. I finally settle on As ready as I'll ever be, which feels both true and untrue.

I clear my throat. 'Do you know how many people are coming tonight?' I ask Declan.

His hand tightens on the wheel. 'A hundred and fifty,' he says.

Brooks' isn't big, but we've organised events in nearby parks that have had up to that many people before, and I feel my shoulders relax a little. *Maybe this will be okay.*

Then Jed turns off the road ahead of us, and Declan follows, slowing a little as the texture of the road changes from gravel to dirt. The car bumps, and my seat belt jerks against my shoulder. I reach out to grip the side of the door.

'Will everyone be driving in this way?' I ask as Declan skirts round the edge of what I'm pretty sure is an actual crater.

'There's another road that leads to the other side of the clearing, but it's too far to carry the books and equipment,' Declan says. 'Jed will meet attendees there and walk them in.' He glances at my hand on the door, but doesn't say anything, and I find his lack of remark somehow more unnerving.

Declan slows down, his hands steady on the wheel despite the rough terrain. Yumi would love this. And, even three years ago, Gran would've been whooping with every bump. But here I am, gripping on for dear life. I'm not good at this, and the realisation is somehow disappointing. Like I've already failed at finding myself in the wilderness.

We finally pull into an area marked by timber posts and logs that might once have been a car park, but now is just pot-holes and dirt. Declan parks the car towards the end, in one of the few places where the wheels can sit on level ground. He still doesn't speak, just unclips his seat belt and gets out of the car. I step out my side to find my legs are shaky from clenching them against the seat. Still, it's a relief to be standing on solid ground.

Jed is already out and stretching. 'Nothing like a few potholes to wake you up,' he says cheerfully, and I manage half a smile.

Declan nods absentmindedly, grabs his bag out of the back of the car and then starts down the path into the forest.

'A man on a mission,' says Jed approvingly, hefting his own bag onto his shoulder. I hurry to grab mine, then fall into step behind them both.

The path in is slightly soft underfoot, as though it hasn't quite dried from recent rain.

I'm still feeling wobbly, and my brain is flicking between Declan's mood and the logistics of carting a hundred books to wherever we're going to set up, but walking into the trees is . . . nice. Declan leads us with steps that barely make a sound, and Jed is whistling softly beside me. We're not far from the 'car park', but the forest feels thick almost immediately, beautiful, tall trees all vying for a place in the canopy overhead and coax-ing the air temperature down.

It feels quiet, but not silent, as though all the sounds of daily life have been filtered out, magnifying everything else:

the thud of my shoe against a tree root, the whispers of the forest surrounding us, the birds that Jed every few steps cocks an ear to listen to – although some of those I would swear *are* actually silence. Or only audible to dogs and superhumans.

After less than a minute, the path opens up into a small clearing. The early afternoon light twists through the trees, speckling it with a warmth that is more visual than physical. Beyond the clearing is a small, raised wooden cabin with a wrap-around balcony, which according to Bri's notes is where we'll be sleeping for the next few nights. Declan makes his way towards it, and Jed and I trot obediently along behind him. Or, at least, I trot. I don't think there's anywhere that Jed doesn't march.

The wood of the cabin is dark and damp, and its scent hits me as soon as we get close – a deep, earthy smell that reminds me of the cubby house Gran and Grandpa had in their back-yard when I was a kid. It feels both unfamiliar and yet like home – one of those smells that you know in your bones, but that is slightly off in a different context. It makes me want to set up a shop to sell pretend ice cream and tea, like I used to in the cubby house. Until I remember that I will be setting up a literal shop – *their* bookshop – and their absence manages to hit me in the gut in a new way. I rest a hand on the thick plank that serves as a stair rail, imagining what it would be like if they were here.

Gran would be bustling around, finding a way to make tea for everyone, and Grandpa would be quietly taking every-thing in. Eventually, though, his eyes would find a way back to her, the way they always did.

'Do you think she knows?' he whispered to me once.

'Knows what?' I'd asked.

'That she's the story.'

Declan walks up the three steps to the deck and I blink back the tears that have gathered at the edge of my eyes. He doesn't pay any attention to me anyway, just stops at the top to look out over the clearing. Jed marches up and across the deck, straight through the front door, although it's not so much a door as a gap where a door would go if the builder of the cabin had been inclined to put one in.

'Excellent accommodation,' calls Jed from inside. 'I'm just going to do a quick snake check.'

He says it very casually. As though snakes are not only a possibility, but a likelihood. I'm not terrified of snakes, but a snake check is not something that I want to actively participate in.

'I'm just going to check something out here,' I sort of mumble, mostly to myself. I'm half expecting Declan to laugh, or to smirk, or at least to say something – but he just keeps staring out into the clearing.

There's a tension in his shoulders that wasn't there earlier; his white T-shirt pulls against his back while his hands rest on the railing in front of him.

'What's wrong?' I blurt out, because *of course I do.*

'What?' says Declan, looking towards me. Like he didn't even realise I was standing beside him. He frowns, rolls his shoulders and looks out at the clearing again.

'Bri's plan was that I speak from up here,' he says, before

I can repeat my question. He points to a space on the other side of the clearing. 'Can we set the sales table up over there?' I straighten my shoulders. Despite the fact that I'm still not sure I want to be here, I *do* want to do a good job.

'Sure,' I say, keeping my voice even. 'I might ask Jed to help.'

'Sure,' echoes Declan.

Then he goes back to staring into the clearing.

Afternoon arrives faster than the snake Jed found in the rafters of the cabin.

My hands are itching to text Bri, to ask what kind of insurance cover they've got for the tour, but Jed assures me that the snake is a non-venomous type whose bite is a bit of a sting and a good story. And while I love a good story . . . I still don't want to get bitten by a snake.

At 3.40 p.m., he and Declan get ready to start down the path towards the alternative entrance, taking spare gumboots and insect repellent in case anyone needs it. They're both going to collect attendees, leaving me alone in the wilderness. Before they leave, Declan asks me if I can set up the call with Bri on his computer.

He's hesitant unlocking his laptop, but he doesn't make any sarcastic remarks about snooping through his private documents, not even when I half raise my eyebrows.

He's been different since he pulled the papers from his bag in the car. Quieter and more distracted. And I'm trying to tell myself that I'm imagining it. Or, if I'm not imagining it, that

I don't care, that it doesn't matter that the man is a freaking chameleon.

So I don't ask him if he's okay, and obviously I don't actually snoop through his computer, because that would be an insane breach of privacy and my eyebrows are all bark and no bite . . .

I'm still staring at them on the screen when Bri's camera comes on.

'Hey, Clarrie!' she says. Then she leans closer to the camera to peer at me down the computer screen. 'Are you okay? You look concerned.'

I drop the eyebrows.

'I'm fine,' I tell her, rubbing my forehead. 'Everything is fine.' And actually, apart from Declan's withdrawal and the yoga stretches I did to avoid stray snakes when I was going to the toilet, the afternoon has run relatively smoothly so far.

'I'm so glad,' says Bri cheerfully. 'Thank you again for doing this. You and Declan are the best. Jed seems great too! What's he like in person? What's the connection like?'

For a second, I think she means the connection between me and Jed, but then I realise she's talking about the computer. Bri is a little like a happy whirlwind.

'The connection seems okay,' I say. 'Are you still going to do the opening?'

Bri nods, and her head sort of freezes in one spot but also keeps moving, trailing a blur up and down the screen.

'I don't think the nodding quite works,' I tell her.

She stops. 'Okay! No nodding!' she says. 'Is the audio

coming through clearly? Can you plug in the Bluetooth speaker so everyone can hear me?'

I look around the deck, where Declan has very neatly set up everything he'll need – a table, notes, a bottle of water, a larger screen that he's connected to both the laptop and a portable generator so people can see Bri . . . but no speaker.

'It's not here,' I tell her.

'I think Declan was going to bring his,' says Bri. 'Maybe check his case?'

Is she asking me to go through Declan's luggage?

'His *suitcase*?' I say, and Bri nods again.

'Damn it, I forgot about the nodding,' she says. 'But, yes, his suitcase. He won't mind.' She waves a hand in the air and it blurs across the screen.

Maybe he wouldn't mind Bri going through his suitcase, but I'm not sure how he's going to feel about *me* doing it. Not that there seems to be much choice.

'Give me a second,' I say. Yumi is going to have a field day when I tell her about this later.

I leave the computer on the deck and walk through the non-door into the cabin. There's a small, rustic kitchenette in one corner of the room, and two sets of bunk beds in two of the others – Jed and Declan are sharing one, and I'm on the other. The rest of the room is just wooden floorboards and snake party space.

Despite my best attempts to pretend I'm someone who is naturally neat and tidy, my bottom bunk bed somehow already looks like I've lived in it for a week. Declan and Jed's, on the other hand, could appear in an advertising campaign for neat beds. Declan's case is leaning against the wall beside his bottom bunk, standing proudly like it wouldn't dare let anyone mess it up.

We'll see, suitcase, we'll see.

I flip it onto the floor and a strange feeling goes through my stomach at the thought of touching someone else's personal belongings. Specifically, at touching Declan Archer's personal belongings. The thought doesn't help make it feel less weird.

I tug open the zip, the sound loud in the quiet cabin. Somewhere in the background I can hear Bri chatting happily to someone on her end of the computer, interspersed with the occasional cry of a very small baby.

The suitcase smells like Declan – warm, clean and subtle – and I try to hold my breath, to search without actually looking.

There's a book lying flat at the very top – surprisingly, not a copy of *Talking to Trees.* It's called *Retelling,* by Francis Coates, and I've never read it, but the name sounds vaguely familiar, which is a level of knowledge I assume everyone is looking for in their local bookseller.

'Clarrie?' I hear Bri call faintly down the line and I seriously clutch my heart.

Smooth.

'Clarrie, I'm not sure if you can hear me, but I'll be back in a minute. My sister just needs me to hold the baby while she goes to the toilet.'

'Okay,' I yell back, hoping that the group haven't already arrived, that Declan isn't standing out there while I rifle through his suitcase and yell through open doors.

I take another breath and try to focus on the task. *It's just a suitcase.*

I move the book aside to see T-shirts and sifting through them feels like it's too much, too intimate, so I sort of pat the top and then . . . *there.* I find the speaker tucked under some socks and yank it out, then zip the bag up as quickly as I can and push it back against the door.

There's only an empty chair on the screen when I get back, which I assume means Bri is still holding the baby. I plug the speaker into the side of the computer and it registers with a beep, but, wherever Bri is, she's either on mute or far enough away from her microphone that I can't hear her. I sort of stand and stare awkwardly at the screen for a few moments, but she doesn't immediately return, so I lean back and rest a hand on the railing.

The table full of books is all set up on the opposite side of the clearing, piles of golden covers and Declan's name in bold, white font.

This is my next two weeks.

The forest murmurs around me and I close my eyes, taking a second to breathe. It's funny, but despite the six hours in the car the day feels like it's gone too fast. There are too many new things, all at once, and the peace of the clearing feels both incredible and oppressive. Weirdly, in a forest full of literal trees, I feel like I need fresh air.

I wish I could call Yumi. I wish I could call Gran.

Not more than a minute or two later, the sound of people starts to filter through the trees. It's not loud by any stretch, but after the quiet of the past few hours the noise is jarring. I glance down at the computer screen. Bri isn't back yet, and a trickle of nerves flutters in my stomach at the thought that the speaker might not work. I try to reassure myself that there's not much I can do about that now anyway.

Then Jed appears through the trees, walking with what can only be described as stern purpose. He nods to me across the clearing, then stops by a tall tree and starts shepherding people in from the path. They come through in small groups, most of them wearing long sleeves and gumboots and looking around with an excitement that slowly begins to feel contagious. More than a few of them look curiously up at me on the deck, and I try to smile with my best friendly bookseller smile. For all that nerves are humming in my stomach, for all that I'm maybe not cut out to be in the bush, I find that I'm also . . . excited. I've always loved the way that so many different people can have a book in common, a private world that they've entered into that can then become a shared experience if they want it to. It still awes me that a book can be both intimate for a single reader *and* a source of community.

The once empty space is quickly filled with the buzz of anticipation, and I find myself unintentionally scanning for Declan. I can't see him anywhere, and I try to meet Jed's eyes to ask where he is, but Jed seems to be busily alternating between reprimanding people for stepping outside their allotted space, and pointing out interesting birds in the trees.

Then the last few people walk through into the clearing, and there he is. He's standing slightly off to the side of the book table, and somewhere between now and when I last saw him, he's pulled on a cap. It's the first time I've seen him wearing one since the day in the coffee shop.

I don't mean to watch him, but before I can look away he looks up.

He doesn't smile, doesn't acknowledge me in any way, but it's like the noise in the clearing pauses, just for a second.

And all I can think is that he looks different. There's something about the starkness of him being alone in this moment that makes me think of all the bookshop events I saw Gran do at Brooks'. Memories of her joking with authors, of sitting with them and asking quiet questions, tug at my conscience. I know Declan doesn't like me, but he's about to speak in front of a hundred and fifty people. What if he's . . . nervous?

I blink and force my eyes to look away. *It's none of my business.* Bri's still not on the computer screen, but the event isn't due to officially start for another ten minutes.

I don't want to linger alone on the deck that is also a stage, so I push myself off the post and start making my way down the steps. I weave through pockets of people, automatically heading for the book table. I tell myself it's just because I need to let Declan know about Bri and the computer speaker.

He glances up at my approach, but doesn't meet my gaze.

'Did you call Bri?' he asks. His voice is sharp, but he sounds slightly winded, like he can't quite get enough breath.

'Yep, all ready to go,' I say softly.

I hesitate. I might've totally misjudged this, but I take another step closer.

Declan's eyes jerk towards me. 'What are you doing?'

I ignore the question. 'Have you ever heard of Gordon Ramsay?'

Declan frowns under his cap, but he doesn't move away. 'The chef?'

'The picture-book illustrator,' I say, 'who happens to have the same name as the chef. But there were about twenty people who apparently didn't know it was possible for two people to have the same name when they showed up to the Gordon Ramsay event at Brooks'. Some of them brought frying pans to sign.'

Declan doesn't respond, and I feel a hot flush of embarrassment. This was a stupid idea.

'Anyway, you're the only Declan Archer I know,' I finish awkwardly, then clear my throat, like doing so might clear everything that just came out of my mouth. 'Bri's just holding her sister's baby. She should be back in a second.' At least, I hope she will.

Declan nods. 'Right,' he says, tugging on the back of his cap. 'Thanks.' Without another word, he turns and walks towards the steps.

Great.

The chatter in the clearing fades when he reaches the stage, and everyone looks up at him. Even the trees seem to hold their breath.

Declan slips his hat off his head. He looks down at the computer screen, then looks back up at the crowd, a small smile tugging at the edge of his lips.

His hands shift on the railing. I feel like I'm holding my breath and I don't even know why.

'Okay, I'm back,' a loud voice booms through the clearing. *At least we know the speaker works.* 'How did you go, did you find it in Declan's suitcase?'

It's another silence that meets Bri's words, and Declan automatically looks to where I'm standing. I feel, rather than see, a hundred pairs of eyes follow his gaze, and there's nothing subtle about the blush that flames across my face.

Excellent.

'Hi, Bri,' says Declan's low, slightly amused voice. 'Declan here. And all the lovely people who have come for the event.'

'Oh crap,' says Bri. 'I guess you've got the speaker then?' She says it cheerfully, because *she's* not the one who has to stand in a clearing with the man she doesn't like, who she just told an awkward story to. Or with the hundred and fifty people who now think she just looked through his suitcase. Then Bri's face appears on the screen, bright and happy.

'We've got the speaker,' Declan says with warm affection and half a lightning smile, and I'm pretty sure everyone in the clearing falls more than half in love with him. At least a handful turn to look at me suspiciously – the woman who clearly went through their darling's suitcase. 'Everyone, meet my publicist Bri,' says Declan, shifting his hands on the railing and drawing attention back to the screen.

Bri laughs, and launches into her introduction.

Chapter Fourteen

We're five minutes into Declan's speech and I have to begrudgingly admit to myself that his book might actually deserve the attention it's being given, and by the end of the forty-five minutes allotted to this section of the afternoon I realise that I might even like it. From what I can tell, it's part memoir, part an exploration of the way we treat others and ourselves, and part a love letter to trees.

Declan speaks calmly, his eyes lit with a passion that isn't forceful or overbearing. It's more like he's going on a journey himself and he's just inviting everyone else to come along. Even thinking the word 'journey' makes me want to gag a little, but . . . it fits. Despite my dislike of him, Declan's love of the environment we're in is so genuine. It's almost like he's forgotten that he's presenting; he's just sitting down with a coffee to talk about something he loves.

The session concludes to rapturous applause.

'Thanks, Declan,' says Bri. Declan blinks, like he'd half forgotten that he was leaning against a railing next to a computer.

Bri smiles, and her brightness really does translate surprisingly well to the screen.

'Declan will be available to sign copies of his book now,' she says. 'If you'd like to purchase a copy, we have more than enough for you to buy one or ten.' The crowd chuckles good-naturedly – honestly, everyone seems to be in a great mood. 'And trust me,' Bri continues, 'you're going to want to buy at least one. Because today, you have the opportunity to not only get a copy of your book signed by the man himself, but you can purchase it from the bookseller who inspired the dedication!'

There's a bit of a buzz from the crowd, and I'm surprised to find that it makes me *nervous*. For the first time I realise that the people who Yumi has been quoting from reddit are actually *people*, not just mythical internet beings.

'Ladies and gentlemen, Clarence Brooks from Brooks' Books!' Bri announces, and then she starts clapping, her arms blurring from one side of the screen to the other.

The light may be softer in the forest, but there is still enough for people to examine the blush that's taken residence on my cheeks.

'Is it the woman that was looking through his suitcase?' an older woman says loudly to her companion, and inadvertently to the whole group. For the first time, I wish that Declan's stack of books was just a little bigger, so I could hide behind it.

The good news, though, is that I'm already blushing, so at least that can't get any worse.

I don't bother trying to defend myself or to deny any of it, and I determinedly don't look at Declan. *This is how we pay our bills.*

If Gran were here, she'd have the crowd eating out of her

palm while she told the story of the disastrous day that she met Declan Archer. Despite my resolution to sell books, I'm not Gran. So I settle for holding up a copy of *Talking to Trees*. Everyone is already looking at me anyway.

'Would anyone like to buy a book?'

No fewer than twenty people ask me what's in Declan's suitcase. I'm tempted to tell them it contained nothing but underwear and a handwritten note outlining all the qualities he's looking for in an ideal partner. I don't, but thinking about the possibility of it gets me through the questioning.

Almost double that number again ask about the dedication and one woman confides in me that she's glad I told him to write a better book because she found the first dreadfully boring. She looks a little nervous saying it, so I don't ask her to loudly repeat the words so that Declan can hear. Although I will almost definitely find a way to tell him later.

Mercifully, there are no repeats of the customers who came into the shop to berate me for hurting their favourite author. Two people actually ask me to sign their copies next to the dedication.

For the most part, people are *nice*. There's an older couple decked out in what looks like brand-new hiking gear who read *Talking to Trees* together and decided to take a trip around the forests Declan references in the book. They promise me I haven't seen the last of them, but in a lovely way, not in an action-movie-villain kind of way. Then there's the man who just quit a job he tells me was slowly destroying him, because reading the book made him realise that life is too short and *holy crap what is in this book?*

There are smaller stories too. A woman who took up gardening. A man who decided to dedicate more time each day to spend with his kids. A giggling book club who I'm pretty sure snuck a bottle of wine past Jed's keen eye.

Then there are about three separate groups of women who spend most of the afternoon lingering near Declan's signing table, taking pictures when he's not looking.

He is pleasant the entire time, smiling, listening to stories, laughing at jokes, but once or twice I could swear I see him take a deep breath when no one is looking. The books I brought in from the van sell out, and an hour later Declan is still signing on the deck. Jed is across the clearing studying a tree. He's been there for about five minutes, and it's entirely possible he will be there the whole night.

Finally, when Declan looks like he's beginning to flag, and when my smile starts to hurt at the edges, it's time for everyone to leave.

Declan and Jed walk them back down the path, Jed waving cheerily to me as they go. Declan doesn't even turn round, just leans in closer to listen to whatever the woman beside him is saying, as though he's attentive and thoughtful rather than confusing. Something I don't care to identify flashes through my chest, and I finish packing up my table with only slightly more force than it needs.

Then everyone is gone and there's silence again. Like the forest is breathing out, just a little.

The sun has just started to set and I turn on the portable light on the deck, then walk the clearing to check for rubbish before night falls in earnest. People were told that everything they brought in would need to be taken out and, surprisingly, most seem to have listened.

My phone buzzes, and I pause to slide it out of my pocket. There's a new message from Ruth.

Gran update: Gave Maggie a new scarf today.
It looks great with the jumper you got her!
We sat and watched people out the window.
Hope your trip is going well.

The phone vibrates again, and a picture of Ruth smiling brightly beside Gran in a hideously bright scarf lights up my phone.

I stare at the picture for long minutes, relieved at the update, but feeling so far away from them that it makes my chest ache.

Thanks, Ruth. So good to see you both, I manage to reply.

I shove my phone back in my pocket, pick up a few receipts and an empty bottle of wine, and then . . . there's nothing left to do. I feel restless under my skin, and suddenly the idea of being there, waiting for the moment when Declan and Jed get back, just feels like too much. I know that today wasn't about me, but I can't help feeling overwhelmed. I don't know what to do with myself.

I duck into the cabin and grab the head torch Yumi gave

me, pulling it over my head. It's not dark yet, and I figure there's time for a quick walk before dinner and bed.

The head torch is snug on my head, and it feels somehow like Yumi is walking with me. The beam is barely visible with the setting sun but I turn it on anyway, feeling my insides uncurl as I start to move my legs.

Gran used to say that everything looked nice in the afternoon light. Sometimes she'd pull a pose and stand in the corner of the bookshop where the fading afternoon sun hits. She'd invite customers to stand with her, so they could all look good together. It never usually lasted for more than a few minutes, but that was the beauty of it, she said. To appreciate the perfect moment and then to move on.

The forest at twilight feels like a deep breath. The last rays of sunlight kiss the leaves, the green different to when we walked in earlier today. Crickets and frogs are chirping in a loud, discordant symphony, and for the first time all day I feel like I can properly inhale. I make it to a small clearing, leaning against a tree and holding on to the moment for as long as it will let me.

Being alone helps, and by the time the last of the warmth fades from the trees, I'm not quite Wilderness Clarrie, but at least I feel a little less off balance, a little more like I can walk back into the cabin and make small talk. For the first time in a while, I actually start to feel freaking *hopeful*. Like maybe I might actually be achieving something here. It's with a renewed sense of optimism that I push off the tree, steeling myself to re-enter the fray.

But the path back through the trees feels different in the dark. Bushes I was sure I'd recognise in the afternoon light are suddenly indistinguishable from each other in the stoic beam of my head torch. I keep following the path, the calm from the clearing beginning to splinter. I'm pretty sure I'm heading in the right direction, but the peaceful trees from earlier are gloomy now, pressing in around me.

Then an owl – or possibly a monster – hoots behind me, and when I spin round to check, my ankle catches on the root of a tree. Sticks crunch underneath my hands as I go down, and a burst of pain shoots through my leg, sharp enough that I cry out. And, still, the most overwhelming thought I have is that Declan Archer would probably laugh his head off if he saw me *literally* stumbling in the freaking dark.

Which is, of course, when he finds me.

'What the hell are you doing?'

His voice is low and tighter than I've heard it. He's wearing a head torch as well, but his has a strong, proud beam that he points at the ground. He kneels down beside me, frustration practically wafting out with the heat of his body, his eyes glinting in the combined light of our torches. I'm struck by a sudden urge to hide under the leaf litter that's currently making my bottom damp.

'I was just going for a walk.'

I'm trying for mature and classy, but instead my voice just sounds small.

'Without telling anyone? In a place you've never walked before? We're in the *forest*, Clarence.'

'Thanks for the tip, Dad,' I say, because he is so damn *condescending*, and I feel foolish enough as it is.

'The cabin is this way,' says Declan tightly, gesturing in the direction I was vaguely heading. And I'd like to say that I proudly limp my way back to the site, but the second I take a step on my ankle a streak of pain curls through it. I don't cry out this time, but Declan still stops.

The light of his torch swings out into the bush, and he bends down again. This time when he stands, he's holding a long stick. He passes it to me without a word, and the unexpected thoughtfulness of it makes me even angrier.

'I'm not a child,' I tell him, even though I quite literally just called him Dad.

'Could've fooled me,' Declan mutters under his breath, and somehow the fact that he doesn't say it out loud is more offensive.

'You're so arrogant.' The words burst out of me before I can stop them. 'I might be "stumbling around in the dark", but I'm not completely hopeless, you know.' The quote from the article lands heavily in the air between us, but I can't see his reaction, and at this point I don't care. 'Perfect Declan Archer, though, right? Never fallen, never made a mistake? I can understand why you're not dating. You're just too good for anyone to live up to your standards.'

I want to snatch the words back as soon as I say them. It's been more than two weeks since he offhandedly mentioned he wasn't dating at Knit, Stitch and Yarn and now it looks like I've been stewing on the information. But Declan doesn't answer anyway, just keeps walking two steps behind me until the light of the cabin comes into view.

Jed is waiting on the front porch when we get back, and I'm bracing for another stern lecture about the dangers of going out in the dark. But he just runs down the steps and takes my hand to help me up. 'She can be a dangerous mistress, our forest,' he says, which is actually weirdly comforting.

Declan's jaw clenches when I take Jed's hand, but he doesn't say anything, just strides inside and takes a first-aid kit out of his perfectly packed bag. Jed helps me to a chair and brings me a bowl of baked beans to eat and a small ice brick from the freezer, then crouches down and takes off my shoe and sock. He holds the ice against my throbbing ankle, and it's both awkward and a relief to have him doing it. Declan starts to pass the first-aid bag to him, but Jed shakes his head.

'You don't want my brand of first aid,' he says, nodding for me to take the ice and then getting to his feet, and I'm not even sure what that *means*, but it sends an uncomfortable anticipation darting through me.

For a second, I think Declan is just going to throw the bag at me, but then he kneels down at my feet. I automatically pull back, the ice cold in my fingers. Declan doesn't look at me, just leans forward to study my ankle, and I can feel the warmth of his breath against my skin. The hairs on my arms tingle, and it's almost enough to make me yank my leg back as well.

Declan reaches his hand out, but looks up before it connects, and I can almost measure the air in the space between it and my foot. 'Are you okay for me to check?' he asks.

No.

But my foot twinges, and I know that I'll probably regret it later if I don't let him look at it. I nod jerkily, and a second later, warm fingers wrap around the arch of my foot. It hurts, but for the first time since I fell it feels *secure* too, and I fight the urge to close my eyes.

Declan holds my foot steady, moving it slightly and pressing his fingers against the sides to check it. 'Tell me if it hurts,' he says. His voice is practical and removed, but his hands are gentle, soft against my skin. Now that it's elevated it doesn't feel as sore, but when he presses the inside of my ankle I wince.

'It's a little bruised,' says Declan. 'But not too swollen.' He takes a bandage out of the first-aid kit, wrapping it decisively and firmly round my ankle, like he wants to be touching my foot as little as I want him to be touching it. Then he looks up. 'Ice it again,' he says. 'But I think with rest and elevation it should be better in twenty-four hours or so.' He takes the pillow from his bed and throws it at the end of mine. 'You can use this.'

'Thanks,' I manage to get out. Declan nods but doesn't look at me again. He moves into the kitchen area to get some food, like he's glad to be away from me.

Then Jed is there again, helping me hobble over to my bed.

My ankle is aching and I am uncomfortably aware that we're all in one space as I pull out the book I brought with me – the one that's not *Talking to Trees*, because right now I can't bear the idea that Declan might see me reading it – and after re-reading the same page three times I realise that I'm half waiting for Declan to speak again.

He doesn't, though, just finishes in the kitchen and then goes outside onto the deck. After a little while Jed goes outside as well. I can hear their murmuring through the open door, but not what they're talking about.

Emotion clogs the back of my throat and I feel tears threaten at the corners of my eyes. I slide my phone out, holding it under the blanket to dim the light while I message Yumi.

Tried to use the head torch tonight and tripped over. Pretty sure I'm not finding myself in the wilderness (my fault, not the head torch's). How was your day?

Boooo. Do I need to message Declan to ask him to catch you next time?

Please don't.

Bookshop was good. Guess which book is no longer in our window display . . .!

For the first time in hours, I grin. Every time that Yumi creates a window display she includes an old, obscure book and tracks how long it takes to sell. Her record is three hours, but the latest book has been in there more than three months.

You sold it??!

Gemma Murphy is now the proud owner of A Fisherwoman's Lover!

She owns the book, I mean. Not a fisherwoman's lover.

Although I suppose she could own a fisherwoman's lover as well. I don't know much about her personal life.

Congratulations, Yumi.

I'm the best! Thanks, boss. Look after yourself xx

My phone screen goes black.

I prop the ice against my foot and lean back, wondering whether it's worth getting up and getting changed. But somewhere after she was reprimanded by an irate author, Wilderness Clarrie deserted me. After a few minutes my exhausted body and brain take the decision out of my hands, and I fall asleep.

Chapter Fifteen

When I wake the next morning it's to more murmuring on the deck, and it takes me a second to get my bearings. *Did Declan and Jed not go to bed last night?* But when I glance over at their bunks, Jed's looks well and truly slept in, and even Declan's is marginally more mussed than it was yesterday.

My ankle is tender, but it's not as sore as it was last night. I manage to pull some clothes out of my suitcase and then get dressed under my covers, feeling a little like a caterpillar getting stuck in its cocoon as it tries to become a butterfly, thankful that at least no one is there to see me emerge.

After a moment's hesitation, I pick up the stick Declan gave me yesterday and shuffle over to the door. The thump of the end against the floorboards is loud, and the murmuring outside stops. I pause, giving myself another second to swallow my pride. We're together for two weeks, whether we like it or not. I'm still mad at the way Declan spoke to me, but in the light of morning I can admit that, well, he wasn't exactly wrong. It *was* a little foolish to stay out in a dark, unfamiliar forest without telling anyone where I was going. Still, my stomach rolls at the thought of facing him after I told him I wasn't surprised that he wasn't dating.

I make myself walk outside.

It's raining, a light sprinkle that makes the leaves on the trees around the cabin look greener. Declan and Jed are sitting on chairs on the deck, three bowls on the table in front of them. They both look up when I walk out, and Jed stands.

'Morning,' I say, smiling at Jed as he helps me into my seat. Declan pushes a bowl towards me, but I don't look at him because, apparently, I haven't fully *digested* my pride yet.

'Porridge,' says Jed. 'Declan made it. It's delicious.'

My smile only falters a little as I make myself turn towards Declan, his eyes as unreadable as they were when we got back last night. Fresh shame trickles through me, and I hate it.

'Thanks,' I say.

'How is your ankle?' he asks, his voice level.

'It's fine,' I tell him. 'Better.'

Declan nods, then picks up his own bowl, which looks as though it hasn't been touched.

The porridge is lukewarm, but filling, and the silence as we eat is broken only occasionally by bird calls, and then by Jed identifying the bird calls. Declan stands as soon as we've finished eating, and carries the bowls back into the small kitchen.

Jed leans forward over the railing and looks up at the sky.

'Time for a walk in the woods, I think,' he says. 'When the rain clears later it will be a good night for spotlighting. We'll get a feel for the area this morning, so we don't have any more accidents.'

'What's spotlighting?' I ask Jed, curiosity surpassing my embarrassment at his casual reference to my ankle.

But it's Declan who answers, walking back outside and shoving his hands in his pockets. When he's not actively yelling at me, he looks relaxed out here, his hair tousled and the beginnings of stubble starting to prickle on his normally clean-shaven face. 'Spotlighting is looking for things in the forest at night.'

It's on the tip of my tongue to say that I must have been spotlighting last night, but luckily Jed speaks again before I can. 'You coming, Archer?'

The two of them walk inside together, leaving me alone on the deck.

My stomach is warm from the porridge and I realise that with Declan and Jed gone I'm going to be alone in the forest. For the first time in a really long time, there's nowhere I need to be. Later, I'll have to find a way to move the books from the van to the cabin, but, apart from that, it's just me, my thoughts and, most likely, a copy of *Talking to Trees*. I need to read it, but after hearing Declan speak about it last night I also . . . want to read it. I just don't want him to see me doing it.

But when Jed and Declan come outside it's only Jed who is wearing wet-weather gear. Declan has his notebook in his hand.

'I'll see the two of you later on,' says Jed with a nod, tipping his hat.

Declan lifts a hand, and I think I manage a half-wave, the porridge churning inside me. *Declan isn't going with Jed.*

Jed marches off in a way that can only be described as gleeful, patting trees and touching leaves as he passes.

'You're not going with him?' There's a slight note of panic in my voice that I can't quite swallow. Declan just shakes his head, not looking at me.

'I want to do some preparation for tonight,' he says.

It's on the tip of my tongue to tell him that I thought it went well last night, that he has nothing to worry about. But the sentence sticks in my mouth. We're not yelling at each other this morning, but we're not exactly friendly, either.

'Right,' I say instead. He sits down again on the deck and I stand to get my book, like we're some sort of pop-up toy. 'I'm just going to get a book,' I announce awkwardly.

'Do you need help?' The words are stiff and strangely formal.

'No.' It's hard enough that he bandaged my ankle and made me breakfast. My messy suitcase would probably give him a heart attack.

I hobble inside and pick up the book I was reading last night. I only hesitate for a fraction of a second before I pick up *Talking to Trees* as well. I'm a professional – it's my job to read it. I take my phone too, in case Yumi needs to call.

I'm tempted to just sit on my bed and read, but the pride that's flared back up won't let me, so I limp back outside and into my chair. Declan is immersed in his notes, his head down and his brow furrowed, and I find that my frustration at him has faded to a soft embarrassment.

I open the first page of *Talking to Trees* but then pause.

I swallow, glancing at Declan. The apology that's been building inside me since I woke up is burning in my throat.

'I'm sorry for the way I spoke to you last night.' I say the words quickly, like ripping off a Band-Aid. I might not want to be friends with the man, but . . . I was rude.

Declan looks up, a flash of surprise darting through his eyes. He watches me for a moment, like he's trying to find some hidden meaning in the apology, and the idea of what he might say makes me feel like cringing. Then his eyes catch on the open copy of *Talking to Trees* on my lap and he freezes.

'Please don't,' he says in a tone I've never heard before.

'Sorry, what?'

He glances down at the book in my hand, and if it had been anyone else I'd have said that his face pulls into a *wince*.

'I can't . . . I don't think I can watch you read it,' he says.

There's a massive part of me that wants to sniff haughtily that he's the one who's been telling me how bad I am at my job for not reading it. But the expression on his face is so uncomfortable that I can't bring myself to.

I close the book, and his relief is palpable.

'Thank you,' he says briskly, and despite everything I find myself glad that I didn't press.

Declan holds my eyes for another beat. Then I open my other book, and he goes back to his notes.

After a while, though, the forest starts to feel too quiet. The book is fine, but I can't get into the story, and the silence slowly begins to itch against my skin the way it did yesterday, giving me too much room to think, and my feet tap with the urge to do something. To call Yumi and check on the shop. To call Ruth and ask if she'd mind going to see Gran again today. I shift in my seat.

Maybe I could get the books for tonight from the car. But then the rain deepens, spitting more aggressively at the forest and I sink back in my seat. Declan clears his throat.

'Are you okay?' he asks.

'Why wouldn't I be?'

'You've sighed five times in the last five minutes.'

'Says the man who has rubbed his head *ten* times in the last five minutes.'

I'm expecting Declan to snap back, but instead he puts his notes down on the table in front of him and rubs his head again.

'How long have you owned the bookshop?' he asks, like he's trying his hardest to make nice conversation with me. Like maybe he owes me for not reading his book when he asked me not to. There's no malice on his face, just curiosity, so I ignore the pang that the question sends through my stomach.

'Almost two years.'

I see the moment that he registers what that means, the realisation that passes across his face that he must have come into the bookshop right after I took over. He doesn't say any of that, though, just looks up to meet my eyes. And it's maybe that which makes me add, 'It belonged to my grandparents.'

'I read that,' says Declan. 'In the article.'

The mention of Elizabeth's article is enough to make my ears heat.

'I didn't tell her, you know,' I tell him. 'About it being me in the dedication.'

'Right,' says Declan, looking down at his notes again. Rain beats hard on the top of the cabin, and I can tell that he doesn't believe me, even when I tell him like this. Not that it matters what he believes. 'I liked her a lot.'

'Who? Elizabeth?'

Declan's forehead creases. 'You know the name of the woman who wrote the article?'

'You don't?'

Declan sighs and shakes his head. 'I'm not going to argue with you,' he says, and I bite my lip to stop myself saying it was *him* who was arguing. 'I was talking about Margaret.'

The sound of Gran's name on his lips is so unexpected that I flinch. Declan catches it and his eyes soften slightly, and it's almost more unbearable than him thinking that I'm a callous bookseller who would do anything for a sale.

'She was my favourite bookseller,' he says, and if I wasn't feeling so raw I might laugh at the fact that I am as far from his favourite bookseller as a bookshop owner can get. 'She always encouraged me to keep writing.'

I can almost hear her saying it, and a lump forms in my throat. 'Did she ever read anything you'd written?'

'Is that a dig at my writing?' he asks. His lightning smile flashes, briefly, before he shakes his head. 'She knew I was writing,' he says. 'But I don't think she ever read *Flight Risk*.' His first book, the book that started all of this. Which she definitely didn't read, because it came in the week after she went into Glenhaven. I don't say that, though. Declan pauses, and the forest feels too small. I want him to keep going. I want him to stop talking. 'She recommended at least half a dozen of the best books I've ever read. She was incredible.'

And there's something about the way he talks about her that makes my chest ache. I know she's incredible. I know that I'm not her. But it's the past tense that really gets me. It's one thing for me to miss Gran even though she's around, but he doesn't even know her, not really. Tension flares in my stomach, and maybe I'm about to undo whatever the apology did, but I can't help it.

'She's not dead,' I say, and it's so blunt that this time I swear *Declan* almost flinches.

He opens his mouth as though to say something else, when the ring of my phone pierces the clearing.

'Sorry, I have to get this,' I say, so relieved at the interruption that I don't even look down at my phone until I'm halfway inside.

And, of course, it's my mother.

There's no way I can avoid the call, given that I just told Declan I had to take it. I slide my finger across the front and hold it up to my ear, hoping maybe today is the day she's decided to call just to tell me she's thinking of me.

'Hi, Mum,' I say.

There's a pause. 'Clarence.' Her voice comes down the line, smooth and so out of place in the basic cabin. 'I wasn't expecting you to answer.'

I can see the back of Declan's head through the open door,

and I hobble over to my bed, wishing I'd had the foresight to bring my stick with me. Wishing the cabin at least had a door I could shut.

'Is everything okay?' I ask Mum, trying to keep my voice low.

'Everything is excellent,' she says. 'I was just calling to let you know we'll be by the store on Thursday.'

I close my eyes, leaning my head against the top bunk.

'Who is we?'

'I spoke to you about this,' says Mum. 'I'm bringing the estate agent to have a look. I think the building could be worth a bit of money, even if the business isn't.'

I don't even know how to process the words right now.

'It's not your building, Mum. It's not your bookshop, and it's not for sale.'

'Darling, I've had a look at the financials, and I really think—'

'Please, stop.'

Unbelievably, she goes silent. I take a breath, trying to gather myself. Hearing that Declan knew Gran has thrown me even more off balance. I feel exposed and confused, like my nerves are too close to the surface.

'I can't sell it, Mum.'

'You can't keep it, either,' she snips. 'It's a black hole. You could be using the money to do something worthwhile. Something that hasn't been unfairly thrust on you.'

'Like you're trying to thrust this sale on me? At least this black hole means something. It was Gran's – does that mean nothing to you?' I snap, before I realise what I've said. There's a pause, and I know she's gathering her ammunition, ready to swoop on my admission that it is a black hole.

'Look, I've got a job to do, Mum. I can't do this right now.'

There's silence again. 'Fine,' she says finally, and there's a distance to her voice that I know I'll regret later. Another step away from each other. 'All the best with the tour.'

She clicks off, and I'm left holding the phone to my ear, wondering how long I can avoid going back outside.

Chapter Sixteen

The rain continues for the rest of the day, pounding against the roof of the cabin so hard that I'm surprised it doesn't fall in.

After returning from his walk soaking wet, Jed strips off with a speed that is both impressive and affronting. Having him in the cabin makes it feel more cramped, but it also means that most of our conversations are about birds and trees, which is a welcome distraction.

By lunchtime, large puddles of water are beginning to gather in the clearing in front of the cabin, and the rain is still bucketing down. The weather forecast says it's due to keep raining for the rest of the day.

Declan watches the sky, his foot tapping softly on the deck until finally he pulls out his laptop to call Bri. The reception is patchier than it was the night before, but her beaming face still feels like sunshine, and when Declan sees her he seems to relax slightly.

He seems to actually *like* her; he listens to what she says and he trusts her judgement. The thought sends a pang of something uncomfortably like jealousy through my stomach.

'It's raining pretty heavily, Bri,' says Declan. 'Do you think we need to call off the event this afternoon?'

For the first time since I've met her, Bri's expression turns serious. 'There are a lot of bloggers coming today, and some people from the bigger online book clubs. Read, Repeat will be there,' she says, and a wave of dread washes over me, so consuming that I barely notice Declan's sharp inhalation. Read, Repeat. The one blog that Declan granted an interview. Tessa Dalton, who helped Declan tell everyone I was stumbling in the dark.

I try to catch my breath, to remember that I am a professional, but it keeps running away from me. *Call it off. Please, call it off*, I mentally beg.

'I know it's only a hundred or so actual book sales,' Bri continues, 'but the reach is bigger than that. Their content will be everywhere.'

Declan sighs and I swear he's about to rub his head, but he glances sideways and then drops his hand, rubbing it on the leg of his jeans instead. He leans further forward. I'm trying not to eavesdrop, but I find myself automatically leaning forward too. A block of dread is sitting heavy in my stomach.

'What does Jed think about the weather?' Bri asks.

'Going to clear up in an hour or so,' Jed booms from inside, which is very much not what the weather forecast says.

Bri nods. 'Okay,' she says. 'Let's send out an alert about the weather, but keep the event on. If there are any dramatic mud rescues, hopefully someone will be on hand to capture them on camera.'

Declan leans forward. 'Bri,' he says softly, and she waves a hand, sending a blur of movement across the screen.

'I know, Declan,' she says. 'But it could make a big difference, if you're up to it.'

No one asks if I'm up to it.

Declan takes a breath and nods. Then he straightens and signs off from the call, like a professional.

I'll be selling books. Maybe Tessa Dalton won't come. She's interested in Declan, not me, anyway. But the words from her article still feel like they're pressing in on me.

'We should check the path,' Declan says to Jed.

'An hour,' says Jed. 'It will clear up in an hour.'

The rain stops – I kid you not – fifty-eight minutes later. Jed is ready and waiting at the door, and he and Declan check the path in from the road. I message Yumi in a panic.

Someone from Read, Repeat is going to be here tonight. Any sage advice?

You should try picturing everyone in their underwear when they arrive.

Pretty sure that strategy is just for when you're on stage.

She sends a shrug emoji. Then, I use it all the time. Bet Declan Archer looks good in his underwear.

Jed and Declan return twenty minutes later with mud-covered boots and splatters of brown up their legs. I resolutely keep my eyes on their faces.

I'm half expecting that the mud will irritate Declan, but instead he just looks like another version of himself – dare I say, *Wilderness* Declan. And I find that I feel almost . . . jealous. He doesn't say anything to me, just takes off his boots and walks inside, and I want to yell something at him, but I don't even know what. Fear and disappointment scratch inside my chest. *I don't want to do this.*

'It's muddy but passable,' says Jed, coming up the steps behind him. 'Should we get the books?' He looks so alive in the mud and the rain that for a brief moment, it's difficult to feel too pessimistic about Declan's attitude, or about book sales. It doesn't ease my dread at the possibility of Tessa Dalton arriving and writing mean things about me, but I'm grateful for his help. Given the rain we set the book table up in the corner of the deck, and I manage to convince Jed to angle it slightly so it's not facing the crowd.

When he and Declan head down the path again at 3.40 p.m., the group they return with is considerably smaller than it was the day before. There are maybe twenty people, all rugged up in rain jackets and gumboots, and I am hoping desperately that all of them buy books, and that none of them are from Read, Repeat.

The rain holds off, but so does the internet. Declan tries to connect with Bri three times before he gives up on the computer. He glances up at the small crowd, then goes back to staring at the computer as though it might work at any moment. I don't even realise that I'm holding my breath until it starts to feel tight in my chest.

A few people shuffle in the crowd.

Declan bows his head. He half shakes it, as though arguing with himself. Then he takes a deep breath and turns to look at me.

His eyes lock on to mine and it's the same as yesterday, but it's also . . . not. There's a rawness in the air between us, like our conversation on the deck earlier never ended. Like we're the only two people in the clearing.

My stomach tightens, and I ignore the defensive reflex to raise an eyebrow, or to roll my eyes.

'Gordon Ramsay,' I mouth.

Declan doesn't smile, but something in his expression eases. He clears his throat and turns back to the crowd.

And he begins.

I finally exhale, my heart beating like I've run a marathon. Or, you know, a hundred metres.

Ten minutes later, Declan's stumble is a distant memory.

Like yesterday, he is magnetic. Unlike yesterday, though, halfway through the presentation he walks down off the deck to stand with everyone, forming a big circle that feels like one big book club. It's hard to believe that two events in one space can be so different, but there's an intimacy to this one that is almost spellbinding. When Declan finishes talking, he asks Jed to speak a bit about the trees, and Jed is so sternly captivating that even the birds stop to listen.

And then, suddenly, it's over. Instead of crowding around the bookshop table, though, people stay crowded around Declan and Jed, chatting until the air grows cold, until they're ready to leave.

I have sold a total of five books, and have been asked a total of five questions – three of which are about why Declan dedicated the book to me ('You'll have to ask him') and two of which are about where the bathroom is ('Nowhere').

If someone from Read, Repeat is here, they haven't approached me, and after an hour I finally start to relax. The bad news is now there's room in my brain to worry about how few books I've sold. The lighting will never be fixed at this rate. *Still stumbling in the dark.*

Even so, I'm managing to hold the smile on my face when Declan approaches with a petite woman with thick black hair.

'Clarrie,' says Declan. 'This is Tessa, from Read, Repeat. It's an online blog that does some of my favourite book reviews.' Tessa looks at him sideways, and there's a familiarity in her gaze that registers through the roaring in my ears. *They know each other.*

Tessa Dalton, from Read, Repeat. Dread pools in the pit of my stomach and I try to tell myself that I'm an adult, but all I can think is that these two people in front of me laughed about me behind my back. No matter what happened between Declan and I earlier . . . he's still the person who told this woman that I was stumbling in the dark, and I can't let myself forget that.

'Clarrie,' I manage to say, taking Tessa's palm in mine. 'From Brooks' Books.'

'I know who you are,' says Tessa breezily, and I want to sink into the deck. 'Did you catch the article I did on Declan before the book came out?'

'Tessa,' says Declan, when words dry up in my throat. I can't look at him, and I feel angry and embarrassed and small.

'I think I saw it,' I say, and I hate how weak my voice sounds but I'm proud of myself for managing to get something out.

Tessa smiles, and it's not mean, but it's not warm, either. 'I was just wondering if I can grab a photo?' she asks.

'Of me?' The words slip out, and a laugh that I swear I have never heard come out of my mouth before bursts into the space between us. Declan frowns behind Tessa's shoulder, and his disdain is enough to help me straighten my shoulders. I clutch on to it, letting anger drown out the embarrassment. 'Sure. Let's do it.'

'Of the two of you together,' says Tessa with an answering grin, and my heart freezes as Declan's head swings towards her. It's a bitter satisfaction that he looks uncomfortable as well.

'It'll take thirty seconds, D,' promises Tessa.

D.

They lock gazes, Tessa's smug and Declan's unreadable. For a second, I think he will actually refuse, but he inhales softly, same as he did with Bri earlier.

'Fine,' he says.

Tessa gestures to the space beside me, and Declan moves into it like he's walking to the gallows. It's the closest he's been since he held my ankle last night, and I feel the heat of his body as he edges behind my table with me. I automatically take a step back, landing awkwardly on my sore ankle. Declan reaches a hand out to steady me, the warmth of his skin on mine sending a tingle through my arm and I jerk away. I turn to look up at him at the same time he looks down, and there's a look on his face that might be an apology. For a second, time pauses.

'Ready?' says Tessa, amusement in her voice, and Declan stiffens, the moment broken. We turn at the same time to face her, and he slowly lifts his arm to rest behind my back. He barely touches me, but I feel every whisper of his fingers against the fabric of my top, and I only just manage to smile.

Tessa holds up her phone. 'Say *trees*!'

I swear Declan closes his eyes beside me.

'Trees!' I repeat automatically, half my attention on the phone and half on the man reluctantly murmuring the word behind me.

Tessa looks at the picture on her screen.

'Perfect,' she says. 'Thanks so much, Clarrie, great to meet you. Looking good as always, D.'

Declan drops his arm and steps away from me, back to the other side of the table. 'Thanks, Clarence,' he says, but he doesn't look at me as he guides Tessa back down the steps, leaving me alone with a pile of unsold books, a confusing ache in my chest and a hundred unanswered questions.

*

Jed is as close to buzzing as I imagine he gets when they return to the cabin, and he strides inside to get ready for spotlighting.

'I heard a powerful owl on our way back,' he says. 'I'm sure of it.'

He gets dressed so swiftly that I barely even need to close my eyes to avoid seeing his bare chest, then marches to the kitchen and starts heating up some baked beans while Declan ducks outside to change. I want so desperately to be alone, to process everything that happened with Tessa Dalton, and with Declan, and with myself. And yet the idea of being with my thoughts in the cabin while they're out spotlighting feels unaccountably lonely too.

Jed passes me a plate of baked beans – just baked beans – and frowns. 'Are you coming like that?' he asks.

I'm slightly offended by his judgement of my clothes, but mostly I'm just confused. 'Coming where?'

'Spotlighting,' says Jed, and I blink back at him like I'm a deer caught in headlights.

'Do you think my ankle will be up to it?' I say, which is not at all what I was expecting to come out of my mouth.

'I don't know,' says Jed. 'Do *you* think your ankle will be up to it?'

There's something about the straightforward and slightly frustrated way he asks that is fortifying. And suddenly, despite the crappy, crappy afternoon, I *do* want to go spotlighting. To experience this thing that Jed is clearly passionate about, to see what it looks like when someone does something they love. I test my weight on my ankle.

'I think it's okay,' I say.

'Good,' says Jed, just as Declan comes back up the stairs.

I steel myself to defend my decision, but when he reaches the top step he barely even looks at me, just passes me one of the two head torches looped around his arm.

'I have a head torch,' I say snidely. 'Are you sure Tessa doesn't need this one?'

It's a ridiculous thing to say and it doesn't even make *sense.* I hate that I'm speaking out of my hurt, that he might know that he hurt me. But Declan just pulls his own torch over his head. 'This one has a more consistent light,' he says, and I shouldn't be hurt, because I'm here for *work.*

Still, I feel nauseous at the sight of the unsold boxes of books next to my bed. I change as quickly as I can, then falter over the two head torches. Part of me wants to wear mine, but when I turn Declan's on the beam is so bright that it lights up the room. *Damn it.* I would be an idiot not to wear it, and it says something about my mental state that I still think about it. But I pull it on my head and wrap the torch from Yumi round my wrist, knowing that she would be in no way offended by me taking the superior light. She would absolutely be laughing her head off at the situation. I take a quick picture to send to her, and then after a beat of hesitation I pick up the stick Declan got me.

Declan doesn't say anything when I come out, but his eyes catch briefly on the torch around my wrist. Then Jed claps his hands three times.

'Archer, I know you've been spotlighting before, but we'll do a bit of a refresher for Clarence here.'

'Right,' says Declan, slightly awkwardly.

Jed begins by explaining the importance of keeping your feet nimble while your eyes are up, the art of spotting eyeshine and the best vantage points at the base of the trees. He runs around the forest near the cabin, demonstrating.

And, even though he is way more committed than I can ever imagine myself being to spotting animals at night, seeing his passion for what he does is kind of incredible. A whisper of want trickles through me – not to be able to spot eyeshine from any vantage point – but to love something so much that you throw your whole self into it. It reminds me of Gran in the bookshop.

Finally, Jed deems us ready to venture out. He gestures to the forest, then leaps off like a lithe jackrabbit, leaving Declan and I little choice but to follow silently behind him, trying to avoid puddles.

There's a soft hoot ahead of us, and I automatically exchange a glance with Declan in the torchlight, as though spotlighting has temporarily erased any barriers.

'It sounds like a powerful owl,' whispers Declan. 'But I'm pretty sure it's Jed mimicking the call of a powerful owl.'

The noise sounds again, and it sounds a lot like an owl . . . but also a little like Jed. And sure enough, when we catch sight of him in our torchlight, he's softly hooting at the trees.

And you know what? Stuff it. I am all in.

I am going to throw myself into spotlighting, and I am going to follow a hooting Jed wherever he leads. For the first time in a really long time, I'm not going to think about what

I'm doing or worry about the bookshop. I'm just going to be where I am.

And where I am is in the pitch black with an enthusiastic park ranger, trying not to break my other ankle by looking up to spot the owls.

Every now and then, Jed disappears ahead and Declan falls behind, and the darkness steals my breath away. I can hear my heart everywhere, can feel it thumping in my skin. I'm alone in a way that I've never felt before. I can't quite tell if it's terrifying or exhilarating.

Then after ten minutes of searching, a loud, screaming sound echoes through the forest and my heart stops for a second. Declan stumbles behind me, his torchlight swinging around the trees, and I hear him softly swear under his breath. I backtrack to find him looking down at his feet, one of which is ankle deep in a puddle.

The screaming echoes through the forest again, and I jump.

'Masked owl,' he says through gritted teeth, trying to work his foot free.

'Sorry, what?' I whisper, wondering where on earth Jed is.

'That sound. Jed is doing a masked owl call.'

A slightly hysterical laugh bubbles in my chest as another scream rings through the trees, but the laugh stops short of my lips at the expression on Declan's face.

'Are you okay?' I ask him instead.

He sighs, adjusting his head torch. 'My foot is stuck.'

I shine both my head torches down at the ground. Mud is oozing out around his boot, fixing it in place. There are no trees close enough for him to use to pull himself out, and if I offer him a hand, I'm just going to end up in the mud with him.

I bend down and pick up the stick he gave me. Declan pauses his struggles to watch me shuffle over to the nearest tree, wrapping my arms around it. Then I hold out the stick; it's long enough to bridge the gap between us.

I'm half expecting him to laugh at me, or to tell me that it won't work, but he just meets my eyes in the torchlight. Then he grabs hold of the other end. I grip the stick so hard that my hands start to burn, but I keep pulling until Declan works his foot free. He lurches forward and a rush of triumph rushes through me, and I honestly can't help grinning. I drop the stick, stepping out beside the tree to steady him.

He looks up, his green eyes dark in the shadows of the torch, his arm gripping mine, a reminder of him steadying me before the photo today. My grin freezes in place.

'Thanks,' Declan says, his voice low.

Then Jed screams like a masked owl and his light appears through the trees. Declan drops my arm abruptly as Jed signals to us, and I pick up my stick again as though the moment never happened.

Five minutes later, we see our first owl. Its eyes gleam white in the torchlight, and a thrill of what I can only describe as sheer joy bolts through me. I've seen owls before, in pictures and at the zoo. But it's never felt like this. There's something about the success and the silence and the realisation that we are the only people here in this moment. For a beat, everything just washes away. Jed, Declan and I stand in silence, and in the light of my torch I can see the whites of their teeth. My ankle has started to throb a little, but there's an adrenaline pumping through me, an aliveness that I can feel prickling on my skin.

I grip Yumi's torch in my hand, and keep moving forward.

Chapter Seventeen

The next morning, I wake at 5 o'clock. It's still dark inside the cabin, but it's dim rather than pitch black, as though the light is just waiting on the fringes of the forest for the perfect moment to announce its presence.

Despite the fact that sometimes I like to imagine I am the kind of person who gets up early and embraces the day, in practice I tend to embrace it best while I'm asleep.

But when I roll over and try to go back to sleep, I . . . can't. I'm just too awake. Too aware that something changed yesterday, even if I can't put my finger on what it was.

The loud snores periodically emanating from the other side of the room aren't helping. As much as I'm hoping they might be Declan's, there's a note in them that's remarkably similar to Jed's masked owl call.

I guess 5 a.m. is as good a time as any to get up.

I unzip my bag and pull out a change of clothes as quietly as I can, but just as I'm about to zip it up again there's a rustle of sheets, like someone is turning over. It's almost enough to make me jump, although I have no idea why – it's my own bag I'm going through this time.

Against my better judgement, I straighten, my eyes creeping over to Declan and Jed. Declan's face is obscured by the ladder, and Jed . . . well, there's something on Jed's back.

Even after walking on it last night, my ankle feels a lot better. I creep a few steps closer to Jed, my heart beating fast. I'm not sure if it's a trick of the light, but the hand-sized lump on his back looks a heck of a lot like a spider.

I'm halfway across the room when I realise that's because it *is* a spider.

I freeze, trying to decide whether to somehow get the spider off Jed's back or to leave it in peace and creep out of the cabin to get dressed.

I'm in the middle of reasoning with myself that Jed probably eats spiders for breakfast, when Declan speaks.

'Are you watching Jed sleep?'

His voice is soft, deep and warm from sleep, and my pulse kicks into triple speed before my head catches up. I look down to see him watching me, and for a beat it's impossible to look away. His hair is mussed, and he shifts slightly in bed, the blanket falling down his chest. My eyes dip automatically, and by the time I manage to swallow and to pull them back up to his face there's a flash of heat in his green eyes that sends a bolt of warmth through my body, from my ears to my toes. Something has shifted between us, and it's almost as terrifying as the hairy thing on Jed's back.

I swallow. 'There's a spider,' I whisper to Declan out of the corner of my mouth. It's entirely possible a full whisper might send the spider scampering up into Jed's hair.

But I'm not accounting for Declan's reaction, which is that in his hurry to pull his sheets off himself and *dive* out of bed, he bangs his head on the top bunk and then thumps his feet loudly against the floor.

Unbelievably, Jed *still* doesn't wake up, and the spider moves to Jed's underarm.

Declan stands beside me, turning to look at Jed's back while apparently recovering his breath. Which I can very clearly see through the rise and fall of his chest, because he *definitely* isn't wearing a shirt. I'm pretending not to notice.

'What the hell was that?' I ask him quietly instead.

'I don't like spiders,' says Declan hoarsely.

'You held a snake a few days ago,' I say, because he did. He carried it into the clearing with Jed, and I swear the two of them were about a heartbeat from naming it.

'Snakes are beautiful,' says Declan. 'Spiders have . . . legs.'

'You don't like legs?'

'I like legs,' he says, almost defensively. 'I just think eight is too many.' His eyes are fixed on Jed's underarm. Then he sighs. 'You have to flick it off.'

There's a pause, and it takes my brain a second to catch up. 'Sorry, what?'

'Jed is terrified of spiders,' says Declan.

'*Jed* is terrified of spiders?' I say, raising my eyebrows at him. Declan clears his throat and nods, and my fingers itch with the urge to touch his ruffled hair. There's something about the dim light and his hair and his obvious fear of spiders and the fact that he's just woken up that make the whole situation weirdly intimate. *Get it together, Clarrie.* I clear my throat. 'You sure you're not projecting?' I ask him.

'I definitely am,' says Declan, his mouth kicking out at one side. 'But we also talked about it. We decided that if there were any spiders to deal with it was going to have to be your job.'

How does that even come up?

'We were talking about animals,' says Declan, in response to the look I give him.

'And you think that I can do it, despite the fact that I'm the kind of person who just stumbles around in the dark?'

The quote from the interview trips out again before I can stop it. After meeting Tessa and everything else that happened yesterday, my emotions feel too close to the surface.

The quote hovers in the air between us, and I keep my eyes fixed on the spider near Jed's underarm. I can feel Declan's gaze on me, and I'm half-expecting, half-hoping he just ignores it, like he did the other times.

'I'm sorry,' he says, and his voice is void of any sarcasm. 'I didn't think she was going to print that.'

Surprise grips my throat, and I look up to meet his eyes. He holds my gaze, unflinching.

'But you said it.' My voice is husky. For some reason, it's not the printing of it that's the worst part.

He doesn't deny it, and I exhale slowly through my nose.

'I regretted it as soon as it came out,' says Declan. 'The situation was . . . complicated. But it's no excuse, and I'm sorry.' He hesitates. 'I'm sorry I accused you of leaking the information about the dedication too.'

'You don't think I did that any more?'

'I've seen your face when you're introduced as the bookseller,' he says with the ghost of a smile.

I look at him then, and his eyes are fixed on me. The moment beats between us; the words that have haunted me, taken back by the man who said them.

'Truce?' whispers Declan.

I inhale, then nod. 'Truce.' I clear my throat before the air gets too tight. 'You decided I would deal with the spiders?'

'Theoretically,' says Declan, like he's relieved to be letting the moment drop as well. He looks at Jed's underarm, then at me again. 'And practically I guess, now that we're in this situation.' He runs a hand through his hair once more. 'If you don't like spiders, I guess we can try to work something out together.'

Even in his whisper he somehow manages to sound genuine, determined and terrified. As though despite having just leapt from bed at the prospect of being close to a spider, he will still find a way to face it.

'Move,' I whisper at him, more grumpily than I need to.

'You're going to do it?' he says, a lightning grin transforming his features in my direction for the first time.

'Go away, Declan.'

He dutifully steps back – as far as he possibly can – but I can see a stupid boyish light in his eyes. I step closer to Jed.

Then I hold my fingers ready in a flick, grit my teeth and send the spider flying somewhere on the other side of the cabin.

Declan jumps and Jed wakes with a start, sitting bolt upright in bed.

'I'm ready!' yells Jed.

Then he registers my presence next to his bed. Frowns, as though that's not the weirdest way he's ever woken up.

'Clarence?'

'Spider,' I explain to him, and he looks like he's going to be sick. 'I flicked it away,' I tell him.

'Excellent work.' Jed nods decisively. 'Thank you.'

'I'm going to get dressed outside,' I tell them both, grabbing Declan's neatly folded T-shirt off the edge of his bed and throwing it to him. 'Put a shirt on, Archer.'

As far as exit lines go, it's a pretty good one, I think.

We're ready to leave by 7 a.m., surrendering the cabin back to the snakes.

Declan and Jed have done such a thorough job cleaning that there's no sign we were ever here, no indication that we called this place home for two days. I feel a strange pang of sadness at leaving.

It's five hours in the car today, driving north to a town called Candon, which is a bit over halfway to the location of the next event – the event itself isn't until tomorrow night. Declan is in the driver's seat, and it's almost like he took a mental map of the potholes, because the trip out is a lot smoother than the trip in.

When we emerge from tree-lined roads onto the open highway it's a bit of a shock to the system. I hadn't realised that I'd grown accustomed to the green and the shade.

We've only been on the highway for ten minutes, though, when suddenly, Jed swerves off the road in front of us.

'What—' Declan swings the wheel to pull in behind him. We both watch as Jed leaps from the van and runs into the thick bush beside the road.

Declan doesn't even hesitate. He unclicks his seat belt and pulls open his door.

'Stay here,' he says, then strides into the bushes after Jed.

Leaving me alone in the car.

Chapter Eighteen

I wait for five solid minutes before indignation at being told to stay catches up with me. Truce or not, I'm not going to sit by myself on a road close to the middle of nowhere with no idea what's going on. What kind of Wilderness Clarrie am I?

I open my door and step out of the car.

The road is silent in a way that even the depths of the forest wasn't, and the crunch of my feet against the gravel feels too loud. The bushes that Declan and Jed ran into are still, apart from the soft rustle of leaves in the breeze. For all my attempts to be Wilderness Clarrie in the last few days, there's something exposing about the crisp, open stillness of the road. Like a rawer version of myself might actually exist here. I can't see any sign of Jed and Declan, and the bush is thick enough that I'm going to have to duck and weave to make it through the treeline.

A hundred more possibilities of what could be happening run through my head, none of them good, and none of which are even remotely close to what actually happens next.

I move forward, tentatively pushing aside one of the

branches and watching where I put my feet. I really don't want to trip again.

'Hello?' I call into the silent trees. 'Declan? Jed?'

There's no answer except for the trees rustling more aggressively, as though they're admonishing me for speaking too loudly. Then a car flies past on the road behind me and the sound of tyres makes me almost wet my pants.

Come on, Wilderness Clarrie.

I push the branches firmly to the side and start forward into the trees, wishing I had breadcrumbs to track my way back to the car. I mean, I know the witch was scary and all in *Hansel and Gretel*, but really things worked out pretty well for them in the end.

I move another branch, pressing forward through the clearest-looking passage. An errant stick scratches my cheek, the sting of it biting and then abating to a dull pulse.

Where the hell are they?

I duck under a branch to keep following the gap, only to run smack bang into a solid, warm chest. Hands come to rest on my bare arms and my heart flips involuntarily at the contact.

I can feel every part where our bodies are a whisper from touching, and I don't need to look to know who it is. I swallow, my eyes travelling up Declan's chest. When they finally meet his, my breath catches. There's a gentle wonder on his face I've never seen before.

'Clarrie,' he whispers, and my stomach jolts at his use of my nickname. He leans closer and for a stupid, strange heartbeat, I think he's going to kiss me.

He doesn't – of course he doesn't.

'You'll never guess what Jed found,' he says.

It turns out he's right – I would never have guessed what Jed found. Because I don't think I could've even imagined that someone would spot a bird – *while driving* – and leap from the car to take a photo of it. Or that my travelling companion's initial confusion would transform into an only slightly less fervent excitement.

But when Declan leads me through the forest it is seriously the closest to skipping that I imagine he gets. His walk seems lighter, his eyes are bright and his voice is full of the same enthusiasm he has when he talks about his book. As though his guard has been stripped away. *By a bird.*

'A regent honeyeater,' Declan breathes in correction the second time I ask him to clarify that we've stopped for a bird. Then he rests a warm hand against my upper arm in gentle warning that we're getting close and I need to be quiet.

His footsteps are light, and when he touches the branches ahead of us, they seem to move without resistance. Like the forest knows him. Forget horse-whispering or van-whispering, this man is a freaking tree whisperer.

Jed is standing so still that if someone told me he was a tall, grey-haired statue in the bush I wouldn't even hesitate to believe them. He has a large camera trained at the middle of a tree, but at the sound of Declan and I arriving he looks towards us.

I'm expecting to see him frowning at the little sound we've

made, but instead, his face is alight with joy. His cheeks are red, and his eyes are as bright as Declan's; you can practically see the excitement pouring out of him.

If you'd told me earlier that a man looking giddy over a bird would fill me with anything apart from mild alarm, I'd have laughed. Or smiled politely, so as not to offend you. But there's something about seeing Jed's raw emotion and Declan's unfettered enthusiasm that is like a stab in my gut, a raw envy that these two men feel so passionate about something that it's tangible.

And, like last night when we were spotlighting, I feel a wave of longing.

I felt like that once.

The thought trickles through me, along with a memory of Gran pulling a box out of the storeroom, her eyes twinkling. 'Something came in today,' she whispered, scissors sliding smoothly along tape. She cracked open a side and we both leaned forward, breathing in the fresh book smell.

I can remember my heart skipping a beat when I saw Kate DiCamillo's name stamped in bold type across the top, then the cover Gran had shown me on the computer a few weeks ago.

'Can I read it?'

Gran opened the box wider, then nodded to the books inside. 'Go on, then.'

I'd spent the rest of the day curled up in the corner of the bookshop, oblivious to the world around me. The next day Gran and I sold two copies. It was the highlight of my holidays.

Declan leans in closer and points to the tree, pulling my awareness back to the present.

'Can you see it?'

His voice is a breath against my ear, and a shiver scatters down my side. I ignore it, instead nodding and doing my best to focus on the beautiful black and gold bird he's pointing to in a knot in the tree ahead of us.

It seems completely unaware that it is causing such a stir, ruffling its wings and pecking at something on its chest.

Jed lifts his camera again, and there's the soft clicks of about a million photos being taken. He takes a step forward and a stick cracks loudly beneath his foot, startling the bird away.

There's a pause – a moment of reverence as we all watch the majesty of its flight.

Then Jed whoops, galloping over to where Declan and I are standing. At the bird's exit it's as though sound returns to the clearing, a show that's been paused for ten minutes on a pertinent moment and then starts playing again.

'A regent honeyeater!' Jed exclaims, wiping his eyes, shaking his head and looking back at the empty tree in wonder.

Declan grins, his whole face breaking open. 'I can't believe you spotted it,' he says, and his voice is so full of joy that it makes my breathing catch again. He reaches out a hand to clasp Jed's in his. Then he turns to look at me, and I'm half bracing for his tone to change, but it doesn't. 'I went on a birding tour a few years ago, and one of the women was desperate to find a regent honeyeater, but we didn't see even a hint of one the entire ten days.'

Ten days? He watched birds for *ten days*? What's weirder still is that I don't even want to find a way to mock him about it, or to message Yumi about this. I want to keep alive whatever this mood is, whoever this person is. I want to have gone on that tour. *I want to read his book.*

'How did you even see it from the road?' I ask Jed, because, seriously, the bird is about the size of my hand.

Jed taps the side of his eyes. 'I'm always watching,' he says. Which I fully believe. He opens his camera and flicks through his pictures, and Declan moves closer to peer over his shoulder. They're both so intent on pointing out the bird's features that I'm fairly certain we could be right here until night falls or the camera battery dies.

We stand there for what might be twenty minutes before Jed eases the camera back into its case and then strides ahead, looking back over his shoulder impatiently as though we're the ones holding him up.

Declan half smiles again, like it's easy.

'After you,' he says.

I follow Jed through the bushes, much more aware of the dark-haired, green-eyed man behind me than I'd like to be. He doesn't say anything else as the three of us walk single file back to the car, but there's an easiness in the air. A joy that feels like a bubble around us.

'Do you want me to drive for a bit longer?' asks Declan when we reach the car.

I nod, because speaking still feels like I might break something, and climb into the passenger seat while he gets in behind the wheel. He glances down at my legs, which fit much more easily around the snack bag than his do.

'Do you have any nuts in that bag?' he asks, and I can't actually hold the silence any more.

'Nuts?' I exclaim. 'Are they to throw out the window so you can lure more birds to look at? Or are you looking for a snack?'

'Shut up,' says Declan.

He starts the ignition and I pass him a packet of pecans, and for the first time since we've been in a car together the quiet is easy.

'Are you working on anything at the moment?' I ask after a while.

'Not right now,' says Declan, 'given the whole driving situation.'

'Very funny,' I say.

He clears his throat. 'Actually, there is this new idea I'm working on,' he says. 'Playing around with the philosophical question: if a tree falls in the forest, but there's no one around to hear it, does it make a sound?' Declan keeps his eyes fixed ahead. 'But, instead of a tree, I was thinking of using a girl snoring, as a metaphor.'

He says the entire thing with a straight face.

'You'll probably need to find someone who snores loudly, then,' I say. 'I'm sorry I can't help you out with that one.'

'You can't?' says Declan mildly.

'This is why your first book did badly, by the way,' I tell him after a moment. 'Your metaphors are terrible.'

'That's not what the *New York Times* said,' says Declan, and I can't help the snort that comes out.

He grins in response, and my stomach somersaults.

He keeps his eyes on the road, his smile gradually fading.

'I'm working on something,' he says softly. 'But it's not going quite as well as I'd hoped.'

I don't really know what to say in response. It doesn't seem helpful to tell him that I'm sure things will get better soon – but it also doesn't seem right to make a joke. So, when he turns to look at me again, I sort of half smile. He doesn't say anything either, just quirks the corner of his mouth and then looks back at the road.

Whatever's been shifting between us crystallises into something solid, and a wave of nausea hits me in the gut.

I *like* Declan Archer.

Before I can even digest the thought, my ringtone bursts into the car. I pull my phone out of the side of my bag to see that it's my mum again.

'You can answer it if you want,' says Declan, when I sit there for more than a few seconds just staring at the screen.

I cancel the call and slide my phone back into my bag. 'It's my mum,' I tell Declan. 'I'll call her back later.'

And I'm not sure what's in *my* tone this time, but he doesn't ask any questions; he just mutters something about mothers under his breath that makes me feel like he might understand a little.

We switch not long afterwards. After double checking that my ankle is definitely okay, Declan takes a nap. He is honestly the most silent sleeper I have ever met in my life. It's like he's not even *breathing.* I consider poking him, just to make sure he's still alive, but despite the ease in the mood between us, that's a level of comfort we definitely haven't reached yet.

I've been driving for almost two hours when we pass the sign for a town called Milson. Someone has crossed out the M and changed it to a W, and I spend a solid thirty seconds trying to work out what the joke is. I've never heard of 'Wilson' being used in a rude context, which makes me wonder if Yumi is right and that, actually, I am old. I'm tempted to ask Declan if we can swap drivers so that I can text her – if anyone knows what a Wilson is, it will be her.

We're right behind Jed's van, and he slows down to a crawl as we pass through the main street. His indicator lights up just as his arm appears out of the window to point to the side of the road. When he's definitely, absolutely sure that I've got the message and I flick my indicator on as well, he pulls into an empty parking space. I want to believe that because we're in the main street of a small town he's not about to chase down an animal, but with Jed it's actually kind of hard to be sure.

I swing in beside him and turn off the car, then send a quick message to Yumi. The second the engine clicks off, Declan wakes, looking exactly the same as he did when he went to sleep. The only concession to the fact that he's just spent almost two hours napping is that he blinks once.

'Where are we?' he asks, his voice normal and conversational.

'Milson,' I tell him. 'Or, as the locals have affectionately re-signposted it: Wilson.'

'Why Wilson?' asks Declan, and I feel a surge of comfort that if I'm old, he's old too. I think about raising my eyebrows like he's missing something, but then I risk the possibility that I'll have to explain what he's missing.

'No idea,' I say instead.

Jed appears by my window, and I swear he's impatiently tapping his foot against the concrete.

'Welcome to Wilson,' he says when I step out of the car.

'Is the town called Milson or Wilson?' Declan asks, looking around at the shops. I follow his gaze to see that at least half the businesses go by Wilson and the other half go by Milson.

'I'm glad you asked,' says Jed, looking . . . well, glad that he asked. His eyes light up and he straightens his shoulders like he's about to give a presentation.

'The town was founded by the Wilson family. Rumour has it, the husband was in his cups when he named the town, and he wrote an M instead of a W by accident. His wife was so mortified that she died of the shame of living in a town that wasn't her name.'

'That seems extreme,' I mutter, but quietly, because I don't want to risk interrupting Jed.

Jed just nods. 'Half of the townspeople still go by Wilson, out of respect to her.' He claps his hands together, then points down the street. 'Most importantly, though, the Wilson bakery has the best salad sandwiches this side of the equator.'

'You're a Wilsoner, then?' says Declan.

'I will always side with the ladies,' says Jed, and then he *winks* and saunters down the street.

'What just happened?' I whisper. 'Did Jed just make me *swoon*?'

'No idea,' says Declan. 'But I think I might be swooning too.'

Chapter Nineteen

Milson or Wilson, Jed is right, the salad sandwiches are phenomenal, and I also add a few baked goods to my snack bag. Declan raises an eyebrow when I do, but the side of his lip twitches, and the next few hours pass in relative peace.

When we arrive in Candon, it's to a motel that is the most hideous shade of orange I've ever seen. The rooms face outwards in two neat rows, as though they've been told to line up neatly and are sort of grudgingly obeying.

Declan jumps out of the driver's seat and makes his way to the tired-looking reception. He returns a few minutes later with two massive blocks of wood, a key dangling from each of them.

'Do you think the wood makes people more or less likely to lose these?' Declan says, holding them up. 'They aren't really pocket-sized.' His eyes are bright with amusement, but it's warm, not mocking, and a jolt of unmistakable attraction twists in my gut. It's so surprising that for a second I just stare at him.

'I might go for a walk,' I blurt out finally. 'Get some fresh air.'

Declan frowns. 'Do you want company?'

'No,' I say quickly. 'Nope. No.'

'I'll take that as a no, then,' says Declan dryly, handing me a key. 'Give me a ring if your ankle gets sore and you need me to pick you up.'

'Thanks,' I manage to mumble, shoving the key into the top of my snack bag. It hangs awkwardly out of the top, but mercifully Declan doesn't comment. 'I'll see you soon.'

My ankle is fine, but I bring my stick just in case. From what I could see as we drove through, the main street of Candon consists entirely of one small row of shops. The air is cool but not cold, and I thump my way back along the highway, pausing to stop at a lone tree halfway and catch my breath.

I pull out my phone and dial Ruth's number. She answers on the first ring.

'Clarrie!' she says, her voice filled with delight. 'Perfect timing! I'm just passing Woodsborough on the train back from seeing your gran.'

I can imagine her exactly where she is, can picture the benches at the fancy, neatly kept station of Woodsborough. I look down the street at Candon – two places for a moment connected by our voices down the line.

'How's she doing?' I ask.

'She slept most of the time I was there,' says Ruth, still sounding cheerful. I wonder if it's ever hard for her, watching the changes in a friend she's known forty years. 'I'll go earlier in the day next time. The nurses say she's been in good spirits, though, and I managed to knit a whole sleeve of Finn's sweater. How's your trip going? How is that lovely young Declan?'

Even the mention of his name makes my stomach tense.

'It's good. He's good, I think.'

I can almost hear Ruth smile on the other end of the line and I clear my throat before she can ask any follow-up questions.

'Thanks for the update, Ruth. Give her my love.'

'Any time, dear. Take care of yourself. It's nice to hear you sounding happy.'

Her words linger with me after I hang up the phone and start my slow walk down the street again.

It's strange to be back in relative civilisation. Maybe stranger, though, is the town of Candon itself. There's a supermarket and a butcher, but there's a speciality bike shop and a printer too, all of which look completely empty. My stick scratches against the concrete, and every person I pass nods hello.

Then there, just before the end of the row, is a small happy-looking bookshop.

At first, I wonder whether I'm imagining it – it seems so improbable that a bookshop would exist in such a tiny town. But when I step through the door a sweet-sounding bell rings above my head. Small children run around the shop, their parents chatting in the corners. An unassuming, casually dressed man moves between them, coaxing one kid off a shelf while passing a book to another.

A large tree-shaped display reaches up in the centre of the store, filled with copies of *Talking to Trees*. There's a poster on the side advertising the book as their latest book-club pick, because of course it is.

The man looks up the moment I walk through the door, waving a hand. 'With you in a moment,' he calls out while ducking to the counter to ring up a purchase.

'Take your time,' I tell him, because I'm honestly still not sure whether this is all actually a dream.

The shop is small, but it's fascinating to look at the book selection. There are a lot of big-name books that we stock in Brooks', but their memoir and non-fiction sections are much broader than ours.

Not long after I arrive, the parents and children begin to leave, trickling out of the shop with noise and laughter. The bookshop falls silent again, pillows and books strewn across the floor, and it's so like Brooks' after one of Yumi's children's events that it tugs at my chest. I take out my phone to take a photo.

'I'd tell you to get its good side, but it's chaos from every angle,' says the man, turning back from where he was farewelling people at the door.

'I'm sorry!' I say, my face already getting hot. The man just waves away my apology, his eyes kind.

'It's fine,' says the man. 'The truth is I like to think that our mess shows the best of us. I'm Alex,' he says.

'Clarrie,' I tell him, moving my stick to my other side and holding out my hand. 'And I love your mess.' I bend down to pick up the pillows beside him. There's something about the quiet of the shop, about Alex's unpretentious manner, that makes me add, 'I own a bookshop back home, so it's a familiar sight.' The admission trips off my tongue, and it's only when it's halfway out that apprehension clenches at my stomach. Somehow, in eighteen months, it's the first time I've introduced myself to a stranger as the owner. I'm struck with the irrational urge to add that it's my grandparents' shop, really. But I don't, and the knot in my stomach tightens.

But Alex is unaware of my internal struggle, and he looks up in delight. 'I knew you had a good vibe about you,' he says, tapping his nose. 'I'm new to it, myself. Opened last year after twenty years as an accountant.'

I have about twenty questions for him, half of which are deeply personal, but I settle on the one I've been thinking about since I walked through the front door.

'How sustainable is running a bookshop here?' The words are out of my mouth before I can wonder about how rude it is to ask someone about their financial situation.

'To be honest, it's better than I expected,' says Alex with a laugh. 'Enough people drive through that we get weekend and holiday trade. My projections had us lasting six months, but we're still kicking along. You'd know yourself that it's a passion project, though,' he says, and there's something about the easy way he says it that gets caught in my throat. 'You want a cup of tea?'

A passion project. The words lodge themselves in my chest.

'Do you have any coffee?' I ask. Of all the things I expected to do in Candon, sitting in a bookshop drinking a warm drink is not one of them, and yet . . . it feels right.

The lights in Alex's bookshop don't flicker when he turns on his kettle, and he sets us up at a table in the middle of the store. In the time we sit drinking coffee and talking about books, four customers come in. One of them – a decisive woman named Sarah who walks in knowing exactly what she wants – even sits down briefly at the table with us.

'What time is the book club tonight?' she asks, staring at Alex intently.

'Seven-ish,' says Alex. He looks at me. 'Have you read *Talking to Trees*, Clarrie?' he asks, and I almost spit my coffee.

'Not yet,' I say. My hands clench round the mug at the memory of Declan's face when he asked me not to.

Sarah gasps. 'You haven't read it?' she whispers. 'You are so lucky. I wish I had the chance to read it for the first time again.'

'It's our book-club pick tonight,' says Alex, pointing to the poster. 'You should come along, if you don't mind the possibility of being crucified by the group members if you haven't read it. We raise aggressive readers in Candon.' He says it with such fondness that it brings an actual lump to my throat.

'I'll see how I go,' I tell them.

I don't tell them that I'm the bookseller from the dedication, and by the time Alex and I finish our coffee I almost feel guilty not telling him – as though me being on tour with Declan is some sort of secret. I pick a book off the shelf, and Alex rings it up, adding a copy of *Talking to Trees.*

'On the house,' he says. 'You'll love it.'

I push another twenty across the table at him. I can't believe I'm actually buying a copy of *Talking to Trees* when I have one in my bag, but I also can't let him give it to me for free.

'We need you to last at least another six months,' I tell

him, meaning the words more than I can express. I might not be sure of much, but in a strange way Alex reminds me of Gran. And even in the half-hour I've been here I can see how much this shop matters to the community.

'Do you ever think about giving up?' I ask him as he rings up the purchase.

Alex doesn't even hesitate. 'At least once a week,' he says. He looks up to meet my eyes. 'But then who would give our community books?'

The words are simple and stark, and I don't know exactly how to answer, or what I was even looking for. So, instead, I swallow the emotion welling in my throat and point at the poster on the side of the tree.

'I think I might have something for you,' I tell him.

Chapter Twenty

'What?'

Declan leans against the doorjamb of his room, his hair scruffier than I've ever seen it.

'You've been invited to a book club,' I repeat, my voice faltering a little. He looks and sounds like he's just woken up from a nap. For the first time since marching all the way from Candon Books to his door, my resolve wavers and my mind flicks back to the earlier jolt of attraction. 'Were you asleep?'

Declan covers a yawn with the back of one hand, then leans his arm against the side of his door and rests his head against it. The bottom of his shirt hitches to reveal stomach and a flash of dark hair and I freeze. I try to tell myself that I saw him without a shirt earlier today, that this is nothing, but it doesn't help. *Don't look down, Clarrie.*

'Maybe,' Declan says. He looks warm and rumpled and he closes his eyes in what is an exceptionally long blink, and of course I automatically look down at the thin strip of exposed skin. My mouth goes dry. 'I'm not going to a book club,' he mumbles, opening just one eye to squint at me.

I yank my gaze back up again and clear my throat. 'That is

going to be a problem,' I tell him. 'Given that I have already accepted on your behalf.' His other eye snaps open and his head lifts.

'You what?'

'It starts in three hours,' I add brightly. 'So there's plenty of time to wake up.'

'Clarence,' Declan growls, becoming more alert by the second. He rubs a hand across his forehead. 'You promised that I would go to a book club? On my one afternoon off this week?'

'Technically you also have an afternoon off the day after tomorrow,' I say. He narrows his eyes at me. 'It's for the local bookshop,' I tell him apologetically. 'Alex the owner used to be an accountant. They all love your book.'

Declan presses his head back against his arm and lets out a long, slow sigh. 'Fine,' he exhales without yelling at me, and my image of him shifts a little further from the arrogant man I thought he was.

Until a smile slowly spreads across his face and my stomach flips again. 'But if I'm going you're coming with me.'

Even from outside, we can hear the buzz of noise in the bookshop. I'm wrapped in about six layers because, damn it, Candon is *cold* at night.

I rub my hands up and down my arms and Declan glances at me, his lips quirking in amusement.

'Do you want my jumper?' he asks.

'Why, are you hoping to show your biceps off to all the

people inside the bookshop?' I grumble, and *oh my gosh what have I turned into?* 'How are you not frozen?'

The words are snippy, but instead of snapping back Declan just chuckles softly. 'I run pretty warm.'

There's nothing remotely erotic about the way he says it, but a sudden flush of heat rushes through me anyway. Whatever this new awareness of Declan Archer is, it's not convenient. We're about to open the door to a room full of people swooning over him. I do not need to add myself to that number.

It's nice to see him at ease, though, and I wonder why he doesn't seem as stressed as he did before the previous two events. But before I can ask him he pushes open the door to Candon Books.

All conversation in the bookshop abruptly stops, and about fifteen people's heads swivel in our direction. They're all sitting around in a loose circle of chairs.

There's a beat of silence. I scan the group. I see Sarah, the woman I met earlier, but there's no sign of Alex.

'Hello,' I say, smiling at the room in general. 'I'm Clarence Brooks, and this is—'

'Declan Archer,' a woman whispers reverently from the back of the group and *chaos* breaks out in the room as every one of the fifteen people suddenly tries to talk at the same time.

Declan looks at me in alarm, and I cough to stop the bubble of mirth rising in my throat.

Alex comes in from the back of the shop, rolling his eyes good-naturedly and clapping his hands sharply three times. 'Ladies and gentleman,' he says with warm affection, 'is this how we treat guests to Candon? He's a person, not just the author of our favourite book of all time.' He strides forward to clasp Declan's hand. 'Although you are also that,' he adds. 'Thanks for writing a banger of a book. I'm Alex. It's nice to meet you.'

'You too, Alex,' says Declan. He looks around the group, his usual warm crowd smile on his lips. *When did I start knowing his smiles?* 'It's nice to meet all of you,' he adds.

'So nice to meet you,' a man says, looking like he might faint.

A woman reaches out to touch Declan's arm, then freezes at Alex's look.

'All right, everyone,' Alex says. 'Move up.'

Everyone in the group obediently picks up their chair and shuffles around to make space in the circle. 'We have an "everyone in charge of their own chair" policy,' Alex explains over the general kerfuffle.

Yumi floated the idea of an in-store book club a few months ago. It was just after the most recent electricity bill had come through, and I put her off for weeks. Eventually, she stopped asking.

She would adore an 'everyone in charge of their own chair' policy, and I find myself mentally calculating how many chairs would fit in the space at Brooks' before I realise that, for the first time, I'm considering the possibility of doing it.

Declan coughs and I look sideways to see him holding two chairs. 'You okay next to me?' he asks.

I nod and he places the two chairs near Alex's.

The noise in the room dies down, and Alex claps again. 'Welcome to book club. We're honoured to have Declan Archer and Clarrie Brooks here with us tonight. I know everyone is excited. Given the author is with us, we might give our standard first question a miss.'

'What's the standard first question?' asks Declan.

Alex opens his mouth then closes it again.

'We usually start with "Who here read the book?" ' Sarah pipes up helpfully from the back.

'*Everyone* would have their hand up tonight,' the man on the other side of Alex reassures Declan, and there's a chorus of agreement from the group.

Declan leans back slightly in his seat and raises his hands. 'I don't want to change the regular flow of the book club,' he says. 'It's totally fine with me if you want to ask the question.' He doesn't look at me, but I can *hear* the laughter in his voice.

Alex looks between Declan and me.

'Maybe you could tell us what inspired the book instead,' says Alex tactfully.

At first, I think Declan is going to answer the way he usually does in front of a crowd, with warmth and charisma. But then he looks around the group, his gaze resting briefly on Alex.

'I was going through a hard time,' he says softly. 'Trees have always been a big part of my life – it was a tree that made me believe in love – and I wanted to explore that.' He doesn't elaborate, but my heart aches with a feeling I can't quite name.

'The silver tree,' someone whispers.

'Ohhh,' the group hums.

Declan's smile widens, but he doesn't confirm or deny it.

'The silver tree?' I say, and I hear at least three outraged whispers on the other side of the circle.

'Has she not read the book?'

Despite Alex's worry, the book club doesn't crucify me for not having read the book. They pepper Declan with questions for more than an hour, and he good-naturedly answers them.

There's a warmth in the bookshop that feels like home.

By the time the official tea and biscuit portion of the evening begins I'm so tired that I can barely stand. I make my way over to Alex by the biscuit table.

'Thank you,' he says warmly. 'I can't tell you how much it means to us to have had you both here tonight.'

'It's really a wonderful shop you've got here, Alex,' I tell him honestly.

'I'll have to come visit Brooks' one day,' he says. 'And not just because of the dedication.'

I meet his eyes and he winks at me.

'If we're still around,' I tell him. His brow crinkles. 'If you worked the dedication out, you probably know there are a few things that need fixing.'

'You'll fix them,' he says with such a calm confidence that, for a heartbeat, I might even believe him.

Declan is deep in conversation with someone, and I try to catch his attention twice before he finally looks up. I mime that I'm going to walk back, and he nods, before returning to his conversation.

Outside is even colder than it was when we entered the bookshop, and the sky is crystal clear. Alex's words and thoughts about the bookshops creep in on me, but once I start walking my lungs are filled with air so crisp it's hard to think about much else.

And when I finally make it back to the motel I'm so tired that it's all I can do to take my trousers off and fall into bed.

Chapter Twenty-one

The knock that wakes me the next morning is loud and decisive.

I glance at the alarm clock on my bedside table, then roll over and pull the pillow over my head. We're only travelling four hours today and I don't need to be up for at least half an hour. Whoever is at the door can wait.

'"It would be great if you could just sign some stock after the book club,"' Declan's voice sounds through the door and every part of me freezes. '"It will mean so much to Alex,"' he says.

A laugh catches in my throat.

'Two hours, Clarence,' says Declan. 'You owe me two hours of my life back.'

I mean, that feels a little excessive. I push out of bed and pull on my trousers.

'As if you didn't love the book club's attention,' I say, ripping open the old wooden door to see Declan leaning on the railing, looking over the parking lot. He's wearing his jeans again, and most of the mud from spotlighting is gone, but there are a few patches near his ankles that he missed in whatever sink wash he did. Rather than his standard white top, his shirt is a soft blue that I haven't seen before, and he's holding a stack of papers in his hand. He raises an eyebrow at me.

'I thought you liked the book club last night,' I say, half defensive, half amused.

'I did like it,' Declan concedes, pushing off the railing. 'For the official hour and a half book-club portion of the evening. But then you *left* me, and I was stuck there for another two hours.'

'*Two hours?*' I can't stop the snort this time. Declan glares at me.

'I'm sorry!' I say, trying to wipe the smile off my face. 'I told you I was leaving. It seemed like you wanted to stay.'

'I thought you were just going to the toilet!'

'I was miming walking out the door! What toilet would I have been going to?'

Declan narrows his eyes, then holds the papers in his hand out to me. I take them automatically.

'What are they?' I ask, natural curiosity helping to push away my inclination to study the man for clues and glancing at the one on top.

'More questions,' says Declan. 'About the book. That I didn't get a chance to answer last night. I told them someone would get back to them as soon as possible. You are that someone.'

I'm filled with a mixture of horror and amusement as I flick through the comprehensive stack of questions.

'You know I don't know the answers to these,' I say, and Declan just raises an eyebrow and leans back.

'Better get reading after the tour,' he says.

But before I can shove the paper back at him a bright voice calls out, 'She's up!' and a second later something pushes past him and barrels into me.

A wave of happy perfume engulfs me, before a way-too-awake Bri pulls back to look into my eyes and then leans in to hug me again.

'It's so nice to meet you in person!' she says after one more squeeze, stepping back to stand beside Declan. She beams at me, and then at him.

'I forgot to mention Bri's here,' says Declan wryly, but he's smiling now.

'My sister's husband came home early so I jumped on a flight,' says Bri. 'I went via the warehouse and loaded Little Blue up with as many books as I could. We'll transfer them over to the van this morning before we leave.' She claps, and despite the fact that I'm not fully awake and I have a stack of very complicated questions in my hand, it's hard not to catch some of her enthusiasm. 'Everyone all right to leave in twenty or so? I made breakfast bowls for the cars!'

If you'd asked me a few days ago if I was looking forward to the four-hour car trip with Declan, I'd have almost certainly rolled my eyes at you. But the sensation that washes over me at the realisation that we're not driving together, that he's driving with Bri, doesn't feel like relief – it feels an awful lot like . . . disappointment.

I can sense Declan watching me, like everything running through me is somehow sitting just beneath the surface. But I want him to see how I'm feeling even less than I want to be feeling it.

This isn't bad. In fact, it might actually be a good thing. Maybe the inexplicable bursts of awareness I have of Declan are just because we're spending so much time in the car together.

I keep my focus on Bri, and pull my smile tighter.

'Can't wait!'

Jed is a surprisingly uncomplicated travelling companion. He drives at a steady speed, he calmly points out every animal we pass and he listens exclusively to jazz. If I miss a certain black-haired, green-eyed arrogant author and the slightly awkward random conversations, I don't mention it to myself.

After half an hour, we pull over to the side of the road to eat breakfast. Declan and Bri are dropping off her hire car on the way, so Jed informs me that we have time for a fifteen-minute stop. Honestly, it's a lot like travelling with my dad, if my dad was marginally more communicative and a lot more into birds.

Jed pulls out the two breakfast bowls and passes one to me. It's filled with granola, yoghurt and every fresh fruit imaginable, and I groan when I take the first bite – Bri is some sort of breakfast wizard. It also has the added bonus of making me think of Yumi, who weirdly hates anything that mixes dairy with fruit.

Jed, on the other hand, espouses in *detail* how good they are.

'I have never had such a good breakfast in all of my life,' he says between bites. When halfway through breakfast he glimpses a spotted wren in the forest, it's a genuine struggle between the bowl and the bird. In the end he stands, bowl in hand.

'I'll be back in five minutes,' he tells me, tucking his spoon into his pocket and gripping the side of his bowl.

He disappears into the trees, and for the first time in days I have reception and ten minutes to myself. I pull out my phone and dial the number for Brooks'.

'Good morning, this is Brooks' Books, why the hell are you calling and not kissing the hunk of a man you're driving with?' says Yumi in a sing-song voice.

'Is that how you answer the phone to all our customers?' I ask her, even as amusement fills my chest. I take another bite of granola.

'Pretty much,' says Yumi. 'Although sometimes I sub "man" for "woman". You would be surprised how many people hang up on me. I'm assuming it's because they've gone to do the kissing.'

I can picture her sitting at the table in the kitchenette and for a second, I feel hopelessly lonely, wishing I was there, listening to the kettle shriek and answering Annabel Stone's endless author questions when she inevitably comes in. I curse Alex and his bookshop, and the things they made me feel.

The side of the road feels too quiet.

'How are the trees?' continues Yumi. 'And by trees I mean Declan. Have you read the book yet?'

'No,' I tell her. I don't tell her that he asked me not to, and I don't know why. Only that now the idea of reading it on tour feels like betraying him, somehow. 'I went spotlighting,' I say instead. 'But your head torch wasn't bright enough.'

'I got your message,' says Yumi. 'I thought it might've been some sort of sex reference. Are you trying to make up cool sex references now? It's not working.'

I tell her about the owls and about Jed, and about the spider, about Alex's bookshop and about the granola and yoghurt.

'That's disgusting,' says Yumi matter-of-factly. Then, more softly, 'It's nice to hear you're having fun.'

The granola sticks in my throat but I don't correct her because even with everything that's happened . . . I think I actually am having fun.

'How are you?' I ask her. We've texted back and forth, so I know she's doing okay, but it feels different on the phone.

'Both me and this old hunk of bricks are doing very well, thanks, boss,' says Yumi. 'Except . . .' She pauses, and my senses go on alert. 'You know what, never mind.'

'What?' I say.

'I didn't say anything,' says Yumi.

I'm silent in response, and Yumi sighs dramatically.

'Your mum came in yesterday,' she says finally. 'She had another woman with her. I think she was an estate agent.'

The words make my blood freeze, and the granola in

my mouth turns dusty. *She went in anyway, even after I told her not to.*

'Are you okay?' I make myself speak, to ask the question that matters.

I can almost hear Yumi roll her eyes. 'I'm fine. The bookshop was quiet – it was just Annabel Stone in, and she always asks fewer questions when you're not here. Your mum was fine, and, honestly, they didn't do anything. Just walked around the shop and then out the back, muttering about your gran being manipulative. They weren't here for long. But I wanted to tell you, just in case.'

'Yeah,' I say, trying and failing not to let my mum's muttered comments get to me. 'Thanks, Yumi. And I'm sorry.' I'm not really sure what else there is to say. I rub my head and the motion reminds me of Declan so I stop.

'Don't be ridiculous,' says Yumi. 'Telling your mum that you're having a torrid affair with Declan was the most fun I've had all year.'

'Excellent,' I say. Then I remember it's Yumi I'm talking to. 'You didn't actually say that, right?'

'Okay, I'm very busy,' says Yumi. 'I'm going to hang up now.'

She does exactly that, and I'm still staring at my phone, trying to untie the emotions in the pit of my stomach at the idea of Mum not listening to me, at Mum muttering about Gran and at her being in the shop with an estate agent, when Jed comes back.

'No more dilly-dallying,' he says, marching round to the driver's seat. 'We've got a schedule to keep.'

There's something about Jed's stern determination that rubs off on me, and I send a quick text to my mum. *Please don't go into the bookshop again when I'm not there.*

I slide my phone back into my pocket. I have other things to think about right now.

Chapter Twenty-two

The next site is not so much an intimate space in the woods as it is a massive field.

Jed shakes his head as we drive into the large parking lot.

'Doesn't really count as wilderness, does it?' he grumbles, leaning forward and looking in both directions out of the windscreen to take it in in its entirety.

'Bri said this was one of the places that inspired Declan,' I tell him, glad to have some information for once. Unlike *Talking to Trees*, I actually did read the itinerary in detail. The event tonight is the biggest we'll do on the entire tour. It's also the first time we'll use the tents Declan and I – or Declan and Bri, now – have been carting around. After tonight, we'll have another two days to make our way further north.

Bri and Declan are already out of the van. They're standing in the middle of the field and Bri is talking animatedly, gesturing with her entire body. She bounds across as Jed and I get out of the car.

'Fancy seeing you two here!' she says when she's in earshot, opening her arms wide.

'Hello, Brianna,' says Jed in his usual semi-formal tone. 'Thank you for the breakfast bowls. They were sufficient.'

I frown and look at Jed, who literally talked for five minutes about the qualities of the bowls this morning. He doesn't meet my gaze, and *this is so weird*.

'They were incredible,' I tell Bri, in what is a direct quote from Jed. I look at him sideways out of the corner of my eye, but he doesn't even flinch. 'Did you make the granola yourself?' I say, turning my attention back to Bri.

Bri nods. 'The baby was up all through the night so I took shifts with my sister. It's amazing what you can achieve with a four a.m. start.'

Jed nods too, like he knows what she's talking about, and Bri tucks a strand of hair behind her ear. Behind her, Declan is approaching slowly, looking around at the field. His hands are tucked into his pockets, and he somehow looks both completely comfortable here and ill at ease.

'There's a great spot just through the trees on the other side of the field,' says Bri. 'We might set up the tents over there?' She smiles at Jed, and he turns to Declan.

'I'm happy to do it,' says Jed. 'Declan will help me,' he adds decisively.

Bri's face falls slightly, but she claps her hands together and nods. 'Excellent,' she says. 'Clarrie, I'll give you a hand with the books.'

My eyes automatically stray to Declan, only to find him already looking at me. He glances down.

'Sounds great,' I say.

'Tents it is,' says Declan, drawing his gaze away and back to Jed, and I don't quite know what just happened, but I'm way too aware of where he is in the field as we both walk off to our respective tasks.

'How is your sister?' I ask Bri, pulling my attention back. 'How's everything with the new baby?'

'She's good,' says Bri. 'Tired.' She shakes her head. 'Her baby Lucy is wonderful, so beautiful and cuddly and warm. But I do *not* want kids.'

'You don't?' I say, unlocking the van and reaching in to grab the table we use for the books. I'm surprised – not so much that she doesn't want kids, but that she's so sure she doesn't. She must be at least a few years younger than me.

Bri shakes her head. 'I love other people's kids,' she says, taking the table from me. 'And I will be the best auntie in the world, but it's really just not for me, you know? What about you? Do you want kids one day?'

She looks at me over her shoulder and I feel a little like a deer in the headlights.

It's funny; I've never thought about it much before. I guess I always just thought that I would have kids one day. But being faced with the outright question, and with the possibility that there's a different choice, makes me pause.

'I do,' I tell her, and it's as if I'm learning the answer even as I say the words aloud. I've never been someone who has a ten-year plan; most days I'm just trying to get through the next ten minutes. But, even if I never have kids, there's something about knowing my answer to a big life question that seems . . . hopeful. I lift one side of the table as Bri lifts the other, and it feels like something has shifted inside me. Maybe I have more answers than I think I do.

I don't see much of Declan before the event. Unlike the previous two afternoons, we have no real indication of how many people are going to show up, and it's as if by unspoken agreement we've decided the best course of action is just to be as prepared as possible.

Under Bri's direction and promise that she'll put it back exactly where it came from, Jed begrudgingly brings in a large rock from the woods beyond the field to place on the small platform we've apparently been carrying with us, 'to look more authentic'. Bri cordons off the area around it with rope, ushers Declan up on top of it, then makes me walk around with her viewing it from every possible angle. Honestly, she's so persuasive that it's a small miracle that Declan didn't give in and tell her sooner who the bookseller from the dedication was.

We all stuff the sandwiches Bri made – which are almost Milson/Wilson quality – in our mouths as we're working, marking out the space people will stand in, setting up banners and organising technology for Declan.

Then, all of a sudden, we're fifteen minutes out from the event and I'm standing at my table, rearranging books, watching Declan going over his notes. There's a frown creased along his forehead, and he's tapping his foot with a restless energy that seems so at odds with who he is.

'He hates doing it,' says Bri, sidling up to me with a cupcake in her hand. The words aren't loud, but I still startle at having been caught watching him.

'What?' I say. 'Hates doing what?' But I already know. I've known since before the first event.

'All of this,' says Bri, waving her arm around and taking a bite of the cupcake. 'He nearly pulled out of the tour about four times,' she says between chewing. 'Then we found you, and he was so mad about the publicity around the dedication that I've never been able to work out if he was going through with it to spite you or to help you. Although, with Declan, it's possible it's both.'

Declan looks up from the rock he's sitting on to meet my eyes and I feel something unfamiliar pulse through me that I don't want to touch with a ten-foot pole right now but should probably examine later. He still hasn't even told me why he dedicated the book to me.

'Is he okay?' I ask softly.

Bri nods. 'He's okay. Sometimes, it's just the starting that's hard.'

I rub my chest, pulling my eyes away from Declan's.

'Enough about him, though,' Bri says, finishing her cupcake and brushing off her hands. 'What's up with you and Jed?' Her eyes flick to where he's coming out of the bushes.

'Sorry, what?' I say, 'Jed?'

'I can see why you're into him,' she says. 'He is hands down the sexiest man I've ever seen in my entire life.'

There is no trace of irony in her voice, nothing to indicate that she is joking.

'Jed?' I repeat a little helplessly, reaching for my water bottle.

Bri nods. 'All those silver threads and the stern-park-ranger-exterior vibe really work for him.'

'I'm definitely not into Jed.' At least of that I'm certain.

Bri's head spins towards me so quickly I'm surprised she doesn't get whiplash. 'You're not?' she says. 'Would you mind switching cars with me tomorrow then?'

My head is pounding.

'Are you trying to avoid Declan?' I say, because I'm not sure if I've descended into imagining things.

Bri frowns, then shakes her head. 'No,' she says. 'Why would I try to avoid Declan? Declan is great, but Jed is . . .'

We both turn to look at where he seems to be counting out how many steps wide the clearing is.

'Passionate. Mysterious.'

'Right,' I say, trying to get my head around the fact that sunny, positive Bri seems to have a crush on park ranger Jed.

Bri wraps her arms round me.

'Thank you so much, Clarrie,' she says.

And, apparently, we've officially swapped cars tomorrow.

There's a crunch of gravel, and we both look over to the car park, to where two burly men are climbing out of a van that has *Arnold's Security* written on the side.

'The guards are here!' she says happily. 'I wonder which one is Arnold.'

'We have security?' I ask her.

'Never underestimate a crowd,' Bri calls over her shoulder.

Chapter Twenty-three

In the space of less than ten minutes, the empty field fills with people and sound, and I can't help but wonder how Declan's feeling about all this.

When I finally spot him, though, it's to see him talking quietly with Bri. Her hands are resting on his shoulders, and he's nodding and breathing deeply. And I know that there's nothing between them, and that it's selfish, but . . . my feet itch to go over there and help if I can. I resolutely turn my attention back to the book table.

Bri is buzzing. She flits between groups of people, chatting and laughing, making sure everyone is comfortable and welcoming a group she tells me are just a few journalists. After his conversation with Bri, Declan seems calm. He fiddles with the AV equipment, occasionally pausing to have a quiet conversation with someone who recognises him.

Jed walks the perimeter of the field with the two men from Arnold's Security, stopping every few steps to look sternly at anyone who is overly rowdy. Then 4 p.m. arrives, and Bri makes her way to the rock that Jed set up. Her introduction is as natural in person as on screen, but without the lag to stop her, her arm movements are much more enthusiastic.

Then she introduces Declan. The roar from the crowd is deafening as he climbs up onto the rock with Bri. The rope she used to cordon off the rock and the two security guards standing beside it suddenly seem strangely, painfully necessary. At a *book tour*.

Declan waves a little to the crowd, and another cheer rolls through. A group of women in the front row start chanting his name, and someone close to where I'm standing shouts, 'Your book changed my life!'

It's . . . a lot, and I'm glad to be standing comfortably behind the book table.

Declan half smiles and the crowd almost loses it again.

Bri holds up a hand for quiet.

'I'll leave you alone with Declan in a moment, but, before I do, I'm very pleased to announce that anyone who wants to buy a book today will be purchasing it from Clarence Brooks, from Brooks' Books!'

Bri points to the table where I'm standing, and it's like the first day, when everyone turned to look at me. Somehow, though, even though she's not announcing that I've looked through Declan's suitcase, it feels more charged. Especially when she whispers in a not-whisper, 'Otherwise known as the bookseller from the dedication.'

A few of the journalists Bri pointed out earlier turn to take photos of me, and my first thought is that it's no wonder Declan hates it. It's like there's a giant spotlight illuminating the table, exposing every part of me. But I channel Gran and

I wave, and the crowd cheers again – though much less impressively than they did for Declan – and I feel a weird sort of rush. I'm left both empty and relieved when they turn away.

As with the two previous events, Declan's speech goes well. There's no sign of the intimacy from last time, but there's a wild energy, a fierce passion for the book. Like these people feel the same way about books that Jed feels about birds. And, while I never jumped passionately in front of an author or yelled out that he changed my life, seeing the crowd . . . I *remember* that feeling. I remember sneaking into the bookshop with Gran early in the morning when the next book in my favourite series came out – she'd never let me read them until release day, no matter how early they arrived in store. But there was always a giddiness. A passionate hope about what might happen next in the story. A sense of excitement that I don't think I've felt about anything in the last few years. But even just watching the crowd . . . it reminds me of that feeling.

I think of what Alex said, and I wonder if maybe life at Brooks' could feel hopeful like that again too.

Then Declan finishes speaking, and the sales table is *swamped.*

We sell out of all the books Bri and I brought from the van. Jed runs back to get another few boxes, and we sell out of those too. Declan signs almost continuously, stopping every now and then to stand and stretch, or to come over to collect a book from the table. He barely glances at me when he does, and it feels a little like the moment the crowd turned away, but it also helps me to focus on my job.

It's after 7 p.m. by the time he finishes, and he and Jed look as exhausted as I feel. The clear sky from earlier has started clouding over, but, thankfully, the rain seems to be holding off. Bri is still bright and cheery, as though she could keep going for another six hours at least, and she bounces over to the table with a pair of women in tow. One looks like she's just out of school, wearing jeans and a yellow T-shirt, a camera bag slung over her shoulder. The other is older, wearing a pair of bright pink overalls, and is somehow about fifty times more terrifying. Her square-rimmed glasses rest easily on her nose and her hair is a riot on top of her head, but her expression reminds me of Elizabeth (of the excellent bun and newspaper article). It feels like she can see all my secrets – even the ones that I don't know about myself. I do not have a great feeling about this.

'Clarrie!' says Bri. 'This is Fiona and Ava from *Behind the Books*.' She gestures to them – Fiona is in the pink overalls – and widens her eyes at me in a move that I'm pretty sure is trying to communicate to me that this is a Big Deal.

But despite being what Yumi calls 'over the hill', I do know *Behind the Books* – it's the most reputable book magazine in the country. They do profiles on the books and their authors, and their write-ups have been known to change the trajectory of authors' careers. If *Talking to Trees* gets in *Behind the Books*, it will pretty much guarantee the book's long-term success. Hence Bri's eyes.

Declan stands from where he's just finished signing, and when he catches sight of all of us talking his body goes still.

He looks as though he's caught between coming over and running off into the forest. Then Bri glances over at him, waving a hand, and his fate is sealed.

'Declan,' says Fiona when he reaches us, her voice low and calm. 'It's a pleasure to see you again.'

'Likewise,' says Declan, reaching out to shake her hand. His eyes flick to where I'm standing behind the table and he shifts slightly on his feet.

'Fiona here is gathering information for a possible article on Declan and *Talking to Trees*,' Bri says to me, her voice just a little more high-pitched than usual. 'She was hoping she might be able to have a quick word with the two of you together.'

The two of us . . . together? *Why?*

'Don't worry,' says Fiona when neither Declan nor I respond immediately, 'I'll be kind to her.'

Declan turns to look at Bri, and the look he gives her is so loaded that I'm surprised it doesn't explode in the clearing, and then everyone sort of turns towards me.

What is happening?

I have an awful, sinking suspicion that I'm not going to like what comes next and there is a very large part of me that's tempted to run into the bushes myself. I'm sick of feeling behind on everything. The profile is on Declan – they're hardly going to include much detail on me, even if they know I'm the subject of the dedication. But . . . it's a way to potentially have Brooks' mentioned in *Behind the Books*. Bri and Declan are both looking at me with varying degrees of panic.

'Sure, that's fine,' I hear myself say, still not quite sure what it is that I'm actually agreeing to, and the girl with the jeans – Ava – snaps a photo.

'I thought maybe you could set yourself up over there,' Bri says to Fiona, pointing to the edge of the clearing where a camping chair and two-seater bench wait expectantly. 'I'll bring these two over in just a moment.'

'Bri,' says Declan as soon as they're out of earshot, his voice low and a little dangerous-sounding.

'It's for five minutes,' says Bri, smile barely slipping.

'What's for five minutes?' I ask, apprehension prickling along my arms.

'She wants us to pretend to be dating,' Declan says in a low, tight voice when Bri doesn't respond immediately.

'*What?*' my voice is so loud that Fiona turns to look at us. Bri waves brightly back, like everything is totally fine.

'I'm sorry,' she says to Declan through her smile, and to her credit she does sound genuinely apologetic. 'She saw the picture of the two of you on the Read, Repeat website and there are a lot of comments under the thread. She said addressing it would add another layer to the profile, that people would love to know just a little more about your personal life.'

'What picture on the Read, Repeat website?' I ask.

'Tessa?' says Declan tersely, rubbing his head.

Bri just nods.

'Can we see?' asks Declan. Bri whips out her phone, like she knew this moment was coming. The photo is already on the screen.

It's Declan and I, the moment before we turned to face the

camera for our posed picture. I'm gazing up at him with what appears to be frustration and desire, but Declan . . . he's looking down at me with what can only be described as tenderness and *oh my goodness what are the comments saying?* I close my eyes and Declan shifts beside me, and I resist the urge to look up, to see his reaction to the picture. *Read, Repeat have done it again.*

'Damn it,' says Declan. It's a direct echo of my internal sentiment, and, impossibly, I'm still a little offended.

'What are the comments saying?' I ask.

'There's a lot of speculation about whether or not the two of you are together,' says Bri. 'Which I believe is what Tessa intended.'

Declan closes his eyes.

'I think saying the two of you are dating is the easiest way to explain it for this interview,' Bri adds carefully.

'The best story, you mean?' says Declan.

Bri doesn't deny it. 'The fans are interested in what's happening,' she says. 'Everyone loves a feel-good story.' She hesitates. 'And it will be best for Clarrie short term,' she says, 'if you look like you're dating. Some people are a little angry at her.'

'Could we just ignore the picture?' I ask, trying to sound calm and reasonable about the whole thing and not to fixate on what people are saying, or on the unease thumping through my chest. 'Surely if we don't address it, it won't affect the *Behind the Books* article?'

'Probably not,' says Bri, but she sounds doubtful. 'But if you could do five minutes . . .'

'Plus a lifetime on the internet,' mutters Declan darkly.

'I can do it,' I say quietly, and Declan glances at me, his eyes unreadable.

'Are you sure?' he asks.

There's no hint of mocking or challenge to the words; he's not trying to goad me into it. I feel like if I say no that will be the end of it. It's the freedom of feeling like that, as much as it is the possibility that Brooks' might get more publicity, that has me nodding my head.

'You have to convince them to credit Brooks' at the bottom of the article,' says Declan firmly. 'And if we do this I'm not doing their posed photo shoot.'

Bri nods quickly; her relief visible. 'I'll sort that out,' she says. Then she stops. 'Thank you, both of you.'

She leads us over to the edge of the clearing, where Fiona and Ava are chatting quietly. The sky above them is heavy, and I find myself rather uncharitably hoping for a sudden burst of rain.

'Fiona is thorough, but mostly nice,' Declan says quietly as we near, his breath warm against my ear, and a tingle darts down my spine. I turn to look up at him and his face is too damn close.

'I've spoken to her on the phone a few times already for the profile,' he explains. 'Are you sure you're okay to do this?' he asks. We're close to Fiona and Ava now, so I can only nod.

'Sorry about that,' Bri says to Fiona as Ava hops up from the double bench to make room for Declan and I. *Excellent.*

I sit gingerly on the bench, trying to look like I sit on

benches with Declan all the time. He slides in beside me, so close that his leg rests against mine. I haven't dated anyone in the two years since Jamie and I broke up, and *how do people who are dating even look?* Fiona watches the two of us, a pen resting lightly between her fingers.

'Thanks for doing this,' she says to me. 'The best profiles are always the ones where we get an insight into the authors' lives. Our audience love the stories behind the books.'

'Happy to help,' I say, my voice only a little raspy. Declan shifts beside me, and a second later his fingertips brush mine on the bench. For a heartbeat I think it's an accident, but then he threads his fingers through mine as though, you know, we're dating, and my stupid breath catches. *Totally normal. This is totally normal.* It feels like every nerve has gathered at the points where our hands touch.

'Can you tell me a bit about how the two of you met?' asks Fiona, eyes flicking down to our joined hands.

I clear my throat, trying to ignore the tingling in my hand, in the pit of my stomach.

'We met in the bookshop,' says Declan succinctly. Fiona taps her pen against her notepad, like she's waiting for more, and Bri clears her throat behind us. But Declan doesn't elaborate, and I get the strangest sense that he's trying to protect me.

'Declan came in just after his first book came out,' I say into the silence. Declan's fingers tighten. He shifts slightly, his arm brushing against mine.

Gran always used to say, *'In for a penny, in for a pound.'*

'I was having a bad day, and we were having temporary issues with our power. Declan very kindly pointed out that we should perhaps look at getting it fixed, and in response I suggested that perhaps he might not have written his best book yet.'

Fiona uncrosses her legs and leans forward. 'How did that go over?' she asks.

'I doubt either of us would describe it as our finest moment,' says Declan dryly.

Fiona almost cracks a grin. 'Fair enough. But obviously the two of you have a different relationship now. Can I ask when that happened? Was it before or after *Talking to Trees* came out?'

'Before,' says Declan.

'After,' I say at the same time.

Crap.

Fiona raises her eyebrows.

'Declan counts from the time we first kissed,' I blurt out.

Holy crap, what did I just say?

Declan coughs, and I hear the click of Ava's camera.

'That's romantic of you, Declan,' says Fiona.

I'm expecting Declan to come back with something cutting, or dry, but he doesn't say anything, and I feel him turn to look at me. I don't look back; I'm not sure I can meet his eyes. But the weight of his gaze is enough to make my ears hot and my palms damp.

From there the interview passes relatively smoothly, and I manage to answer the rest of the questions without dropping any more made-up bombshells into the conversation, and without pulling my much-too-hot hand away from Declan. His description of Fiona as kind but thorough is surprisingly accurate. By the time we reach the end of the interview, I am more than ready to be done.

'Two more questions,' says Fiona, and I almost sigh in relief, until she directs the first of the two to me. 'What is it that makes Brooks' special?'

It's more focus on Brooks' than I might have thought possible, and somewhere in my brain I register that it will be great for the bookshop if I have a good answer. Instead, the question makes me freeze. Gran was what made Brooks' special.

'Booksellers are like matchmakers,' I say finally. My palms go damp again, but I don't pull my hand from Declan's. 'The good ones can set you up for life.' Gran was one of the best.

Fiona nods, and I know it will be enough to leave it at that, but then I think of Alex. Of his bookshop, and all the people who showed up last night to talk about a book together. Of Yumi and her bets with the customers. Of the kids who came in proudly dressed as sea creatures. Of Annabel Stone.

'And the community,' I blurt out, just as Fiona opens her mouth to ask the next question. 'Our community is what makes Brooks' special.' I swear all the other sound in the clearing fades, and I feel heat rush to my face. *Was that too much?* I don't know if I even answered her question.

But then Fiona smiles. 'I look forward to visiting one day,' she says. She leans forward.

'Last question. Did he write a better book?'

Time pauses for half a beat. Declan squeezes my hand, so lightly that it might be an accident.

'Excellent question,' he says. 'Did I write a better book, Clarrie?'

I do meet his eyes this time. He raises an eyebrow, his eyes bright with a wry amusement. And there's something about the moment that makes my breath catch again.

'I'll tell you when I finish reading it,' I say, and that side of Declan's lip curves up.

Fiona chuckles, a low, warm sound. 'I like that,' she says. Then she pushes to her feet.

I slip my hand from Declan's to shake hers. If she notices my palm is wet, she's classy enough not to comment on it.

'Thanks so much for your time today, Clarence. Declan, Brianna, I'll be in touch.'

She tucks her glasses into her pink overalls and walks back across the field. The air feels cold on my palm, and I rub my fingers against it.

'That was great,' says Bri seriously when Fiona is out of earshot. 'Thanks, Declan; thanks, Clarrie. I'll follow up with Fiona to make sure they mention Brooks'.'

I nod, because it feels like all my words have been swallowed up by the interview, and by the heat in my hand. But before Bri can say anything further Jed arrives, his eyebrows furrowed.

'Everything okay, Jed?' Bri asks.

'The double tent has fallen down,' says Jed, and I *see* Bri and Declan straighten, the interview forgotten. But those words still feel like they're thrumming along my skin, beating in my brain – *What makes Brooks' special?*

'Is it salvageable?' asks Declan.

Jed shakes his head. 'There were a couple of poles missing earlier and I thought I'd found a workaround, but it hasn't worked around. Looks like you and I will be outside tonight.'

I force my attention to the present. I don't know much about tents in general, but I do know we've only brought three – Bri and I were going to share the double, and then Jed and Declan have a single each.

The darkening night sky is heavy with clouds now. Bri pulls out her phone and the bright light of the screen illuminates her face. 'We can drive to the nearest hotel,' she says. 'It looks like there's something about forty-five minutes away, but I can't tell if there's any vacancies.' She frowns at the screen, tapping like it might make the connection faster. 'Otherwise, Clarrie and I could squish onto one mat in a single, and you two can share one? They're big singles.' She looks at me for confirmation that I'm okay with that, and I nod.

The suggestion sits unobtrusively in the air for less than a breath.

'We'll be all right,' says Jed. 'You two take a single each. We've got the tarp. And it shouldn't be more than a little damp – those clouds are all bark and no bite.'

Chapter Twenty-four

I'm honestly not sure I ever in my life want to see a cloud that Jed considers to have bite.

The storm rages overhead, pouring water in sheets over the whole campsite. The fire Jed built that we ate dinner around is not even smoking embers any more, and from inside the tent I can hear what sounds like a bucket of water tip from the top of the tarp every five minutes.

Inexplicably, I can also hear someone snoring. It sounds like it's coming from beside me, so it must be Bri. The tarp covers both of the tents and about two square metres in front, which is where the men have set themselves up.

I can't sleep. I keep telling myself that it's just the rain, but it feels like my skin is buzzing. And I'm not sure if it's because of the interview, or because of the crowd today, or holding Declan's hand, or knowing that there are comments about me on the internet, but it's the same feeling that crept up on me in the forest a few days ago. The restless urge to do something, to discover what's at the end of the stillness. And I swear it's probably just Yumi rubbing off on me, but, for a stupid second, I want to feel the rain on my face.

Before I can overthink it, I unzip the tent and climb out.

Only to almost run into a dark shape right by the door. My chest leaps in shock and I barely manage to stop myself from squealing. *Wilderness Clarrie strikes again.*

Declan reaches out to steady me, his hand cold and wet.

My heart feels like it's going to pound its way out of my chest, and he unfurls himself from where he was crouched by the door of my tent.

'What the hell are you doing?' I hiss at him, my voice harsh from shock.

Declan drops my arm and runs a hand through his hair, flicking droplets of water between us. As my eyes adjust to the dark, I can see that he is saturated. His hair is dripping, his clothes wet.

'Apparently this tarp isn't quite big enough for two,' he says dryly, his teeth chattering slightly.

He nods to the ground in front of the tent. Jed is completely sprawled out across the space, his arms and legs fully extended in every direction.

'Sitting up straight by the tent door seemed preferable to the other option, which was out in the rain,' says Declan conversationally. 'Though I'll admit to having tried both.' He shivers, the movement racking his body again. 'What are *you* doing?'

'I wanted to feel the rain on my face,' I say, which sounds ridiculous now that I can *see* the rain on Declan's face and the impact that it's clearly having. More ridiculously, I want it more. Like something in my chest is aching to feel the moment of shock, to at least stumble on purpose. I want to take a deep breath, to be right where I am. *I want to know the right thing to do about the bookshop.* I push the last thought down.

Even in the dark, I see Declan's raised eyebrow. 'It's really more of a waterfall,' he says, another shiver running through him, but the pounding has softened to less torrential drizzle against the tarp now. I steel my shoulders. I take a step towards Declan and he stills. I'm close enough now that I can smell his skin, the scent of him mixed with rain. Then I take a breath, and step around him, out into the rain.

And it is so freaking cold. Something between a squeal and a laugh bursts out of me, my chest pounding and swelling. I close my eyes and take a breath, and it's somehow both stupid and freeing. Like for just a second, anything is possible. Like there's still hope in the unexpected. When I step back under the tarp a moment later, I'm shivering too. Declan just watches me, the whites of his eyes bright in the dark.

'Was it everything you dreamed it would be?' he asks dryly.

'It was,' I say.

The air prickles against my skin, the relative warmth of the tent beckoning as cold seeps deeper under my skin. I'm seconds from stepping back inside and changing my top and I *pause.* I'm pretty sure I'll be able to warm up again. But Declan will be out here all night. Whatever I'm feeling, Declan has been feeling for two hours at least. And there's space in the tent; Bri has most of the bags in hers, so it's just my bag and me in mine.

'Doyouwanttosleepinthetent?' I ask quickly, before I can second guess myself.

Declan is silent – like I've literally stunned the words out of him.

'It's not because I'm into you,' I blurt out, shivering again. 'But I'm just cold. And I thought that you might be cold too.' I realise what I've said. 'I mean, not that we'll warm each other up, just that it will be warmer for you inside the tent.' *What the actual hell am I doing?*

'Makes sense,' says Declan, and there's that amusement in his voice even as he shivers again.

Jed murmurs something in his sleep and rolls, one arm shooting up in the air and landing with a thud on the other side. Then, like his body has realised it's not taking up enough space, it kicks a leg out behind him.

It's enough to dampen the awkwardness slightly.

'Seriously, Declan,' I say, my teeth chattering now. 'You can't spend the night like this.'

Declan hesitates. He glances down at Jed again, then looks back up at me. It's hard to see his eyes properly in the dark, but we stand like that, frozen for a moment. I don't want him to say yes . . . I don't think. I also don't want him to die of hypothermia.

Then finally, he nods, and my throat closes.

'Just let me get changed first,' he says.

Even with the rain hammering against the tarp, the sound of the tent door opening feels loud and my spine stiffens. I burrow further into my sleeping bag. The rest of me feels like it's starting to warm up, but my hair is still damp, and the lingering smell of rain is strangely hopeful.

'Hey,' whispers Declan.

'Hey,' I whisper.

'Are you okay if I come in?' he says. I can just make him out, crouching in the dark.

I nod, then I realise that he probably can't see me nodding.

'Fine,' I say. 'That's fine.'

He moves slowly, like he's giving me the opportunity to yell suddenly that I've changed my mind about sharing the tent. The 'extra-large single' that felt ample ten minutes ago doesn't even have enough room in it for a second sleeping mat. My hand tingles with the memory of his.

Then Declan is inside, tugging the zip closed. The sound of the rain muffles, just a little, and when he turns back round to face me the air is so still that I swear he must hear me swallow.

He doesn't say anything, just lowers his body carefully down beside me, as far on the other side of the tent as he can. Which is not very far.

'Did Bri say that this is an extra large?' he asks after a moment, his voice too warm and too close.

'I think she might've been overselling it a little,' I say, and he huffs out a laugh that I *feel*.

We both stop talking, but the silence is heavy. Every whisper of movement, every intake of breath pulses in the space between us.

This was a terrible idea.

The sleeping bag I'm burrowed inside starts to get hot, and I try to slowly wriggle my shoulders out, but it's not enough. I slide one arm out just as Declan turns over, and my bare skin brushes against his.

His skin is like ice, and this time I actually do squeal, piercing the tension.

'You're freezing!' I tell him.

'I wanted to feel the rain on my face,' says Declan.

'Hilarious.'

'Also, my sleeping bag got wet,' he says.

'Did you also find a freezer somewhere and sit in it for a while?' I say, wriggling all the way out of my sleeping bag before I can overthink it. I unzip the side and open it so it spreads out like a blanket.

'Clarrie,' says Declan, his voice low and firm. 'I'm fine.'

'You're really not,' I tell him, settling the sleeping bag over the top of us.

'I'm . . .' Declan groans as it covers him, and it dissolves the lingering tension in the air. 'Oh, it's so good,' he says. 'I had forgotten what it was like to be warm.'

He tugs on his side of the sleeping bag, sliding it away from my side, and I pull it back.

'You can't have the whole thing,' I say.

'Do you not remember that I'm dying of hypothermia?' says Declan, tugging it back again.

'You didn't even want it a second ago!' I say, pulling on my side.

It lands almost evenly, and it stays like that for what might be five minutes.

I've closed my eyes and am just starting to imagine that I might be able to forget the large, solid male in the half-a-person tent with me and actually get to sleep, when the sleeping bag starts moving infinitesimally, creeping over to the other side of the tent.

I hold the corner tightly, tucking it under my side so there's no way he's going to be able to get it out, and the sleeping bag pauses.

'That's rude,' says Declan, his deep voice warm.

'I have no idea what you're talking about,' I say.

There's another pause, and then Declan yanks. The sleeping bag slides out from underneath me, rolling me to my opposite side and making me gasp with startled laughter as I scramble to stop myself.

I land against Declan's chest, and we both freeze, the laughter dying in my throat.

The material of his shirt is soft, and I can feel the heat of his body through it.

For a moment we both just lie there. I can see the bright of his eyes in the darkness, and the shadows playing along his cheeks. His hair is still wet. I moisten my lips, and Declan shifts beneath me, the muscles in his body taut. He doesn't take his eyes off mine.

And maybe I'm still feeling a little reckless from the rain, or maybe I just can't contain whatever has been building in me for the past few days, but I run my hand lightly along the hard plane of his chest. Declan inhales sharply. Then he slowly, tentatively reaches up a hand to cup my cheek. His eyes dip to my mouth, and my pulse flutters in my neck.

I can feel the whisper of his breath against my lips. My heart is beating so loudly that I'm sure he must be able to hear it.

Stuff it.

I lean forward, my eyes fluttering closed.

But before my lips touch his, Declan shifts beneath me. *Away* from me.

'Clarrie,' he whispers apologetically.

The rejection is like a knife in my gut. I push myself immediately off him, trying to get as far away as humanly possible in a one-man tent.

He's not interested. Whatever I've been feeling the last few days . . . it was one-sided. Embarrassment burns hot and cold through my body, and I seriously consider climbing out of the tent and back into the rain just to get away from him. *What the hell was I thinking?*

'Clarrie,' Declan says again, his voice soft. 'I'm so—'

'It's fine,' I mumble into my pillow, even though it's clearly not. 'I just misunderstood the situation. All good here, though. Totally, absolutely good. Night, Declan.' I inch deeper into the corner, like my whole body isn't burning up with mortification.

'Thanks for doing the interview today,' Declan says quietly after a while.

'You're welcome,' I say, as cheerily as I can.

I don't tuck the sleeping bag under me, and he doesn't pull on it again.

But I'm pretty sure we both lie there for what must be hours, pretending to sleep.

Chapter Twenty-five

Declan is gone when I wake up in the morning, and the tent seems emptier than it did before he came in last night.

There's condensation gathering on the roof, my pillow somehow smells like him and the sleeping bag is squarely on top of me, like he might have moved it to cover me when he got up.

The mortification of last night feels as fresh now as it did then. All I want to do is burrow under the sleeping bag and hide, but I can hear movement outside: our day has already begun. So instead of closing my eyes and pretending I'm still asleep, I push myself up to a sitting position, stifling a groan when all my muscles protest. I unzip the tent, and I step blinking into the light.

Jed is packing up Bri's tent, humming cheerfully as though he's never had such a good sleep in his life, and Bri is kneeling by a rock chopping fruit. They both look up when I emerge.

'Morning, Clarrie!' says Bri with a wave as Jed nods.

The tarp is gone, and the sky above the trees is a clear, crisp blue. There's no hint of the storm from last night in the sky, like I might have imagined the whole thing. But the grass is soggy, there's a lingering scent of rain in the air and the droplets glimmer on the leaves. There's no sign of Declan.

But, just as I'm pretending to myself that his absence wasn't the first thing I noticed, he materialises from between the trees. His hair is scruffy and his clothes look rumpled, and the sight of him makes my heart stumble. I go to tuck my hands in my pockets before realising I don't *have* pockets, so I cross them across my chest instead.

Good one, Clarrie.

Declan looks up, and he hesitates ever so slightly at the sight of me.

'Good morning, Clarrie,' he says, and the sound of his voice sends a stab of something to my gut.

I lift my hand and smile tightly, but then he's still moving closer and I swear I can feel the heat of his body even though he's at least two metres away and suddenly it feels like I have too many hands. Or too many feet. Too many or too much of something.

I turn round to busy myself, to start packing up the tent and, miraculously, I actually manage to avoid tripping over a rope.

'Well done,' says Jed cheerfully. 'Tripped over that rope this morning myself. This is the one Declan put up.'

I can't help glancing at Declan, and his eyes dance, but he just nods.

'I think it was,' he says gravely. 'My apologies, Jed.'

Jed nods, and I want to hug him because it feels like it would be safe and warm. I don't hug him, though, because it would also be super weird to do that. I just pull the pegs of the tent Declan might-have-but-probably-didn't put up, stay as far away from him as I can and listen to Jed resume his humming.

The rest of the pack-down goes smoothly, but I'm grateful that we're not doing it every day and that we'll be in a motel again tonight. The mood at the campsite is . . . strange. Declan and I barely talk to each other and when we do it's painfully polite. But I'm always aware of where he is and what he's doing, like my subconscious can't help keeping track. Is this the state of play now? Did I send the truce that had developed between us backwards?

I mean, either way, it's fine. That's fine.

Not that Jed and Bri seem to notice anyway. If I'm not mistaken – and it's entirely possible I am, given my preoccupation with the situation with Declan – they are *flirting*. At one point, I would swear that Jed is flexing his muscles while he's washing the dishes, but it seems so impossible that I'm assuming I must have imagined it.

When everything is packed away, we load up the cars.

And, honestly, I'm actually looking forward to travelling with Jed today. I am ready for consistent, reliable silence punctuated by the occasional bird chat. No tension-filled silence, or looks that I spend half an hour trying to analyse. Hell, after my nature-embracing moment in the rain last night, I even feel like I might be able to take the lead on pulling over and running into the forest to find birds.

But when I walk round to the passenger seat of the van, Bri gives me a meaningful look, and the memory of our conversation yesterday pours over me like icy water, colder than the rain on my face last night.

Crap.

After the interview and the tent last night, I totally and completely forgot that I'd promised her we could trade cars. Bri is wiggling her eyebrows at me, a massive smile on her face, and there's no way I can pretend I don't remember the conversation.

I prise my fingers from where they're gripping the van's door handle – apparently not all of me is quite ready to give up on the idea of an easy, uncomplicated car trip – and I step quietly back.

Declan looks up from where he's unlocking the 4WD, and when he sees me very much not getting into the van, his expression freezes. Jed rests a hand on the top of the van and frowns at me over the top.

'Everything okay, Clarence?' he asks.

'Clarrie and I are trading today,' says Bri brightly, totally and blissfully unaware of the tension that's grabbed hold of the car park.

She swings a bag over her shoulder and smiles sunnily at Jed, and despite the frown that deepens across his face he also looks like he might be secretly overjoyed. *Excellent. Good for them.*

I automatically return Bri's hug when she bounds forward and wraps her arms round me, meeting Declan's eyes over her shoulder. He seriously looks as though he might be in physical pain. Cool. Cool, cool cool.

I can feel his eyes on my back as I walk round behind the car, the gravel loud beneath my feet. It's a lot like walking into a particularly unpleasant doctors' visit. Albeit one where you might be attracted to the doctor, who has explicitly told you he doesn't date and pulled away when you tried to kiss him.

Bri and Jed both hop into the van and Bri honks the horn three times before they peel out. From where I'm standing at the passenger side of the 4WD I can see Jed turn to frown at her. A spark lights my chest at the sight, and I have half a smile on my face when I finally get into the car. Declan climbs in at the same time, and there's a matching laughter in his eyes when they meet mine. He clears his throat and looks straight ahead again.

After a beat of hesitation, he pushes the radio on and reverses out of the car park. I slide my sunglasses onto my face and rest my head against the side of the window. At least it might be a good chance to catch up on some rest.

What feels like twenty hours but is probably only one passes, and Declan and I exchange a total of three sentences.

The first is when he asks if I mind if he switches the radio station (I don't), the second is when I magnanimously ask if he would like a snack from my bag (he doesn't) and the third is when he points out a bird on the side of the road and I don't see it.

Thankfully, the tension simmering in the car is cordial

enough that we can both at least pretend to ignore it. We're both reasonable adults. No big deal.

I know that I, for one, am very much not wishing that I could sink into the car seat every time Declan's hand shifts on the wheel, or when my attention drifts to the heartbeat pulsing in his neck and I remember last night.

I open my mouth to say something – *anything* – when Declan suddenly brakes, swerving off the side of the road and then back on again.

There's an audible bang from the front of the car, and almost immediately the driver's side starts to dip and drag, clanking along the road. Declan's arms tense and he curses under his breath. He flicks on the indicator, easing on the brakes this time and pulling over.

We both sit there for a second, saying nothing. Declan closes his eyes and takes a breath.

'I'm so sorry,' he says, his voice low. 'There was an animal in the middle of the road.'

'It's okay,' I tell him, because even though I'm shaken too, he was the one driving and that's . . . awful. 'I'm sure the animal had a nice, long life.'

Declan huffs out a laugh, his eyes still closed. 'It probably still will,' he says. He opens his eyes and meets mine, and there's an apology there. 'I missed the animal, but I think the cost of that was our tyre. It sounded like something punctured it.'

'I'm sure our tyre had a nice, long life too,' I say solemnly.

'I'm just going to change it,' Declan says, stretching his arms on the wheel. 'Unless you want to?'

He's not being facetious, or joking. He is genuinely asking me if I want to change the tyre. Yumi's offered to teach me how to change a tyre at least ten times, but I drive so little that I've never taken her up on it. I will, when I get back, I decide. But right now . . . I shake my head.

'I'll let you get this one,' I tell him.

Declan nods and opens his door, and I lean back in my seat.

We're on a two-lane highway, but the road is silent and still. There's scrub and bushes out of the window, but not much else.

Declan walks round the front of the car, then makes his way to the back. The boot creaks open and I hear him rummaging around, then it swings closed again, and when Declan reappears beside me it's with trepidation on his face.

A feeling of foreboding settles across my skin.

'There's no spare tyre?' I say.

Declan's jaw tightens. 'There's no spare tyre,' he says. 'And no phone reception. Unless yours has some?'

I pull my phone out of the side pocket of my bag. There's less than twenty per cent battery remaining and . . . no reception. I shake my head and almost in unison we look towards the road, where a total of zero cars have driven past in the five minutes we've been stopped.

Declan sighs.

'There was a petrol station a couple of kilometres back,' he says. 'I can walk until I get there or at least until I find reception.'

'I'll come with you.' It's a near thing, but it turns out

I want to avoid Declan less than I want to sit alone in the car on the side of the road.

Declan doesn't question me, just pulls his water bottle out from the side pocket of the driver's door and nods.

I unpack half of my snack bag and then jump out of the car, lifting my pack and the rest of the snacks out with me.

Declan watches me and he raises an eyebrow at my snack bag.

'Don't complain to me when you have so little energy that you can't keep going,' I tell him.

'I'll be sure to keep all complaints to myself,' says Declan, before shutting the door.

I start walking back in the direction we came from, and Declan falls into step beside me, clicking the key fob to lock the car. The beep is loud on the silent road.

'Jed would have words with you about that beep,' I say. 'It probably scared away at least ten different kinds of birds.'

Declan doesn't respond, and the joke falls awkwardly flat.

'I'm sorry,' he says after a little while, and my stomach lurches uncomfortably at the possibility he's apologising for last night. But then he adds, 'I shouldn't have swerved like that.'

'I mean, I don't really think it's your fault,' I tell him, relief making my knees weak. 'But I'll forgive you if you forgive me for Alex's book club in Candon.'

'Right,' Declan agrees. 'You did leave me at a book club.' Then he falls silent. He definitely doesn't tell me he forgives me.

I turn to look at him pointedly. He meets my eyes, his expression carefully bland.

'Did you have anything you'd like to say, Declan?' I ask him.

'Not that I can think of, Clarence,' he says.

I push him into the bushes and the element of surprise is enough to catch him off guard.

He yelps as his arm scrapes on an errant branch, stumbling awkwardly.

'I'm not sorry,' I call back to him, marching ahead.

Declan jogs to catch up to me, a smile hovering at the corner of his lips despite the fact that his arm is scratched and I am actually, in fact, a little sorry. The good news is that the exchange seems to have lightened the tension that was lingering between us.

We walk in silence for a little longer, but it feels different; less charged. The highway remains empty and still, and after a while I find myself relaxing. Maybe we won't see each other after the tour, but we can at least be semi-comfortable for the rest of it. The occasional chatter of birds punctuates the silence, and Declan lets me set the pace.

We've been walking for maybe ten minutes when he clears his throat and, whatever I'm expecting him to say, it's not what he actually does say.

'My mother wrote the dedication.'

Chapter Twenty-six

'I'm sorry, what?' I say.

'My mother wrote the dedication,' Declan repeats, and the words are still no clearer than they were two seconds ago. He keeps walking, but when he realises that I've stopped he pauses a few steps away.

He rubs a hand through his hair and looks out across the bush.

'I . . .' he starts, then he tucks a hand in his pocket and pulls it out again, like he's not quite sure what to do with his body. It's the same way he looks sometimes before he speaks in front of the crowds, and even though I have no idea what he's talking about and I still feel stupid after last night it cracks something inside me.

I don't want him to feel like that.

'Should we walk again?' I say.

His eyes cut to me and there's an honest gratitude in them, but he still shakes his head.

'No, it's fine,' he says. 'This is fine.' He takes a breath, looking at the trees. The road is silent, stretching out in either direction.

'I don't . . . like people,' Declan begins finally, and his

voice is a little dry, a little raw and a little self-deprecating. 'I mean, I don't *dislike* people,' he adds. 'I am doing a terrible job explaining this.'

I don't move. I'm not sure I'm breathing.

'Being on stage, the events, the interviews . . . I know it's all part of the job. I'm lucky to be able to do it.' He looks at the road. 'And I hate it. Or rather, more accurately, I find it soul-destroyingly terrifying.'

His admission is unsurprising, given what Bri told me yesterday and what I'd already gathered myself. But it's difficult to reconcile it with the Declan who is so settled once he gets started on stage.

'How do you do it?' I ask. 'How do you make yourself stand up in front of people?'

'It helps when I'm passionate about something,' he says, meeting my eyes, and a thread of want pulses in my stomach. I push it down. 'It also helps when someone distracts me beforehand,' he adds softly. 'I never said thank you,' he said, 'for the first two events.'

'Is that a thank you?' I say, trying for levity.

'That's a thank you,' says Declan. He doesn't laugh, his eyes unwavering on mine.

I clear my throat. 'So your mother wrote the dedication.'

Declan sighs, finally breaking eye contact. 'She reads romance,' he says, like that explains everything.

'What's wrong with that?'

'Nothing,' says Declan emphatically. 'It's just . . . with my first book, I really didn't do any publicity. I hated the idea of putting it out there. Although, again, I realise it's part of the job. But Mum loved the idea of going into her local bookshop and picking up a signed copy. She was begging me to go in and sign books for weeks.'

I stare at him in horror, bile in my throat. *His mum wanted a signed copy of his book and I sent them all back and then basically told him his book was crap.* I cover my face with my hands.

'I'm sorry,' I tell him, my voice only mostly muffled by my hands.

But, just when I'm about to sink into the ground in mortification, he takes a step closer. 'Don't,' he says, his voice fierce. 'Seriously, Clarrie, I don't know how to explain it, but there was something surprisingly liberating about you telling me to write a better book that day in the bookshop. It . . .' Through my fingers I see him look away briefly before he continues. 'It took me outside my head. Freed me from my own expectations. Made me realise that *I* liked *Flight Risk*, no matter what anyone else thought. I started writing again after that.'

Declan pauses. He's far enough away that I have space, but close enough that the hair on my forearms is prickling at his warmth. 'Months later, when I'd submitted the manuscript, I made the mistake of telling Mum what had happened,' says Declan, the deep rumble of his voice catching between us again. 'And she became convinced that it was the start of an epic love story.'

Oh my gosh. A flush starts in my *nose* and spreads everywhere.

'She came over to my house for dinner one night,' says Declan. 'I was in the middle of working on something, so my computer was open. She . . .' He hesitates, and I crack open another two fingers to look at him. He's not looking at me, but the corner of his mouth kicks up, like he knows I'm watching. 'She wrote an email to my editor on my computer when I went to the toilet.'

I rip my hands off my face to meet Declan's eyes, because there is no way that he can be telling the truth about this. 'Your mum hacked into your computer?'

Declan nods.

I narrow mine. 'You're lying.'

Declan lifts up his hands. 'I promise you I am not,' he says.

'You're telling me that your mother wrote a dedication and sent it to your editor, pretending to be you?' I say, and it sounds so ridiculous coming out of my mouth that I'm half expecting him to laugh. He doesn't.

'I am telling you that my mother wrote that dedication and sent it to my editor, pretending to be me,' repeats Declan. 'And then I didn't speak to her for two weeks.'

'Why the hell didn't you tell your editor that it was your mother?'

'Because I was embarrassed,' he says, and after a beat he rubs his hand through his hair. 'But I also didn't want to embarrass her,' he admits.

'You didn't want to embarrass her. Your mother, who thought we were in a romance novel, who illegally posed as you.'

'Is it illegal?' says Declan.

'Probably,' I tell him. 'My brother is a lawyer,' I add.

'What kind of law?' asks Declan.

'It's not really relevant,' I say.

Declan laughs, and the sound catches me in the gut.

Stop it. He rejected you.

As though he can hear my thoughts, Declan sobers.

'She's a bit of a *closet* romance reader,' he continues. 'She buys all her romance novels on the internet. She would have felt awful if I'd told my editor the truth. And . . .' He closes his eyes and I can hear the sharp inhale of his breath. When he speaks again his voice is barely above a whisper. 'Maybe there was a very small part of me that wanted to know what a certain bookseller thought of the new book.'

My heart skips painfully in my chest.

'I'm sorry that I didn't stop the dedication,' he says, opening his eyes to meet mine straight on. 'And I'm sorry about last night.'

Mortification floods through me. 'Declan—'

'I wanted to kiss you,' he says, barrelling on. 'But my life is complicated right now. I'm complicated. And, despite how I might make it seem sometimes, I *like* you, Clarrie.' He exhales slowly. 'I really like you.' My eyes feel hot, but I can't look away.

'I don't want to hurt you,' Declan whispers. 'No matter how much I might selfishly want to kiss you.'

I take a step towards him, and I see him swallow.

'What if we kept it simple?' I say. I know it's foolish, to offer myself like this again. I need to work out what on earth I'm doing with almost everything in my life. But, right now, I want this moment outside of time to last just a few beats longer. To tell reality to get stuffed. I want to kiss him once, so

I can stop thinking about what he might taste like. 'What if we paused reality for just a moment?'

'Paused reality?' says Declan.

'I promise I don't want to date you,' I say, and the ghost of a smile flickers across his lips. My mouth is dry. 'But if we both wanted to kiss each other – just this one time – maybe we could do that. Like standing out in the rain.'

'If we wanted to kiss each other,' repeats Declan, his tone even, and for a moment I think he's going to reject me again. But then his eyes drop to my lips. When they meet mine again, there's a desire in them that snatches my breath away.

For a heartbeat we just stare at each other, like this invisible string between us is pulling tight.

Then it snaps.

I'm not sure who moves first, but one second we're breathing the same air and the next his lips catch mine.

He groans, reaching up to touch my cheek and pulling me closer. Heat floods every part of my body and I grip his shirt with my fist.

He tastes like warmth and sunshine, and all I want to do is press closer. The moment stretches and lengthens, and I'm so consumed with the feel of his lips, soft against mine, that I barely even notice a sound creeping into the quiet.

Until the first car in twenty minutes roars past, tooting its horn in a way that would make Jed have a fit.

'Woohoo!' a man yells out the window. 'WOOOOOO HOOOOO!'

Declan and I spring apart, both panting slightly. My lips

feel hot and my body is struggling to catch up with my brain. I feel mortified and amused and frustrated by the interruption.

I meet his eyes, and there's a warm laughter in them, and maybe I'm imagining it, but it feels like there's a fraction of disappointment too. Then he turns to look at the car. We're both silent, watching it scream off into the distance.

Well, that's that. I shift my snack bag on my shoulders.

'It might've been nice if they'd stopped to see if we were okay,' I say, trying to act natural. Like I didn't just kiss Declan Archer on the side of the road. Like every part of me is not aching to do it again. Declan is quiet, his eyes still on the highway.

'One kiss, right?' he says finally, his voice hoarse.

'Right.' I push the word out of my throat, which feels unnecessarily tight, and turn to start walking. Declan falls into step beside me. My lips are still tingling, and he's silent as we walk down the road, the air taut with the lack of sound.

I clear my throat, as though that will help. 'How are you so okay with the beeping? Is that not the same as standing on stage?'

'I'm pretty distracted,' says Declan.

I turn to look at him, and there's that heat in his eyes that makes me want to stop again, one-kiss plans and people with car horns be damned.

But we agreed – it was just a pause. I keep walking.

'Distracted by the urgent task of changing a tyre, you mean,' I say.

'Yes,' says Declan dryly. 'That must be what's distracting me.'

We make it another ten steps before Declan stops suddenly.

'Stuff it,' he says, grabbing my hand and pulling me off the side of the road to a tall tree. Then, like he realises what he's just done, he pauses, and drops my hand. He clears his throat, his eyes on the tree. 'How would you feel about maybe two—'

But before he can finish, before he can think, I lean back against the tree and yank him closer.

When our lips meet again, there's nothing tentative about it. Fireworks explode in my chest and my body is on fire. I wrap my hand up round his neck and press closer, and when our tongues meet it feels like it's always been like this.

After what might be minutes, or hours, Declan pulls back. He leans one hand against the trunk of the tree, watching me.

'I have to admit something,' he says, recovering his breath. 'It wasn't the changing of the tyre that was distracting me.'

A laugh catches on my lips, and Declan's lightning smile flashes across his face. His hand strokes along my cheek, sending warmth cascading through me.

And it feels so much like the moment in the rain that I don't think about my next words, not until they're out of my mouth and in the air around us.

'What if the pause lasted until the end of the tour?' I whisper.

Chapter Twenty-seven

Declan stills, his other hand tightening at my waist. Something flares in his eyes, but he doesn't say anything.

'I mean, obviously, we couldn't pause everything,' I say quickly. 'Given that I'll still have to sell books and you'll have to stand terrified in front of large crowds of people. But maybe we could . . . not fight with each other. In a completely uncomplicated way.'

Even as I'm speaking, there's a tiny part of me that suspects that it's a terrible, terrible idea. But I'm not ready to step back under the tarp yet. In a week, I'll go back to reality, and Declan will go back to his complicated life, but what if we stretched the moment just a bit longer? Maybe Wilderness Clarrie isn't about finding myself in the bush. Maybe it's more about a break from the real world, to give me perspective when I get back. We can spend the next week together, and then we can go our separate ways. I can do this without getting emotionally involved. I didn't even like this man two weeks ago.

Declan clears his throat. 'You want to . . . not fight with each other this week?' he says.

'Right,' I say, swallowing. 'I don't want anything beyond

this week,' I promise. 'We go home, we go back to our lives and maybe one day you come in to sign books and I smile at you pleasantly. But I just . . . I want to breathe, for a little bit. To maybe find a part of myself by not looking.'

'That's not really how finding things works,' says Declan.

'It definitely is,' I say. 'I wasn't looking for my shop keys and they just turned up.'

Declan barks out a laugh, and the sound of his deep chuckle is so unexpected that my breath sticks in my throat. Then he hesitates, and my stomach twists.

'To be clear, I am aware that I would be an idiot to say no,' he says, holding my eyes. 'But I'm still not sure if it's fair to you.'

Frustration gathers in my chest, in my head, and I'm so damn tired of not getting to choose.

'And who decides what's fair to me? You? Am I not allowed to make a decision about what I want?'

The words pour out of me, because arguing someone into . . . I don't even know what – a book-tour fling? – is obviously the most effective solution. Declan pauses, but he doesn't look away from me. The bark of the tree is rough against my back, and there's an internal part of me that is squirming with discomfort, but I don't take the offer back.

'If you need to say no, I will respect that,' I tell him. 'And I will try my best not to make it awkward. But don't say no for me.' Something opens inside my chest at the words, a freedom that I haven't felt in a long time. 'I want this, Declan. It's okay if you don't.'

Declan studies me for another minute. Then he closes his eyes, and I'm pretty sure he mutters something under his breath, but there's one word that is clear.

'Yes.'

'Sorry, what?' I say.

'You know what I said,' he says, opening his eyes again. 'I would really like to . . . not fight with you for a week.'

'To be fair, you start most of them,' I say, nerves tingling in the bottom of my stomach and through my chest.

Silence falls between us again, and I honestly didn't even think about what pausing everything else for a week might look like, but I can hear my heart beating in my ears. *What happens next?* I lick my still swollen lips and Declan's eyes darken. He leans forward.

'So, for the next week I can kiss you any time I want?' he asks, the first to break the silence for once.

'What is this, *Sweet Home Alabama*?' I say, and when his lips touch mine again I feel his laugh against my lips, and the metaphoric freaking rain on my face.

It's after lunch by the time we make it to the petrol station. We're walking side by side, a few centimetres of space between us – not that I'm hyper aware of them or anything. But despite having stopped to kiss more than once, holding hands again feels too . . . intimate. Not a part of whatever the agreement is between us. Still, it's nice to walk together without arguing.

The small, dusty petrol station is just in sight on the horizon when Declan's phone beeps. He slides it out of his pocket and reads the message. 'It's Bri,' he says, clicking to call her. I hear the phone ringing against his ear, and at the reminder of the outside world the niggle of unease rises again in my throat.

But, even as I'm trying to think of all the questions that I probably should be asking myself, Declan reaches down with his free hand, absentmindedly folding his fingers between mine, and my heart stops. *It's just a week, Clarrie.*

'Hey, Bri,' says Declan. 'I just got your message. I'm sorry we missed the lunch meet-up. We got a puncture this morning, so we've been on our way to a petrol station to see if we can sort it out.'

I hear Bri gasp on the other end of the phone, and Declan pauses while he listens to her.

'No, don't worry about coming back. We're almost at the petrol station now. Yeah, we've been walking all morning,' he says. 'Clarrie's a slow walker,' he adds. He looks down at me and I raise my eyebrows at him and he raises one back. And I honestly have no idea what comes over me, but I lean forward and lick the side of his neck and he coughs.

'Sorry, Bri, I missed that,' he says.

I smile not a little smugly as Bri speaks again.

'No, I was just a bit distracted, because Clarrie licked me,' Declan says into the phone.

My jaw drops open and Declan grins, a massive, all-out smile that takes over his entire face. I let go of his hand and snatch for the phone, and he switches it to the other side. I don't even know what I was expecting when I suggested pausing, but it wasn't this. There's a lightness in my chest, and I can feel a laugh at the back of my throat. Because of *Declan Archer*.

'No, I'm serious,' he says. 'It was almost a bite.'

He looks back at me. 'She doesn't believe me,' he says to me, letting me snatch the phone from him. 'Bye, Bri,' he calls.

'Hi, Bri,' I say, ignoring Declan.

'Clarrie! I don't know who that man on the phone was, but it wasn't Declan Archer,' says Bri. There's a male voice in the background, and Bri must turn away from the phone slightly because her voice changes. 'No, no, Jed, it was just an expression. I mean it was Declan, but he sounded different. We don't need to go back and get Clarrie,' she says – I'm assuming to Jed. Then her voice moves closer to the receiver. 'Actually, do we need to come back and get you? Declan said no, but he also sounded like he might've had heatstroke or something.'

It makes me snort, and Declan just raises an eyebrow again.

'No, we're fine,' I tell her. 'Hopefully we'll get the tyre sorted and we'll see you later today.'

'No rush!' says Bri brightly. 'Just call us if you need us. We're happy to come back.' Then she pauses. 'Jed says to tell Declan if he sees an orange-bellied parrot to make sure he stops and takes photos.'

'Thanks, Bri,' I tell her. 'We will.'

I disconnect the call and turn back to Declan.

'She didn't believe me, did she?' he says.

'She's worried you might have heatstroke,' I tell him.

'And Jed said to take a picture of an orange-bellied parrot if we see one.'

'As if we'd see an orange-bellied parrot and not take a picture,' mutters Declan, and it's me who reaches out to take his hand this time.

Thankfully, the petrol station has spare tyres. It also has a friendly mechanic named Merry, who offers to drive us back to our car, and then changes the tyre for us more quickly than I even knew was possible before wishing us a happy Wednesday.

At one point Declan turns round to meet my eyes, and there's so much light in them that I swallow. *One week, Clarrie.*

Then Merry is gone with a beep and a wave, and Declan and I are both sitting in our seats again, silent on the side of the road. And despite our earlier agreement, for the life of me, I have no idea what happens next.

'I have never seen someone change a tyre so fast in my life,' says Declan.

He starts the engine, but doesn't fasten his seat belt yet. He leans forward to look out of the front windscreen at the position of the sun. He takes a breath, and when he turns to look at me it's with hesitation on his face, like he's about to take the last few hours back.

'What?' I say. 'Are you about to confess something?'

He smiles, but it's a distracted smile that doesn't quite quench my apprehension.

'Merry mentioned that today was a Wednesday,' he says, like it means something.

'Right.'

Declan looks out of his window again, and the car engine continues its steady, pulsing idle. 'I know we need to be another five hours from here tomorrow, but how do you feel about a small detour? It'll add about an hour to the trip.'

'Because it's a Wednesday?' I say.

'Because it's a Wednesday,' says Declan.

'Where would the detour be to?'

'If I told you, it wouldn't be a surprise.'

'I didn't know it was a surprise detour.'

'You didn't ask,' says Declan.

I frown, and he raises his eyebrows at me. His face has settled, as though now that he's announced the day of the week, he's made whatever decision he was pondering when he looked out through the windscreen. And, even though it was me who made the decision to let go for this week, the amount I want to say yes scares me.

'There might be snacks,' he says seriously.

A week, and then back to reality.

'You should have led with that,' I tell him. I reach over my shoulder and fasten my seat belt.

Declan grins, and clicks on his own seat belt. Then he takes out his phone.

'I'll just let Bri know,' he says, typing quickly.

Then he chucks his phone into the side pocket and pulls

out into the empty lane. After a few minutes, his hand snakes across the empty console to take hold of mine.

Warmth pools in my stomach, and I look out of the window, enjoying the sensation.

And maybe my heart flutters a little, but that's fine. It's totally fine.

Chapter Twenty-eight

The sound of a ringing phone wakes me, but it's not a tone I recognise.

I open one eye to see that we're surrounded by open fields, and we're driving steadily but slowly uphill. There are few trees around, but the sky looks endless and open above us. On the far horizon I'm pretty sure I can see mountains.

Declan glances over at me and the phone keeps ringing, but he doesn't answer it on the car speaker or pull over to take the call.

'Do you want me to cancel it for you?' I ask, yawning.

'You can if you want,' he says. 'But it's not my phone.'

I'm about to joke that maybe Merry planted some sort of burner phone on us when realisation dumps over me like cold water. It's my phone, and it's my mum. I changed her ringtone after she called a few days ago, so I'd know when she was ringing without looking.

Idiot.

Declan glances over at me again. 'Are you okay?' he asks. He looks down at the snack bag, where we both know my phone is. 'We're almost there, but I can pull over if you need to take it?'

I haven't heard from her since I sent her the text about not going into the bookshop yesterday. But speaking to her feels like inviting reality back in after Declan and I have just agreed to pause it. I'm not ready to listen to her justify her actions.

I shake my head. 'No,' I tell him. 'It's okay. It's my mum. We have . . . a complicated relationship.'

'Is she a Brooks?' asks Declan.

'She is,' I say. 'Though she wants to sell the bookshop.'

So much for completely ignoring reality.

'Sorry,' I say. 'That's definitely breaking the rules of the pause.'

'What?' says Declan. 'I thought the only rule was that we weren't fighting?'

'You thought wrong,' I say.

'I did not,' says Declan. Then, 'Sorry, I couldn't help myself.' He's silent for a moment. 'Do *you* want to sell?' he asks.

There is no judgement in his words. He's giving me space to answer however I want to.

'I don't know,' I tell him honestly, but as soon as the words are out of my mouth, I know they're not true. My heart thumps painfully, and my breath catches in my chest, and the knowledge that's been building in me for the past week finally comes to the surface.

'No,' I whisper, the word making my throat ache. I shake my head. 'But I'm scared.'

I know, intrinsically, that Declan will let me leave it at that. And it's that knowledge as much as anything that makes me continue.

'I've never known what it's like to not have a bookshop in the family,' I say, the words trickling out at first and then picking up speed. Sharing this feels dangerous in so many ways. It's different to knowing small, random facts about each other. Different even to Declan admitting his own fears about being on stage, though I'm not sure why. But, now that I've started, I don't want to stop. 'My grandparents started Brooks' fifty years ago and they were always there. I feel like most of my childhood memories are at Brooks'.'

'With your mum?'

'Sometimes.'

She used to sit out the back and work while I was in the bookshop with Gran. It's a detail that somewhere along the line I've unconsciously edited out, that until this moment I honestly haven't thought about in the last ten years.

Declan waits.

'Gran let me help out in the shop, and it always made me feel so grown up. We used to play a game where I'd name a book and she had to recommend something similar, and if she couldn't do it I got to pick the next window display. One of my greatest nine-year-old achievements was the installation of a life-sized *Charlotte's Web* window display.

I swallow at the memory of Gran talking about it just a few weeks ago, telling me it was one of her best. At the time, she'd complained for days about having to papier mâché a life-sized pig and Grandpa had told her that at least it meant they didn't have to clean the cobwebs out for a little while.

Declan still doesn't say anything, and I wish he would. I want him to make a joke or change the subject. But he doesn't, and I keep going.

'They lived a block away from the bookshop, and it was their life. They ran it together up until he died a few years ago. Gran kept going by herself for a little while after that, but when I left my degree she decided to pass it on to me. We were going to do it together, at least for a little while. But then just after that she . . . well, you know that she left.' My throat closes, and I swallow past it. 'She has dementia. She's in a nursing home now.'

The words are stark and somehow empty of everything that they mean. The joy I feel when I see her; the relationship built from years of memories that are now both solid and mist. The familiar pain of the moment she doesn't recognise me; the gratitude that she's still here. The way that the bookshop feels empty without her.

'I'm sorry,' says Declan quietly.

I turn to look at him and I regret it almost immediately, because the sight of his face and the care in it *hurts*, and a few of the tears that have been gathering at the corners of my eyes threaten to spill. I can feel Declan's eyes on me, but I keep my gaze fixed on the window because this is over in a few days and he can't be more than a moment to me. And because maybe I'm not ready to fully look at what wanting the bookshop for myself means. I wipe the sides of my eyes.

'Did you always want to be an author?' I ask after a while, silently willing him not to try to circle back to me.

'It was either that, or a professional soccer player,' says Declan, and I exhale in relief.

'Both good options. What made you choose the writing over the soccer?'

'*Bend It Like Beckham*,' says Declan immediately, and I am so legitimately surprised that for a few seconds I don't say anything.

'The early 2000s film *Bend It Like Beckham*?'

'That's the one,' says Declan. 'It came out when I was maybe eight. I was so excited that there was a soccer movie coming out. I planned my birthday around it.'

'You planned your birthday around *Bend It Like Beckham*?'

'I did,' he says. 'Five eight-year-old friends and I went to the first possible screening to watch what I was expecting to be a solid soccer film.'.

'It's not really a soccer film,' I say tentatively.

'Not really a soccer film,' says Declan, his lips quirking. 'Some might even call it a romantic comedy.'

'You took five of your friends to see a romantic comedy when you were eight?' I say, a laughter I didn't think was possible ten minutes ago bubbling in my chest.

'I did. After that, soccer was never quite the same for me,' says Declan. 'Great movie, though,' he adds a second later, and I can't describe the feeling that rushes through me, this fierce, warm affection. It's bright and it's terrifying and I'm fairly sure I could drown in it. I clear the warmth from my throat.

'Did anyone say anything afterwards?' I ask, and Declan grins.

'Not much,' he says. 'Everyone sort of just went home.'

'Do you still play?' I look at him.

Declan nods. 'I'm not as good as Keira Knightley though.' He lifts one hand off the wheel to point out of the front window. 'We're almost there,' he says, and I look forward to see we've reached the top of the hill.

A town sprawls out below us: a thatch of old buildings nestles in a sparkling green and yellow valley that is literally glowing in the afternoon sun, and there are rolling hills in the distance. You could put a picture of this place next to 'quaint' in the dictionary. It's so peaceful and idyllic-looking that I let out an audible sigh, and Declan glances over at me.

'Shut up,' I say without looking, and he smiles.

We start the descent into the valley, the road meandering down until we eventually pass a bright yellow sign announcing that we're entering Mayfield.

'What's in Mayfield?'

'Telling you would ruin the surprise.'

'Is it a good surprise?' I ask. The car bumps over a small bridge and I catch a brief glimpse of shady trees and a winding river sparkling underneath.

'I guess that depends,' says Declan, flicking on his indicator and turning right like he's been here more than once before, 'on how much you like snakes.'

'Ha,' I say. Then I pause, because I'm not actually sure whether he's joking. I mean, they wouldn't be the first snakes we'd seen this tour.

I look at him, but his gaze is fixed on the road. We drive

straight ahead at the roundabout, away from a sign pointing to the town square.

Declan indicates again and turns down a narrow one-way street with terraced houses on one side and a playground on the other. He looks at home, driving here. The street is full of parked cars, but Declan finds a place to pull in right at the end.

He turns off the ignition and the car stills.

'Are there really snakes?' I ask him.

Declan unclicks his seat belt, then reaches across me to open the glovebox. His arm brushes against mine and despite the threat of snakes my stomach clenches. He hovers there for about ten seconds too long – which I swear is on purpose – before pulling back with something in his hand, his eyes *dancing*.

It's a packet of snake lollies, and I cough on a surprised laugh. The tension at being in this place with Declan eases a fraction.

'Those look suspiciously like snacks, Declan Archer.'

Declan reaches into the packet, his expression still serious but for his eyes. He pulls out a green snake and pops the whole thing in his mouth.

'They're not really snacks,' he tells me, holding out the packet to offer me one. 'You find snakes in the wild, so these are really more like research into the wilderness.'

'Have they been in the car the whole time?' I ask, and he just grins. I break eye contact and pull a purple snake from the packet.

'Any other secrets I should know about?' I ask lightly.

Declan hesitates for a moment. 'That day in the deli, the reason I found your keys is that I went back to buy a brownie,' he says.

'Did we drive to Mayfield to eat a packet of snakes?' I ask instead of kissing him again like I want to. I look around the street. The sun is glinting off the tops of buildings and the trees are green, and I can hear the sound of kids playing in the park back down the road. 'Not that I'm complaining,' I add. Then, more honestly, 'It's lovely.'

'Not just the snakes,' Declan says, but he looks apprehensive.

'I'd hope not,' I tell him. 'Given that I was promised snacks, and I have it on good authority that snakes are not snacks.'

'I would hate to disappoint you,' he says gravely.

'Your choice of green snake was already disappointing,' I say. 'It can pretty much only go up from here.'

'Good news,' says Declan. 'A man always likes to hear he's hit rock bottom and that anything above that is a bonus.' His takes a breath, kisses me so quickly that my head spins, then opens his door.

He's at my door and opening it before I can finish sorting my bag.

'Leave the snack bag,' he says, grabbing my hand and pulling me outside.

He makes a quick stop by the boot of the car to collect two sleeping bags, and when I look at him quizzically he raises an eyebrow back at me.

'How do you feel about sleeping outside tonight?' he asks. 'It's safe, I promise.'

'Bri pretty explicitly told me there was only one night of camping,' I say, following along beside him anyway.

'I did try to warn you that day in the deli,' says Declan, tucking the sleeping bag under his arm. 'But you can back out if you want to.'

His expression is warm, and I shake my head.

'Come on, Archer.'

We walk back the way we drove in, Declan with the sleeping bags tucked under one arm. The street is lined with parked cars, and after a little while we run into other people walking along wearing beanies and jumpers. A family piles out of their car just in front of us, their two young girls dressed in tutus and snow jackets. On the other side of the road, a man helps an elderly woman out of the car into her wheelchair.

Everyone smiles and waves, or nods hello, and we smile back, and I can't help thinking about how much Declan looks . . . more like *himself* here. His fingers are threaded through mine the entire time, his palm steady and warm. We go right at the roundabout this time, heading towards the town square, moving with the gentle stream of people. It's busy but not crowded, and there's something relaxing about walking with so many other excited people. Even if I have no idea where we're going. Then we turn the corner to walk through a covered alleyway filled with shops and . . . *Christmas music?*

'Is that "Jingle Bells"?' I whisper to Declan, just as we step out into what can only be the town square. But Declan doesn't answer; he doesn't need to.

At the centre of the square is a giant tree, covered from roots to tip in decorations and lights. A bright golden star perches proudly on top. Christmas-themed market stalls line three of the sides, facing the open shops in the old buildings surrounding them. On the final side of the square is a narrow road that seems to be blocked off, and just beyond it is a massive green slope. People are setting up picnic mats and sleeping bags with views of the trees and stalls below.

I look at Declan, who is already watching me.

'What the hell is this?' I say, but I can't keep the wonder out of my voice.

'This is Mayfield,' says Declan solemnly. He waits, and I narrow my eyes at him. He gently steers me forward towards the stalls, stepping closer to avoid a teenager running past.

'Years ago, there were floods in the area on Christmas Day,' he says, his voice close to my ear. 'And after the recovery and the rebuilding the town decided to hold a Christmas celebration, to commemorate what they'd done, and what they'd missed. Apparently, someone joked that they should have Christmas every month. To find a reason to celebrate whenever they could.'

We reach the first tent, which is filled with trays of meat, roast vegetables and loaves of bread. Declan collects two plates and passes one to me.

'I have no idea how everyone agreed to it, but that was the beginning of Christmas in Mayfield,' he says. 'It happens on the third Wednesday of every month – different groups from Mayfield and the surrounding towns take turns to organise it.'

He passes me the sleeping bags and reaches into his pocket to pay the man at the exit for the food. When I start to protest, Declan says that I can buy a copy of *Talking to Trees* to pay him back, and I am seriously going to end up with about six personal copies of this book that I haven't read. The next tent is desserts, and a lovely woman packs Christmas pudding and mince pies into boxes for us, wishing us 'Merry Christmas' as she does. The sense of community pours out of every millimetre of the town square. The warmth of Declan's hand is steady in mine and, more terrifyingly, there's a growing warmth in my chest. This is dangerous.

We pass stalls filled with Christmas decorations and novelty advent calendars, and I have so many questions, like *how on earth do these people stay in business?* and *what are the advent calendars counting down to?* But when I whisper them to Declan he whispers back that the town is full of world-class burglars counting down to their next robbery, and I want to push him into some bushes again, but I can't find any, and also: I'm carrying a lot of food.

We make our way across the road to the hill, and find a spot close to the top where we'll also sleep tonight, which Declan promises is legal. From where we're sitting, we can see all the way down to the base of the tree, where a group of carollers are beginning to set up.

'This is incredible,' I tell him.

Declan nods. 'I find it a good place to breathe,' he says, a kindness in his voice that I haven't heard before, and I don't know if it's because of what I told him about the bookshop, but neither of us brings it up. I look out over the crowd. *He's helping me have a nice break from reality.* I swallow down the roast potato that's stuck in my throat, pushing down the uneasiness in my gut.

The food is warm and filling, and Declan and I alternate between eating and guessing what the first song is going to be based on the relative enthusiasm of the carollers as we watch them arrange themselves in front of the tree.

'"Jingle Bells",' says Declan. 'They'll lead with something upbeat.'

'They'll definitely start with "Silent Night",' I counter. 'And "Jingle Bells" to finish, to leave the crowd on a high.'

Gradually, the light begins to fade from the sky, and after a while the entire square begins to twinkle with different colours. Hundreds of fairy lights, woven through the Christmas tree, along buildings and across the tops of the market stalls. A hush falls over the crowd, like everyone knows what the lights mean.

Someone taps on a microphone. 'Good evening and merry Christmas, Mayfield!' the voice booms out into the night.

'This is how you should start your events,' I tell Declan.

'Yes, I can see how that would really make me less nervous,' says Declan. 'Telling a group of people who have come to hear about a serious fiction book that it's Christmas.'

'Our first carol this evening is going to be "Jingle Bells",' says the woman at the microphone.

'Damn it,' I say loudly. The people on either side turn to look at us, and *crap*.

'Sorry,' I whisper to them, while Declan laughs silently beside me. 'I'm so sorry.'

They finish with 'Silent Night', which Declan refuses to call a draw despite my insistence that first and last are basically interchangeable. The air seems to ring with the sound of carols when they finish, like the last note is still being sung as families gradually filter out of the space.

People unzip sleeping bags and roll out mats all around us, and the buzz of earlier settles into a quiet chatter. Declan wanders to where the market stalls are packing down and returns with two hot chocolates. He settles in beside me, and we watch as the carollers farewell each other by the tree.

He looks back down across the thinning crowd in the town square.

'My dad lived here,' he says finally.

'He doesn't live here any more?' I say, averting my eyes from the couple in front of us saying a particularly passionate goodbye.

'He passed away last year,' says Declan, and I pause to look at him. He's not watching me, though; his eyes are still fixed on the glowing tree ahead of us.

'I'm so sorry.' The words are hopelessly inadequate.

Declan shakes his head. 'I spent most of my life mad at him. He and my mum separated when I was ten. He'd always dreamed of being a musician and he was so disappointed in what life had dealt him instead.

'I think when I started writing was the first time that I felt like I understood him, even a little. I was lucky to have a month up here with him, before he passed away, and I edited most of *Talking to Trees* here. My next book – the one I'm working on – it's about him, in a way.'

A lump forms in my throat, thinking about Declan and his father, but also about my own disappointments in my relationship with my mum. How much of that is because we don't understand each other? *How much effort have I made to know her?* It's a sobering realisation. I need to have a proper conversation with her in person when I get back.

I want to ask Declan questions about his new book, but I don't want to push him. Once, I remember seeing an author cry after a bookshop visit, and I asked Gran why they were so sad when they'd made something that people loved. *'Every author is different,'* she said, *'but for many of them the process of creating and then letting go is . . . delicate. We get to be the safe hands that help the books on their way.'*

I clear my throat. 'This is the tree you were talking to, then?' I say, pointing to the giant Christmas tree still twinkling in front of us, and Declan softly exhales. 'Not exactly wilderness, Archer.'

'Sometimes stepping outside your comfort zone is its own kind of wilderness,' says Declan.

The sentiment lodges itself in my chest, and I swallow.

'You didn't include it as part of the tour, though.'

'No,' says Declan. He pauses, takes a sip of his hot chocolate. 'I've heard not everyone appreciates my metaphors.'

I snort, and Declan almost smiles. He shifts, angling his body slightly so his arm is curved behind my back. We watch the fairy lights twinkling and the tents being dismantled, and I drink the rest of my hot chocolate and I'm pretty sure Declan's goes cold, but he doesn't move his arm.

It's just a week, Clarrie.

Chapter Twenty-nine

The next four events pass by relatively smoothly; everyone arrives on time, it doesn't rain and, despite my best attempts to convince him it's a good idea, Declan doesn't lead with any Christmas carols.

Bri still hasn't managed to persuade Jed that they should ride off into the sunset together, but we don't switch cars again, and the long drives that I was dreading before the tour become my favourite part of the day.

One afternoon, Declan tells me that he stole a wishing stone from a school market when he was a kid.

'What made you do it?' I ask, looking at him sideways as we pass fields and cows and sheep out of the window.

'It's like you've never even seen a wishing stone,' says Declan, shaking his head. 'They're mesmerising.'

'And your mum wouldn't buy you one?'

'No,' says Declan. 'She still doesn't know I took it.'

I gasp in mock horror, and Declan ducks his head. 'I had to leave it at least twenty years,' he says. 'If she found out any sooner, she'd have made me track down the stallholder and take it back.'

'Do you still have it?' I ask.

'I will neither confirm or deny that,' says Declan.

'Colour?'

'Blue,' says Declan, sounding affronted. 'I wouldn't steal a *yellow* wishing stone.'

As well as a stolen wishing stone, I learn that Declan has a dog called Fido, that he loves cooked tomato but is apathetic about it when it's fresh. I also discover that he is strangely passionate about people not indicating at roundabouts.

I tell him about my crappy toaster, and Yumi, and about how I accidentally lost my pet chicken when I was eight. I buy snacks almost every time we stop, and Declan doesn't comment, but he does sneak my nuts.

Ruth messages me twice with picture updates. One is her and Gran and another scarf, and the other is the two of them with a copy of *Talking to Trees*. I went shopping at Brooks'! she proclaims.

It's still the bestselling book at Brooks' by a long margin, and Yumi tells me that she moved it to the second spot on our bestseller wall yesterday, just for fun.

We've stopped at three bookshops in the last five days, and in each place *Talking to Trees* is sitting happily at number one. I've overheard enough conversations between Bri and Declan in the past week to know that the book is going well. For my part, I've sold more books than even our best estimates, and yesterday I called Mike to confirm that we wanted to go ahead with the electrical repairs. And it feels . . . good.

Having gone into this tour expecting it to be a disaster, it's hard to believe that there's a part of me that now doesn't want it to end. There are things I'm looking forward to about being back, but I'm already missing the open skies and the feeling of rain on my face. Declan and I don't talk about the end of the pause and, in real Wilderness Clarrie style, I figure that I will just spot that owl when I come to it. Or something like that.

When we climb back into the car after the final bookshop on our way to the final event of the tour, Declan lets out a long sigh, leaning back in the passenger seat.

'Are you upset because they didn't have the most recent Francis Coates?' I ask lightly, and he opens one eye at me, a flash of surprise and something else passing through them.

'How do you know I like Francis Coates?'

'I've seen your suitcase,' I whisper, and Declan laughs, a low, even chuckle.

'He's a really good writer,' he says.

'I've heard that.' Honestly, I only know he exists because of Annabel Stone.

'Are you okay?' I ask. 'There was quite a crowd at the end.'

He nods. 'Part of the job,' he says, like this is something he tells himself often. Then he sits up and rubs a hand through his hair. 'And it really is incredible, the people I get to meet,' he says. 'There was a man in there . . . he said his son gave him the book for his birthday, because he'd read it himself and loved it. He's going to give the signed copy back to his son next birthday.' There's a wonder in his voice when he says it – like he can't quite believe that his book has meant that to someone. 'I'm lucky, to do what I do.'

I reach down to touch his hand, and he turns his palm so he can lace his fingers with mine. 'Did you send Yumi some pictures of the window display?' he asks.

They had built a literal mountain out of books, complete with a jolly-looking hiker on the side. 'I did,' I tell him. 'She said we should try doing the Eiffel Tower. She asked if you can please write a book about Paris so we can pretend that was our motivation.'

'I'll work on it,' says Declan.

It's such an innocuous exchange, but there's something about planning even an imaginary future that stalls the conversation. *Tomorrow. We go home tomorrow.*

'How does the mountain compare to your *Charlotte's Web* display?' asks Declan.

'How dare you even ask,' I say solemnly. 'Nothing will ever top the *Charlotte's Web* display. It was perfect. Apart from when Grandpa broke his finger trying to get the papier mâché pig out of the window.'

'He what?' Declan laughs.

'He spent four hours in Emergency,' I say, laughing as well. 'Though Gran said it was still worth it.'

'She told me once that *Charlotte's Web* was her favourite book,' he says softly, and my heart cracks, just a little.

And I try again not to think about tomorrow.

Chapter Thirty

It's a pleasant surprise that, after two large events, the last stop on the tour is the smallest. Still, Bri tells me that the eighty tickets sold out in two minutes.

All four of us are carrying books and equipment in, though Jed has offered to make a quick trip back for anything we can't manage. When Bri tries to explain that it will mean double trips on the way back out as well, Jed cheerfully starts listing all the birds that have been sighted in this forest.

And honestly, if I was a bird, this is probably where I'd choose to be too. The trees are tall and green, and they stand like they know what they're doing. There's a stream nearby that runs close to the path, and our walk is accompanied by the steady trickling of water.

In what has become typical over the past two weeks, there's also no phone reception – at least, not with my provider. Two days ago, I had a conversation with Yumi that almost entirely consisted of me just saying, 'Can you hear me?' and, 'What about now?'

Declan leads us down the path, his back straight like he

barely even notices the box of books he's carrying. We're all walking single file, because the trail isn't wide enough to walk side by side – at least, not without someone falling in the bushes. Luckily, the path is flat and straight.

'You know,' calls Declan conversationally, 'we're just going to have to carry these back out again.'

'But we'll have fifty helpers,' calls Bri from the back of the line. 'And they'll each be hugging their copy to their chests! We're giving them the experience of buying the book in a place no one else has.'

It's the third time they've had the same discussion, and it was obvious from the first that Bri was going to win. She never seems to descend into arguing, but she is unbelievably convincing.

We traipse quietly down the path, listening to the water and the birds. Then we turn and the route opens up into a clearing that the path winds alongside.

'It's just through there,' says Declan, pointing to a gap in the trees.

Jed marches ahead, and Bri skips to catch up with him, tucking Declan's computer under one arm. Declan waits to fall into step beside me.

'How are you feeling?' I ask. He's quiet, but he doesn't seem as stressed as he has the past few events, or even as he was in the bookshop earlier. I wonder, not for the first time, what it must be like – to steel yourself to talk in front of people when you hate doing it as much as he does.

'I'm fine,' he says. 'Glad this is the last one.'

There's a beat and, for a second, I think he's going to say something else, but then Bri and Jed make it through the bushes up ahead, and I hear Bri *squeal.*

She drops her books on the ground and then runs back to us.

'Declan Archer, I can't believe you didn't tell me!' she yells. 'People are going to lose their minds when they realise that this is the spot with the silver tree. You know they're going to lose their minds, right?'

Declan just smiles. 'I thought it might be a nice surprise,' he says. He turns to me.

'The silver tree? From book club?'

'It's the location of a scene at the end about love and hope,' he says.

'The best scene from the book!' says Bri. 'Apart from the scene at the Christmas market in April,' she says. 'Maybe you can recreate that one on the next tour.'

Declan doesn't look at me, but I can feel his attention shift to where I'm standing. 'Maybe,' he says, and I'm left feeling both warm and a little empty as we follow Bri through the trees at the edge of the clearing.

Not far into the forest is a smaller, more intimate collection of trees that stand in an almost perfect circle. There's a massive rock at one edge of the space, and just beside it is a two-metre tree with bare branches. There are no leaves on it – it doesn't look like it's had leaves on it in a long time – but the entire thing is painted silver, and wrapped round the trunk is a neat green vine covered in vibrant flowers.

'It's a nice tree,' I say, while Bri moves closer and totally loses her mind over the scene that apparently takes place here.

When I look at Declan it's to see him watching me with amusement. 'The scene is really more about the internal discovery of the main character than it is the tree,' he pauses. 'But it is pretty great.'

I shrug my bag of books off and rest it next to the rock, leaning in to look at the silver tree. I run my hand along the bark, and there's something so heartbreaking and hopeful about it, about the flowers and vine brightly adorning it. It feels so out of place in the rainforest, but there's a different kind of beauty to it.

'No one knows who tends to the flowers or the vine,' says Declan, 'but they're always alive, and they never encroach on the rest of the forest.'

I look up at him, and he reaches out to rest a hand on one of the low branches.

'My stepfather proposed to my mother here,' he adds, his voice so soft that only I can hear it.

We haven't talked much about Declan's birth father since the day in Mayfield almost a week ago now, and I don't know his mother's full story, apart from that she adores his stepfather and writes Declan's dedications.

But the place means enough to him that he included it in a book and on the tour, even with everything that happened with his dad. My fingers itch with the urge to take his hand, but I don't, and I can feel the end creeping up on us like the moss at the base of the silver tree.

Bri is right – the fans who arrive eagerly down the path at 1.45 p.m. adore the silver tree.

Jed and I watch from the sidelines as groups take photos of the tree, of themselves with the tree, of Declan with the tree. Several people even ask to buy copies of the book early, so they can take photos of it with the tree.

'It's all pretty weird, isn't it,' says Jed, watching them with a frown on his face.

'It is,' I say as a girl walks into the clearing and comes to a dead stop, her jaw dropping open. She stands like that for a full ten seconds, then literally pinches herself. 'But there's also something sort of magic about it, don't you think?' I say. 'That something so many people read alone becomes a shared experience.'

Jed nods uncertainly, then mutters something about how real magic is a regent honeyeater in flight.

When 2 p.m. comes round, Bri climbs onto the rock, pulling a more reluctant Declan up beside her. The crowd that has been squealing and taking photos falls silent. I think a few people even stop breathing.

The anticipation that fills the air is like a hum. All these people's lives have been touched and impacted by something that someone created from nothing. And it's warm and it's sweet, but it's also poignant, and something about the moment makes my breath catch and my eyes sting.

Like he's heard my thoughts, Declan looks to where I'm standing. I can see the pull of nerves along his jaw, and I give him a thumbs up. He shakes his head at me, a small smile on his face, and I feel like I am about a heartbeat away from sobbing irrationally.

I love this.

The thought is more solid than it's ever been, and I feel it harden to something that feels a lot like resolve as Bri finishes her introduction. Then she angles her body slightly towards me, and I straighten, because I know what's coming. And, since it's the last stop on the tour, it's pretty likely she's going to go big.

'Ladies and gentlemen, I would also like to introduce you to Clarence Brooks, our wonderful bookseller and . . . according to some . . . Declan Archer's muse.'

Far out, Bri. I'm so focused on trying to stop the familiar blush that it takes a second for me to realise that some of the people at the front are booing.

'She's not good enough for you, Declan!' someone yells, their voice bolstered by the loud agreement of people around them.

Declan's head snaps up.

What?

The booing gets louder, and it's probably only five people but it feels like the entire crowd, and then something flies through the air towards me, smacking me in the chest. I look down to see half an apple roll along the book table in front of me, a dull pain echoing through me. My mind blanks.

There's a murmur of confusion through the crowd, and people start pushing into each other as Jed moves towards the source of the missile. My heart is beating in my ears, my chest, my nose, and Bri is saying something but I can't quite hear her.

Did someone just throw an apple core at me?

The thought, though, is muffled by the sight in front of me, which is Declan ignoring Bri's protests, climbing down from the rock and into the jostling crowd. Where his face was impassive and closed before, now it's alive with barely masked fury. It's that as much as anything that seems to pave a way for him as he stalks across the clearing.

I'm vaguely aware of the volume rising, but Declan's eyes find mine and hold them, like he's asking me to stay with him.

And then he's in front of me, eyes scanning my face. I try to smile but it sticks a little at the edges, and Declan takes a small, imperceptible breath.

He reaches out hesitantly to take my hand, and his palm is warm against mine, jolting me back to the present.

Someone threw a freaking apple core at me.

I feel hysteria rise in my throat, but I swallow it down, and Declan squeezes.

'Are you with me?' he breathes, just to me.

I feel like I am and I'm not, like I'm outside of my body watching this weird thing happen. But I also feel *angry. Because someone threw a freaking apple core at me.* Beyond Declan, the crowd still feels out of control, but he doesn't rush me.

I nod, and he pushes the books I've spent the afternoon neatly stacking to the side, which – of all things – somehow manages to penetrate the shock that I can still feel thumping through my body. I glare at him, and his face finally relaxes.

Then he climbs onto the table. When he speaks, his voice is warm, but it's sharp enough to cut through the noise of the crowd.

'Like Bri, I'm very happy to have you all here today. *Talking to Trees* is the book of my heart, and it's an honour to share it with you and to hear your stories. I can promise you access to me – both today and in every word of the book. But for anyone who feels like the dedication also gives them access to the bookseller, to Clarrie – it absolutely doesn't. That's an error that's on me, and I'm sorry. But respectfully, whoever threw that, I'd like you to leave. Now.' He looks down at me, his eyes bright and fierce. 'We are a team.'

Declan looks over at Bri, who is still standing open-mouthed on the rock. 'Bri, do you mind if we move the stage over here?' he asks. Bri shakes her head, and Declan smiles a lightning smile at the crowd, who for the first time since the event started are genuinely silent. Like someone could drop a pin and you'd hear it. 'We'll be with you in just a moment, everyone,' says Declan. 'I promise that in exchange for the delay I'll even tell you why this place is special.'

For all that he's warm and self-deprecating on stage, it's the most I've seen Declan give of himself – and as though he's not even thinking about it.

A small, awkward cheer goes up from the crowd, but Declan barely seems to notice. He crouches down on the table as Bri makes her way towards us.

'Do you want to leave?' he asks, and in this moment, I fully believe that he will call off the event if I ask him to. His expression is wide open, and despite the apple core and the confusion that's beating in my veins I shake my head.

'I'm okay.'

He reaches out a hand as though to touch my face, but he doesn't. Then he stands on the table again, and starts telling the crowd about his mother.

On the other side of the clearing, I can see Jed guarding a few people like a hawk, and Bri squeezes my arm before she melts into the crowd to deal with them. And though they are warm and genuine, Declan's words feel like a dagger in my chest. *We're a team.*

At least, until tomorrow.

Chapter Thirty-one

I manage to stand through Declan's entire speech without bursting into tears. There's no sign of either Bri or whoever threw the apple, but my nerves still feel strung like an out-of-tune guitar. Declan finishes to rapturous applause, and steps down off the table.

He glances at me, and for a moment I think he's going to ask if I want someone else to sell books, but he doesn't and, somehow, that helps. Instead, he just picks up the copies he knocked off earlier and places them carefully back on the table.

I take a small, steadying breath, then make myself turn and face the first customer who tentatively approaches. This is my job. An elderly man stands in front of me, holding the hand of a woman I presume is his wife, and my first thought is to wonder if they seriously walked all the way in here.

'I'm so sorry about what happened,' the elderly man says, his face all warm concern.

'Thank you,' I tell him automatically, trying to smile at both of them, and the desire to not just cope but to *do something* pulses through me. 'It felt a bit more like a rock concert than a book signing, didn't it?'

The man laughs, a deep, vibrant chuckle that seems at odds with his wiry frame, and for a second he reminds me of Alistair from Knit, Stitch and Yarn.

'I could tell you some rock concert stories that would make your toes curl,' confides the man.

'You could tell stories from anywhere in your twenties to your seventies that would make her toes curl,' says the woman next to him. She turns towards me. 'I can barely wear shoes any more my toes are so curly,' she confides.

It startles an unexpected laugh out of me, and from the corner of my eye I see Declan pause his signing. I lean forward to look at the woman's shoes. They're gorgeous, blue with neat white bows.

'You wear them well, in any case,' I manage, and she winks.

It gets both easier and harder after that. As though they've all taken Declan seriously, no one hassles me about the dedication, but every few customers someone offers me their support. A young woman gives me a whole apple, which I think is either symbolic or in case I need to return fire. Never in my life have I had my hand squeezed so many times, or so many people tell me that I'm so brave to sell books after what happened.

I can feel tears prickling behind my eyes, and a tingle in my nose that makes me have to sniff every minute, but I manage to hold it together. I listen and I talk, and when it gets to be too much I direct people to Jed for a bird fact.

Declan signs more quickly than he has previously, and it's

much earlier than anticipated that Jed starts gathering people to walk everyone back down the path.

Bri arrives just before they set off, and she talks quickly to Jed before striding over to Declan and me. Her face is set; her eyes serious. For the first time, it's like Bri has dimmed her lights.

'Are you okay?' she asks me immediately.

'I think so,' I say, surprised to find that it's true. I don't feel quite as on edge any more – the other people in the crowd went a long way to easing that feeling in my chest – but there's a lingering anger, and confusion.

'What happened, Bri?' asks Declan.

'Tessa,' says Bri, and Declan exhales loudly.

'What did she do?' he asks.

'She wrote another article,' says Bri, pinching the bridge of her nose. 'The *Behind the Books* piece comes out tomorrow, so I suspect she was just trying to play off that. But it was a bit of her own version of . . . behind the scenes. Of how she imagined your interaction in the bookshop with Clarrie might have gone.'

Apprehension knots itself in the pit of my stomach. *What the hell? What did she say? And why would she even do that?*

'It's pretty ridiculous, really, but apparently it was enough to convince a few of your fans that Clarrie was your enemy.'

'I'm sorry,' says Declan, his voice heavy. And it's a crappy, crappy thing, but it's not his fault. I half smile at him, but his expression doesn't change.

'I'll see if I can do anything about it,' says Bri.

'I can speak to her if that helps,' says Declan.

Bri nods. 'Thank you.'

Silence falls in the clearing, and it suddenly occurs to me that this is officially the end of the tour. It feels both intense and anti-climactic, and all I want to do is curl up in bed. I don't know how I imagined this going, but . . . it wasn't like this.

I'm sure the walk back down the path is the same distance as it was on the way in, but it feels infinitely shorter, like time is speeding up, racing us home, and before long we're back at the cars.

We still have to drive three hours to get to the airport hotel we're staying in tonight; then we fly home tomorrow morning. Back to reality.

Finally, the trees thin and we arrive back at the cars. Jed is leaning against the side of the van, listening to a bird call on his phone. Declan looks up at the sound, but doesn't comment, and somehow the lack of conversation about birds indicates more starkly that it's all ending than anything else.

I'm about to turn towards Declan to say – I don't know what – but then everyone's phones start beeping with messages, bringing the world to the edge of the forest.

I glance down at my phone to see I have three missed calls from Ruth.

My blood goes cold.

It might be nothing; she could've called me once and then redialled twice by accident. But my fingers are shaking as I scroll to her name.

The dial tone feels loud in my ear and the long, slow breaths I'm trying to take keep catching in my chest. Then the ringing stops, and Ruth's warm voice comes down the line.

'Clarrie?'

'Hi, Ruth,' I manage to push out. 'What's happening?'

'It's your gran,' says Ruth gently, and my heart stops. 'She's had a fall.'

Ruth keeps talking, and I'm vaguely aware of her telling me that Gran has fractured her hip, that she's going into surgery. She's giving details and information that is probably important. But I only hear snatches of it. And I don't know if it's because it's so unexpected, or because I'm already feeling bruised, but darkness prickles at the edges of my vision, and when I try to breathe it catches in my throat.

Then Declan is there. His voice sounds like it's coming down a tunnel, but I hold on to it. And when I don't answer his gentle questions he doesn't keep pushing.

'Do you want me to talk to her?' he asks, and I somehow manage to nod. He takes the phone that's slipping from my fingers and I hear him speaking calmly and quickly to Ruth. Then he slides my phone into his pocket, wraps his arms round me and holds me while I sob against his chest.

Chapter Thirty-two

It's funny, the things you can know with your head and not with your heart.

In my head, I know that Gran is old, and that one day she will die. But I think there's also a part of me that is fully expecting her to live for ever.

I know that she's made it through surgery, because Ruth tells me when I phone her back. I know that she's in hospital recovering. But I'm still picturing her in Glenhaven. Like my brain can't quite process the idea that she's somewhere else again.

I know that things change, but my heart hasn't quite caught up.

Declan drives us to the hotel. For the first hour, he is quiet, as though knowing instinctively that I'm feeling too overwhelmed to engage with anything. After a while, though, he begins to talk.

'One of the first times I came into the bookshop, I found your gran sitting on the beanbag in the corner,' he says slowly, as though giving me time to react. I don't say anything, and he glances at me again before continuing. 'She looked up as the bell rang, and when I opened my mouth to speak she told me I had to wait until the end of the chapter. I just stood there.' He shakes his head and laughs softly. 'For five full minutes, I stood there. And when she'd finished she looked up and told me it was a cliffhanger and that I should probably grab a book to read next to her because she was diving in for another chapter.'

A tear tracks down my cheek, but I don't wipe it away.

'She shuffled over and we read side by side on that beanbag for almost twenty minutes,' he says.

He falls quiet again, and I reach out to rest my hand on his leg. He doesn't look down, just loops his fingers through mine.

It's like that for the rest of the drive – moments of quiet, interspersed with stories about his experiences in the bookshop.

In a corner of my brain, I realise that our last minutes are trickling away. I haven't really processed what happened in the clearing, or the fact that the tour is finished. That our pause is almost over. But there's no space to dwell on any of it; I'm too consumed by my worry about Gran.

It's late afternoon when we pull into the airport hotel. Declan checks us in, then walks with me to the room. He hesitates outside.

'Do you want me to stay with you a while?' he asks softly. 'Just to sit?'

I know it will probably make everything harder tomorrow, but right now I don't care. I don't want him to leave. 'Yes, please.'

I'm too tired to do much apart from climb into bed with my clothes on. Declan hesitates again, then sits on the bed beside me. He rests a hand on my back, making small, soothing circles with his fingertips. After what might be five minutes or an hour, he clears his throat, then he starts talking about the different types of trees he knows until I fall asleep.

When I wake, it's dark outside. I can feel Declan's warm, solid presence behind me, and his arm is wrapped across my body, as though shielding me from the outside world.

I should get up. I should go and sit in one of the awful red armchairs in the corner of the room. I promised I only wanted a pause, but I know that at this point every moment I spend with him is only going to increase the heartache when he's gone.

I wriggle back into his warmth. He murmurs something in his sleep, pulling his arm tighter round me and I drift back into sleep.

It's early morning when I wake again. I can see the sun beginning to peek over the horizon. I don't know how long I lie there, watching as activity begins, as planes begin to take off. It's so neat, so efficient. The plane gets ready to leave, it flies away and the airport waves goodbye then moves on to the next plane. Once the plane is gone, the airport isn't thinking about it any more. It becomes another airport's problem.

At least, I think that's what happens. To be honest, I'm not really sure how air-traffic control works.

I'm desperate to be in the hospital with Gran. But it's also the last place I feel like being. I don't want to see her hurt, to see another slice of her vulnerability. I want to hold on to the memories I have of her running around the bookshop and telling stories, of asking people questions, not to have them slowly erased with this new reality. And even that thought feels horribly, hideously selfish.

When Declan wakes just before six, he sits bolt upright. 'Sorry,' he says, his voice husky and his hair a mess. 'I didn't mean to fall asleep. How are you doing?'

'Fine,' I tell him, but we both know it's a lie.

He nods, squeezes my hand, then stands up and starts packing. As though ten seconds is all he needs to be a fully functioning person. We're ready to go fifteen minutes later, like he knows without talking that I'll want to be at the airport early, no matter that our flight doesn't leave for another three hours.

I fall asleep on the plane and Declan doesn't tease me about snoring when I wake up. He doesn't even raise his eyebrows at me. It makes things more real somehow, and the hollowness in my stomach widens.

'You didn't mention my snoring,' I say hoarsely, and it's the first thing I've said since we got on the plane. It's such a ridiculous thing to say, and Declan just studies me for a while. There's a tenderness in his expression, and I wonder whether he's called Tessa about the article in Read, Repeat yet. Yesterday feels like a lifetime ago.

'I didn't realise you were sleeping,' I think I hear him say before I drift off again. 'I thought there was a bear on the plane so I was trying to be as quiet as possible.'

Declan and Jed are collecting the luggage while Bri and I wait by the door. She's organised a car to take me from the airport to the hospital and when I try to thank her, she hugs me so tightly I think my ribs might crack.

'I'll call you next week,' she says. 'Declan will be packing for his move, so I should have plenty of time in the next few weeks.'

My brain is so foggy that it takes me a second to register what she's said. 'Sorry, what?' I say. 'What move?'

Bri frowns. 'You know, to Mayfield?' she says. 'I thought he said he took you there?'

Mayfield. Where his dad lived. Where Declan held my hand. A twelve-hour drive from here.

'Declan's moving to Mayfield?' The words feel sluggish, like I can't quite get them out.

Bri freezes, her eyes going wide. 'Crap. Oh crap, I'm sorry, Clarrie, I thought you knew.' There's pity in her eyes, and my head is spinning. It's too much, all at once.

Declan's moving. I can't process the information; I don't have space to work out what I even think about it. But he doesn't owe me anything. He said his life was complicated. This was a *pause*. It was never going to be anything more.

I still feel it like a punch in the gut.

'No, I . . . I didn't realise.'

I can already feel the tears prickling at the corner of my eyes.

Gran's in hospital. I just have to focus on that right now.

'Oh, Clarrie,' says Bri. 'I'm so sorry.'

'It's fine, Bri,' I say, in response to her horrified expression as Jed and Declan return with everyone's bags. 'I'm fine. I just need to get going, to see Gran. I'll talk to you soon, okay?' I manage a watery smile and turn to Jed, trying to push aside my thoughts about the man beside him.

The stern affection on Jed's face is a relief. His farewell is less effusive but no less warm, and I manage to hug him without bursting into tears. Then he opens the bum bag he was wearing on the plane that I probably subconsciously assumed was carrying his travel documents and valuables. Instead, it's just filled with feathers.

He pulls one out and presses it into my palm, and the tears that were threatening spill down my cheeks.

'I'll take you spotlighting around here sometime,' he says. 'There are a few great spots an hour out of the city.'

I nod. 'Thanks, Jed,' I say, my voice only cracking slightly, and he gives me a brisk hug.

Then it's just Declan standing in front of me, green eyes sharp on mine.

The airport flickers and fades for a second, and Declan's eyes feel like a waypoint, the same as they did in the crowd yesterday.

But this was just a pause.

We're not dating. The pause is over, and he doesn't owe me anything.

'Bri told me you're moving,' I whisper.

Declan inhales sharply. He closes his eyes. 'Clarrie, I—'

'I think it will suit you,' I continue. 'Mayfield.'

Declan searches my eyes. His expression is unreadable. He opens his mouth, but before he can speak I cut him off again.

'I have to go,' I say. 'But thanks for the tour. All the best with the move.'

Then I turn round and walk back out into reality.

The hospital smells the same way that all hospitals seem to smell. As though someone mixed cleaning products, sadness and hope and invented a hospital-scented air freshener that's distributed worldwide.

The corridors are white with bright lights and faded paint, and when I enquire at the front desk they direct me to the fourth floor.

I take the stairs, because I can't stand the idea of being stationary, and I'm pretty sure that two weeks in the forest doing moderate amounts of walking qualifies me as the kind of person who takes the stairs.

The fourth-floor ward is quiet but not still, footsteps and soft voices and beeping machines all rolling together in a constant soundtrack. Gran is in the last room on the left.

The first thing I see when I walk in is a posy of cheerful, bright-coloured flowers on the table beside her bed. I wonder how many bouquets of flowers a hospital throws out each week.

Gran is in bed, tucked under crisp, white sheets. She looks small in a way that I've never seen her, even in the last two years since she went into Glenhaven. She's hooked up to a few different machines, but her face is peaceful.

I put my bags on the floor and sink slowly into the chair beside the bed, one that I could swear is the exact same brand as the chair in the airport hotel.

I want to take Gran's hand, but I don't want to wake her. Instead, I sit and stare at the lines of her face, like I might be able to remember all the expressions I've ever seen in them.

The animation in her features whenever she told a story or listened to one of mine. The joy when she listened to a song she loved. Frustration when she heard about something broken that she couldn't fix. And then both pulled down by the heaviness of grief and buoyed by her endless determination after Grandpa died.

I miss her so much.

It feels like such a stupid, selfish thing to say. *She's still here. Her face still dances through all those expressions. You still have time with her.*

But I miss the lost moments too.

Gran wakes not long after, and it's with a confusion that the nurses tell me is normal but that breaks something afresh in my chest. I stay for a few hours, trying to be as consistent as possible, but after a while, she needs to rest again.

And while it's awful seeing her in the state that she's in, my mind is more settled at having seen her. At being close.

I stretch my legs in the corridor, and pull my phone out of my pocket to see missed calls from Yumi, and my heart stops when I see there's one from Declan too. The urge to call him washes over me like a wave. But I don't. *He's moving away. It was just a pause.*

I need to call Yumi back to tell her what's happening, but

I don't want to talk on the phone right now. I want to be somewhere familiar. Somewhere that feels like Gran.

I'm walking out through the hospital doors before I can question the decision. Going to Brooks' will get me out for a few hours, and I can talk to Yumi in person.

Navigating my way through the train station with my luggage feels overwhelming, so I do something I never do, and I order an Uber. The driver is blessedly quiet and the traffic on the road still hasn't peaked. It's not long before we arrive in the familiar tree-lined street.

I ask to be dropped off a street away.

The sound of the door shutting feels loud, and when the driver pulls away in his electric car the tyres peel along the road. The footpath is wet, like it rained recently.

My stomach twists and knots in anticipation as I walk past the deli, and Ruth's antique shop, where I can see a hand-drawn sign on the door saying that she's closed for the afternoon.

And then there it is.

Brooks' Books.

I don't know what I'm expecting. A lightning bolt. A punch in the gut. A feeling of overwhelming joy. Tears, streaming down my face, like my body knows what's really in my heart when it comes to the bookshop.

None of those things happen. It's just Brooks', the same as it's always been. More familiar to me than the back of my hand, and stamped with memories both good and bad.

The bell chimes happily above the door, like it's welcoming

me, though not any more enthusiastically or warmly than it welcomes any of our customers, and not as sweetly as Alex's bell. *I'll have to ask him where he got that.*

'With you in a minute,' Yumi calls from out the back, and for the first time in twenty-four hours I almost feel like smiling, because I know that she's probably just sitting down for a cup of tea and her afternoon cookie and will be annoyed by the presence of a customer.

I put my bags behind the counter and note the small changes Yumi's made while I've been away. She's rearranged a few bookshelves. Updated the display table. All the small things that she knows she can do without me freaking out about the change.

'Clarrie!' Yumi's voice sounds behind me, and I turn round, half expecting to be met with a million questions about the tour, teasing about Declan or a picture graph explaining why we should implement something new.

But the smile on my face drops as it takes in the tense look on her face. I've literally only seen Yumi stressed once in her life – when her neighbour phoned to tell her that her snake, Lucky, had somehow escaped from her apartment.

'Where have you been?' she says, her voice strained. 'I thought you'd be here earlier.'

'Hospital,' I say, my heart tripping over itself to know what's going on. 'Gran had a fall. What's wrong?' I ask. 'Yumi, has something happened?'

'Your gran had a fall?' says Yumi, her face falling further, if that's even possible. 'Oh, Clarrie, I'm so sorry.'

'It's okay,' I say. 'She'll be okay.'

Yumi reaches out to squeeze my hand, and I try to smile. 'What happened here?' I repeat.

Her eyes search mine, and I raise my eyebrows. She raises hers back, but her heart's not in it, and it makes me feel like my stomach is closing in on itself.

'Yumi,' I say.

'Your mum came in again today. She was with the same woman as last time,' she says finally. 'The estate agent.'

'Again?' I say. I'm exhausted, and confused, and I don't understand what's going on. But I'm also not particularly surprised that the woman was an estate agent. I should have called Mum back. I should have stopped letting Wilderness Clarrie try to pause things.

Yumi nods. 'I think . . . Clarrie, it seemed like she's found a loophole. She was talking about contesting your grandmother's decision to give you the bookshop, given it was so close to when your gran was diagnosed. Apparently, she's been collecting evidence to put together a case that your grandmother wasn't mentally fit to make the decision.'

'What?'

Yumi's words feel like they're filtering through me in slow motion. I don't even know whether what she's saying is possible, or legal, but the thought of Mum selling Brooks' out from under me feels like a blunt force to my gut.

But apparently my gut hasn't quite finished bottoming out, because when I look at Yumi's face, there's still hesitation there, and Yumi *never* hesitates.

'There's more?' I ask, my voice ringing in my ears. Yumi nods once.

'There was also an article on Read, Repeat,' she says finally, and my stomach unclenches fractionally, because at least this is a familiar drama.

'I know,' I tell her. 'There were people at the last event who were motivated to throw an apple core at me based on the imagined bookshop conversation Tessa Dalton wrote.'

But Yumi is shaking her head even as a frown blossoms across her face.

'That's hideous and let's please shelve it for a few minutes, but . . . not that article.'

'What?'

'It was a new post. Announcing that the bookshop is for sale.'

'*What?*' My head is buzzing and my knees are threatening to sink me to the floor. It's too much. Too many things, all at once.

'Honestly, it was really more of an advertisement,' says Yumi, but her posture seems a little more relaxed, the revelations out of her bones now.

'Who would have even told her?' I say, but dread is already trickling through my bones. *I told someone my mum wanted to sell.* 'Declan,' I whisper.

'Probably,' says Yumi. 'They used to date, right?'

Chapter Thirty-three

They used to date, right?

'What?' I repeat again – because I can't seem to say anything else – but it's a whisper this time. As though my settings have been tampered with. 'Declan and Tessa?'

I've literally been on tour with the man for two weeks . . . I've been *kissing* him for half of that. And, apparently, I never really knew anything about him at all. *It was just a pause.*

Yumi frowns. 'You didn't know? It was referenced in that article you were talking about, the one about the bookshop conversation.'

'I didn't read it.' Bri didn't say anything. And Declan sure as hell didn't, either. But then . . . he didn't say anything about moving, either. *Because we're not friends.* We're not anything. But I trusted him. I told him things I hadn't told anyone and, even if that was never part of the deal, it still *hurts*.

I try to remember what happened yesterday – did I just miss it? But even in the haze of the past twenty-four hours, I know that I didn't.

'I'm not sure what the look on your face is,' says Yumi. 'But . . . coffee?'

I don't know. I don't know what I want. I just feel so stupid. And I feel ridiculous for feeling stupid. Declan doesn't owe me details about his life plans, or his relationship history.

Except that he did an interview with her. Except that now my failure is on display. Again. How could he tell her about Mum trying to sell?

I close my eyes, trying to reconnect with the version of myself that felt confident in the dark. But whatever I felt in the moments I was spotlighting must have stayed in the forest.

Then the bell to the shop rings and my heart sinks, but my body turns automatically towards it, like it already knows who is there. As though it would know him anywhere.

Because of course he'd show up now.

Still, I'm not properly prepared for the sight of his green eyes and his black jeans and his stupid cap.

Declan slides it off the second my eyes meet his, and somehow in the last two weeks his face has become so familiar that it makes my heart clench.

'I was waiting in the deli,' he says, his voice low and hoarse. 'I saw you walk past.'

We stand and stare at each other, and I see him note my luggage on the floor and the bags under my eyes.

'I'm going to make that coffee,' blurts Yumi.

'Thanks, Yumi,' I say, my eyes on Declan.

He takes a step forward the second she leaves the room, and I take a step back, because I don't even know how to be close to him any more. Something whispers across his face, but he stops moving.

'How is your grandmother?' he asks, tucking his hands into his pockets, like he did at the airport.

'Why are you here?'

Declan's eyes are steady, searching mine.

'I don't really know,' he says. 'I just . . . I wanted to see if you were okay.'

'So you can talk to your ex-girlfriend about it?'

Declan flinches, but he doesn't look away.

'I should have told you about Tessa.'

'Told me what? That she might have a heightened awareness of your love life because the two of you used to date? Or that she was planning to announce to the world that Brooks' was for sale?'

'What?' says Declan, his brow furrowing.

'Don't act like you're not the one who told her,' I say. 'I confided in you, Declan.' My voice breaks in a way that it didn't earlier, and I hate it that it does. Declan looks like he's going to take a step closer, but he doesn't.

'I didn't tell her the shop was for sale,' he says, and my heart twists in my chest. 'When did she post it?'

'I don't know,' I snap. 'I've been busy visiting my grandmother in hospital. While my bookshop is falsely advertised on the internet.'

The words hang in the air between us. *My bookshop.*

Declan's watching me, as though he noticed what just

happened, and I harden my expression. I'm not sharing this with him.

'I spoke to Tessa last night,' he says, his eyes on mine, and it shouldn't hurt but it does. 'She apologised for the article yesterday and what it caused. It's off the site now. I don't know anything about the new article, but if she thought the shop was for sale . . . I think posting about it would have been her trying to make amends.'

His tone is measured, and I want to scream, because I don't want to hear about how perfectly reasonable Tessa is.

'And is she going to come down and help when my mother walks through with potential buyers?'

I take a breath, try to steady myself. None of this matters right now. I have to get back to the hospital. I have to deal with whatever the fallout of the announcement is. But there's a big, ridiculous part of me that's distracted by thoughts of him and Tessa together. I want to ask when they broke up. I want to ask whether he loved her, whether he still does. I want to ask if she's the reason he thought I'd leaked the dedication.

I close my eyes briefly, like I might be able to block the thoughts out.

None of that is my business. We were never anything more than a moment out of time.

'I can help,' says Declan.

'What, from Mayfield? Come on, Declan, we're back to reality now.'

'What if I want *us* to be reality?'

His voice is so soft, but the words are sharp in my chest

and I have a feeling that if I breathe they'll destroy me. *How freaking dare he?*

'And how would that work? You'd send me Christmas-themed postcards once a month? I don't want your pity, Declan, and I don't want your help.'

'What do you want, Clarrie?' he asks.

I have to focus on Gran. I have to deal with Mum. I have to forget about this man who is moving a full day away.

'I just want you to leave.' I hold his gaze. He watches me for another second, and when I don't say anything, he just nods once, then turns round and walks out again.

The doorbell jingles, and he is gone.

My chest feels broken and sore, and my eyelids prickle, but I don't cry.

Yumi creeps out from the kitchen, and some part of my brain notes that she has absolutely zero coffees with her.

'Must have been some tour.'

Going back to the hospital feels overwhelming, but I don't want to go home, either. And I sure as hell don't want to talk to my mother yet.

Plus, I promised Gran.

The nurses on the fourth floor nod to me like they already know me, and I wonder how many new people they see every day, in their most vulnerable moments. They tell me that Gran is still resting, and I reassure them that I won't wake her.

But when I sit in the chair next to her bed – the one that already feels moulded to my butt – the room is too quiet.

There's too much space for the past few hours to come crashing down on me.

I clear my throat softly, and the sound is loud in the white room, but it makes me feel less hollow inside.

'I went on a book tour, Gran,' I whisper. 'To help save our shop.'

Gran doesn't move, and I shift in my seat, opening my mouth again before I really know what I'm going to say – trying to fill the gaps in the room and in myself.

'It was two weeks in remote locations,' I begin, trying not to think about Declan's face when he asked how she was, but I didn't answer.

And I tell her about the tour. About Declan Archer and the book that I haven't read, about Alex the bookseller and Merry the mechanic. About Bri and the layers that give life to her endless positivity. About Jed and his passion for birds. About how I think that there's the smallest possibility that I might have accidentally fallen in love with a man who is moving across the country and didn't even tell me. I tell her about Wilderness Clarrie. About spotlighting, and about being alone in the dark, and the rain on my face. I tell her about how the tour has given the bookshop a much-needed boost. That we're going to have new lights, and that I don't know if it will be enough, but that I am determined to do everything I can to keep it alive.

I tell her about the bookshop. About the things that have happened recently that I know she would love. I tell her about the community, about the people whose stories have touched me. The things that I missed while I was away. And then slowly, more hesitantly, I find myself telling her all the things that I hate about it.

I whisper until my throat is sore, and I feel like there's nothing left inside me. Gran just lies in bed, breathing steadily.

When I hear a soft knock at the open door, my heart tries to punch its way through my chest and I almost jump out of the chair.

I turn round, my stupid heart dropping when I see it's not Declan. Of course it's not.

It's Ruth, watching me through her blue-rimmed glasses.

And, oh my goodness, how much of that did she hear?

'Ruth,' I say, standing up and walking forward like she didn't just hear me spill my guts out to my sleeping and injured grandmother.

'Hi, sweetheart.' Ruth smiles. 'I won't interrupt you. I just wanted to come in and check how she's doing. How you're both doing, actually.'

'Come in,' I say, pulling up a fresh chair for her. Gran stirs in the bed, but doesn't wake.

'Are you sure?' asks Ruth slowly, doubtfully, but at my emphatic nod she smiles kindly and takes the chair I've pulled up next to mine.

We both sit there for a minute, watching Gran sleep, and I can feel awkwardness crawling across my skin. It's been a hell of a day.

'How was your trip?' says Ruth. 'I so enjoyed all of your updates about it while you were away.'

'Fine,' I manage, my throat dry. 'It was fine. Thanks for checking in on Gran for me, Ruth.'

Ruth waves my thanks away. 'Any time you need to go away, consider me your woman on the ground,' she says.

It's nice, sitting with Ruth, but I'm so tired. I'm wondering how soon I can make my exit when she speaks again.

'Your grandmother told me once that she hated the wonky shelves in the bookshop,' she says. 'She said that it drove her mad, the idea that the books weren't straight.'

For a second, I just look up and blink at her. At this piece of new information.

'I didn't know that,' I say. But then I realise – *that's not true.*

Gran rearranged the books on the wonky shelves regularly, and more than once I saw her measuring them with a ruler, muttering. It's just that those memories – the mundane, everyday moments – are never the ones I associate with Gran.

I realise that for all the time I spent in the bookshop with her I never got to see what the grind of it was like. Not until it was just me, running it alone. I never imagined that there might be things that she hated too.

I have so many questions for Ruth, and she waits patiently for me to speak. But none of what's in my head is what actually comes out of my mouth next.

'What do you hate about the antique shop?' I ask her.

If she's surprised by my question, she doesn't look it. She doesn't even pause long before she answers.

'I don't particularly like having people buy things,' she says. 'I rather like the way it's all arranged.'

The words make me laugh. And then suddenly, irrationally, the tears that paused earlier are leaking down my cheeks, and I'm sobbing again. I'm sobbing about the bookshop and about Gran and about Declan Archer and about how I don't know what I want, but that, actually, I might also know exactly what I want, and right now is a terrible time to realise all of that when I've just done my best to give up on it all.

'Oh, sweetheart,' says Ruth, patting a hand on my shoulder.

'Sorry,' I tell her, sobbing harder. 'I'm so sorry.'

When my tears finally subside, Ruth is looking both kind and sort of stressed.

'I didn't mean to make you cry,' she says. 'I've made a bit of a mess of this, haven't I?'

I shake my head, because she really hasn't.

'You know her so much better than I do,' says Ruth. 'But if I know anything about Margaret, it's how proud she's always been of you, Clarence. I'll never forget the day she told me that she found a trail of books on the floor and when she followed it, she found you, tucked up and asleep on the empty shelf. She said seeing the bookshop through your eyes is what earned it the place it had in her heart.' When I look at Ruth, she's watching Gran, a sad smile on her face. 'She might not be able to express it in the same way now, but if she thought for a second that it wasn't what you wanted, she would be the first person to tell you to sell it and use the money to do whatever you want.'

Tears prick behind my eyes, but they don't fall down my cheeks this time, because she's right. I know it in the same way that I know that Gran would find Jed's passion for birds inspiring. But the thought of selling the bookshop with Gran's permission doesn't fill me with relief – it fills me with dread. Not because I don't know what to do without it, but because I don't want to do anything else.

I love being a bookseller. The realisation is like a train that's been coming down the tracks and, when it arrives, it's without fanfare or tears. But it's there: waiting calmly at the platform for me to step on.

'Peggy?' says a voice beside me on the bed, and Ruth and I both turn to look at Gran, blinking and stirring, calling my mum's name. 'Are you here?'

I reach out and take Gran's hand, papery and thin, in mine.

'I'm here, Gran.'

Chapter Thirty-four

My parents' house is at the top of a hill that overlooks the water. It stands shoulder to shoulder between two other grand houses, as though the three of them are competing to see who is the tallest.

It's not easily accessible by public transport, so Yumi lends me her car. Her only two rules are that the radio must be played at full volume and that I promise not to get distracted by falling leaves.

After two weeks away from the bookshop it feels strange to be back home and to not be behind the counter at Brooks'. It feels stranger still to drive across the city. But it's long past time that I speak to my mother. I finally listened to her voice-mails last night, both of them basically repeats of the same message – that she's made progress on the sale, and can I please call her.

There is no mention of the fact that she is trying to dismantle and reassemble my life. To take away the bookshop. I could call her, but the conviction that began in me on the hill in Mayfield has taken root. I need to see her in person.

The salt air is fresh against my skin when I step out of

Yumi's hatchback. Mum and Dad's house stands tall and silent, casting shadows even in the morning light. I mean, to be honest, the position of the sun means that every house on the street is casting shadows.

It's such a contrast to the places where we've been the past couple of weeks that, despite the fresh air, I feel like I can't breathe. The glue on the pieces that I've been trying to patch together since yesterday feels so fresh, but there's something about knowing that Brooks' Books beats in my blood, about the love I rediscovered on the tour, that gives me confidence.

No matter how nervous I feel . . . I have to do this.

I push my legs up their front steps, ringing the doorbell before I can talk myself out of it. I can hear it echo through the house, and the click of my mother's heels against the timber floors. She opens the door dressed in a pencil skirt and blouse, which means she's probably getting ready to go out.

I see the surprise light her sharp brown eyes before she covers it.

'Clarence,' she says. 'Lovely to see you.'

'Do you have time to talk?' I ask her.

She stands for just a second, taking me in. Then, 'Of course,' she says, moving gracefully to the side to let me in.

I follow her through the spotless house to the sleek white couches by the front windows that look out over the water. I don't sit down, and Mum doesn't either.

'Would you like a cup of coffee?' she asks, ever the hostess.

'I would like to know what the hell you're doing, trying to

sell the bookshop from under me,' I say, my voice as mild as I can make it. I curse myself almost as soon as the words are out. I wasn't going to lead with this. I was going to be calm and reasonable, and at least ask how she was first. But I can't take my words back now, and . . . maybe it's better this way.

Mum holds my gaze, her eyes unreadable. She doesn't bluster or stiffen or pretend that she's not trying to do the exact thing I'm accusing her of doing, and I ignore the disappointment that trickles through me. As though there was still a part of me hoping that I might be wrong.

'I'm trying to help you,' says Mum. The words are such a vivid reminder of Declan yesterday that pain slices through my gut, spilling anger out with it.

'To help?' My breath catches in my throat. 'Are you kidding me? Having Gran declared mentally unfit? Taking away my career? Constantly judging me and finding me wanting? Selling my freaking home? Tell me, Mum, how is any of that helping?'

I'm breathless by the end of it, and I hate that I am. She's just standing there, immaculate and entirely unruffled.

'Home?' she asks, her perfect eyebrows raised. And that's it. That's all she says.

'What are you talking about?' I say. I go to rub my head, but it reminds me too much of Declan and I really don't need to be reminded of Declan right now. I clench my fist by my side.

'You said I was trying to sell your home,' says Mum. 'Is the bookshop really your "freaking home"?'

'You know it is,' I say, and my voice sounds broken, like it's coming from someone else. Because, no matter how sure I am about the bookshop, Mum talking about it like this *hurts.*

'No,' says my mother, and her voice is sharp, clipped. She smooths down her skirt, and the action freezes something in me, because she *never* fidgets. 'I know that the bookshop was my parents' home. They poured themselves into it, but that was okay for them because they loved it; it was their dream. But I will never forgive my mother for the burden that she placed on you by giving it to you. I cannot believe that she actually had the gall to ask you to leave university – to leave behind *your* future and *your* dreams – just so that you could pour all of yourself into hers.'

My mother's voice is fierce in a way that I've never heard it, and when I look at her there's fire in her eyes too. 'I will be the bad guy in your story, Clarence, and I will find a way to sell the bookshop if it means that you can finally find your way back to doing the thing that you love, rather than the thing that she loved. You might be her granddaughter, but you are *my* daughter, and I won't let that place destroy you.'

My legs feel shaky, and I take a step back to sink into the couch. I can't take my eyes off her, though, off the bright fury in her eyes. Trying to process the words that she's saying.

'What?' I whisper. 'What are you talking about?'

Mum delicately arranges herself on the couch opposite me, her face set with determination.

And, as her words filter through me, all I can think about is Declan, sitting on the hill and saying he felt like he spent his life mad at his father without understanding him.

'Is that really what you think?' I ask, searching her eyes. 'That I left university because she asked me to?'

I try to read her, but she's silent and still.

'I didn't leave my degree because Gran asked me to. I left because studying law made me feel like I was drowning.'

My mother doesn't move a muscle, apart from to shake her head.

'No,' she says. 'She told me that she was giving you the shop. That if I was going to be mad at anyone for you leaving your degree, it should be her.'

Oh, Gran.

'She gave it to me *after* I left,' I say, all of the residual anger draining out of my body. My mother has seriously spent the last two years thinking that Gran asked me to give up my degree?

But why would she think otherwise? I never told her. I spoke to Gran about everything that had happened, not to Mum. And, for the first time in my life, I wonder how that must have felt for her.

'She gave it to me so that I had a home, while I was working myself out.'

My mother's face freezes, and when she smooths her skirt again, her hand is shaking.

'You hate the bookshop,' she says, and there's a rigid certainty still hanging on to her voice, like she's rereading the story, trying to understand the pieces. 'Every time I speak with you, you sound so stressed. You called it a black hole.'

I rub my hands across my face, because I can't even deny

it. Because of course she thinks I hate the bookshop. I've never given her a reason to think otherwise. Up until the tour, up until I thought it might be taken away from me – I didn't know that it was what I wanted, either.

And I realise that by not talking about how I feel about it, all I've given her is space to imagine the worst. I can't change everything that's happened between us, but maybe . . . maybe I can talk to her.

'Some days, running the bookshop is really hard,' I tell her. She's watching me, but she doesn't say anything. 'But some days . . . it's like magic. The idea that I can give someone a story that means something to them, or opens up new worlds for them, or that just helps them escape for a few hours is powerful. I know that I'm not fighting for the law to be upheld, or bringing people to justice, but what we do in the bookshop matters. I might not always have good days, but it's home, Mum. And it's not for sale.'

Mum turns to look out at the water, and for a moment she doesn't speak. In the kitchen, I can hear the faint tick of the wall clock.

'I used to hate it when she said that me not loving reading was the ultimate act of teenage rebellion,' she whispers finally, her gaze still fixed out of the window. 'It always made me feel as though I'd failed, somehow.' She smooths her skirt again. 'I told myself it was okay, that I was good at other things. I didn't need to love reading. I made a good life for myself, Clarence. A successful life.' She takes a breath, then turns to look at me. 'But I was so jealous that reading gave her that relationship with you.'

The words are stark in the space between us.

'Mum,' I whisper.

She holds up a hand. Then she inhales sharply, and stands.

No matter what has shifted in the past ten minutes, her ability to pull herself together hasn't, and by the time her knees straighten, she looks exactly the same as she always does.

'Are you sure?' she asks. 'About not wanting to sell?'

It's not an apology, but the fact that she asks lodges itself in my throat, and, at my nod, she types something into her phone and slides it onto the coffee table beside her.

'I was always going to give you the money from the sale,' she says, and her use of the past tense relaxes something in me.

'You'll stop the process?'

'I've just messaged the agent,' she says, slightly irritably, as though it's ridiculous for me to even ask. 'I'll speak with your brother this afternoon.'

'I'm sorry that I wasn't more open with you,' I say. 'About the degree, or anything that came after it. About the bookshop. I want to change that. Maybe . . . maybe we can schedule a lunch, once a month.'

She swallows and nods, something that looks suspiciously like tears shining bright in her eyes.

'And maybe I can pick the place sometimes,' I add.

She raises an eyebrow.

We sit there in silence for a moment. It's not comfortable, but it's not uncomfortable either, and maybe there's hope in that.

*

In my first move as someone who no longer has a bookshop up for sale against their will, I sit on a bench by the water, then call Yumi and ask if she's okay to manage for the rest of the day by herself.

'Don't expect the shelves to be the same when you get back,' she warns.

'Okay,' I tell her.

There's a pause at the other end of the line.

'Sorry, boss,' says Yumi. 'I think the line cut out. Did you just say "okay"?'

A whisper of a smile almost passes my lips at the tone in her voice. 'I did,' I confirm.

'Did your mother drug you?' she says. 'Are you still there? Do you need me to send the police?'

'No drugs,' I say. 'And no sale.'

Yumi cheers, then I hear her apologise to the customers in the store.

'But, seriously, did you mean it about the shelves?'

I think about the crooked shelves in the bookshop. About preserving Gran's memories, and valuing the new ones. About misunderstandings, and about seeing new things in the dark.

'Go for it,' I say.

'No takebacks,' says Yumi. Then she adds, 'By the way, Tessa Dalton phoned the bookshop and I told her you'd call her back. I'll send her number through. Battle all your demons at once and all that. Okay, bye.'

She hangs up before I can reply, and I stare at the phone in my hand for a few seconds, wondering if I can throw it into the ocean. It beeps with a message from Yumi, sending me the number, and my stomach turns. *If I can confront Mum, I can call Tessa Dalton.*

I dial the number before I can talk myself out of it, closing my eyes and imagining spotting a masked owl. It's weirdly therapeutic.

'Hello?' Tessa's voice comes down the line, and I manage not to screech like the masked owl.

'Tessa,' I say. 'It's Clarence. From Brooks' Books.'

'Clarence,' says Tessa, and I clench my fingers against the seat of the bench. 'Thank you for calling me back.' The line goes quiet for a beat, and I wonder whether it's disconnected. 'I was just ringing to apologise.'

'Sorry?' The word slips out, because whatever I was expecting from Tessa Dalton it wasn't a straight apology.

'Yes,' says Tessa. 'That's what I was trying to say. I'm sorry for printing something that incited people to act like idiots, and I'm sorry for the error yesterday.'

It's like all my words were used up in my conversation with my mother, because I honestly don't know how to respond.

'Declan told me that the bookshop isn't for sale,' Tessa continues. 'He – rather forcefully, I might add – requested that I remove the post. We've not had great luck with articles, the two of us. He says I overshare, but, honestly, that man is a vault. Six months we were together, and he never told me who you were or why he wrote the dedication. Though, I'll admit, publishing something that he said about you in the heat of an argument wasn't my finest moment. I can see why he broke up with me over that one.'

My head is reeling from the revelations, but her casual mention of Declan makes my breath catch. *He broke up with her over the first article.* 'Right,' I manage, and I can almost imagine Tessa's amused look. 'The article was pretty good, apart from that.'

I'm not sure who is more surprised by my words.

'Thanks,' says Tessa.

'I'd rather not see more articles about myself, though,' I tell her, watching a man cast off his boat. I cannot actually believe how strange this conversation is.

'Declan said the same thing,' says Tessa. 'You try to set people up, and this is the thanks you get,' she sighs.

'Set people up?'

'Declan is like a snail when it comes to moving on things,' says Tessa, by way of explanation. 'I thought a few extra articles might speed up whatever is obviously between you. And I owe him,' she says softly. 'Even if the fool *is* moving to Mayfield,' she adds, the softness vanishing like mist.

I want to ask her more about Declan, to keep talking, but it's a slippery slope, and I'm not sure it's one I can climb back up from at the moment.

'If Declan didn't tell you the bookshop was for sale, who did?' I ask instead.

'Oh, I can't tell you that,' says Tessa breezily. 'Protecting my sources and all that. I have to go, Clarence, but call again soon?'

The weirdest thing is, I actually might.

I call the hospital next to check on Gran, and they tell me that she's doing well, but that she might need a rest after all the visitors yesterday. They're hopeful that they'll be able to move her back to the nursing home tomorrow to recover there.

The news leaves me feeling both relieved and a little lost, and I walk by the harbour for a while instead, watching the sparkle of light along the water. It's beautiful, but there's no shade anywhere, and it's so strange to imagine that two days ago I was in the forest.

And, just like that, I know what I want to do with the rest of the afternoon.

I get back across the city without crashing Yumi's car, and I pretend not to see Mrs Potts telling me I can't park in the visitor space in front of the apartments.

I make myself a coffee and a crappy piece of toast, and I pull my snack bag out from where I dumped it last night under my dining-room table. I can still smell the whisper of Wilson/Milson bakery treats when I unzip it open, and I push aside crisps and apples to find what I'm looking for.

The copy of *Talking to Trees* that I bought from Alex.

The sight of Declan's name on the cover hurts, and the desire to call him, to talk to him about everything that's happened over the last few days, pulses through me.

But I don't. Instead, I do something I haven't done since the first time I saw Declan's dedication. I open his book.

*

I stay up until I finish it. It's filled with hope and warm humour and fifteen different kinds of trees. There are way too many references to the wilderness. But I can hear him between the lines of wisdom: the wry, teasing Declan of whom the book has flashes, but never really sees fully.

Then, on page three hundred and sixty-eight, his character visits a bookshop. It's small and warm and it feels like home, and the bookseller who serves him has grey hair and a laugh so loud that you can hear it even when the door is closed. I rest my hand along the page, like that might bring me closer to it. And if I hadn't heard that same laugh a thousand times in my life it would be just another interesting character in an intelligent, interesting book. But I know that it's so much more than that.

He wrote about Gran.

It's not in a way that would identify her to anyone else, and it's not about me. He didn't even tell me. He wrote about her because she's his favourite bookseller. He wrote about her because he *saw* her. Because, for all his fear on stage – he loves people. He sees people.

And, like all the men and women on the tour, I just want more of him.

It's a really freaking great book.

It's after 1 a.m. when I take my phone out to message him. I don't stop to ask whether it's a good idea, or to think about the fact that it's probably a bit rude to message someone in the middle of the night.

Instead, I think about how twelve hours isn't that far,

really. About how maybe I'm confident enough to handle that distance.

I finished the book.

I stay up until 2 a.m., irrationally waiting for him to message back. But he doesn't and, like a sucker, I fall asleep with my face pressed against the cover.

Chapter Thirty-five

One week later

The first thing Yumi did after I gave her permission to rearrange the shelves was to move the horror section in next to the children's fiction. For a half a day I had to explain to customers why there were masks, missing limbs and a varied assortment of undead people side by side with the picture books.

'I thought it would be funny,' Yumi said solemnly.

'And also nightmare-inducing?'

'Building resilience in the younger generation,' she replied.

She waited a whole half a day before she showed me the section at the back of the shop that she'd cleared, suggesting we turn it into a book cave for kids, complete with torches.

'You rearranged an entire bookshelf as a joke?'

Yumi shrugged. 'I wanted to lower your expectations before I showed you the cave,' she said. 'Besides, when you agree to it, I'll have to move the children's books anyway. The look on your face was definitely worth it.'

The book cave is already a huge hit, and the rest of the changes Yumi's made since have been small and practical. And while I feel a small pang every time something in the shop changes, there's also been something . . . hopeful about the process.

Every day for the past week, we've drunk coffee at the worn table at the back of the bookshop and she's taken me through her spreadsheet of ideas – the one she apparently started six months ago. There's no way we'll be able to implement everything, but talking about all the possibilities feels so damn nice.

So nice, that it's not until the end of each day that I check my phone. It's been almost a week since I messaged Declan, and he still hasn't messaged me back.

I've spoken to Bri, and to Jed, both of who called to check on Gran. Neither of them mentions Declan, and I feel the absence like a scar.

In a moment of weakness, I message Tessa Dalton, who tells me that he's moving in a week.

'Come on,' says Yumi when I'm still sitting at the table staring blankly at the papers, and I look up to see that the store officially closed an hour ago. Yumi catches the look. 'Don't worry, your master apprentice has it covered.'

'What are you still doing here?'

'It's Knit, Stitch and Yarn night,' Yumi says, like it's obvious.

'I am not going to Knit, Stitch and Yarn. I have to get up early tomorrow to visit Gran.'

They moved her back to Glenhaven today, which meant I didn't see her. And while I don't feel like I need to run the changes we're making to the shop by her, I just . . . I want to spend time with her. To take her books, even if she can't read them.

Plus, my plans for the evening basically consist of waiting by my phone for Declan to not message me back.

Yumi, though, is having none of it.

'You are young, and vibrant, and you cannot spend the evening feeling sorry for yourself at home,' she says. 'Besides, you promised Ruth,' she adds with a pointed look, and it's the thought of letting Ruth down that gets me over the line.

'Fine,' I tell her. 'But you know it's mostly just a bunch of elderly people sitting around talking and pretending to knit?'

I feel disloyal even saying the words, but it's a last-ditch attempt and I'm feeling a little desperate.

'Perfect,' says Yumi happily. She wraps a scarf round her neck – a bright blue and yellow creation that I've never seen before – then picks up what I think might actually be a giant knitting bag, and marches out of the bookshop.

I pull the door closed and lock it, and I'm about to take my phone out of my pocket – just to check – but Yumi turns round to look at me, as though she's got some sort of sixth sense.

She waits until I catch up with her, then raps smartly on the door of the antique shop. A second later, a warm, smiling Ruth opens the door.

'I love your scarf,' she tells Yumi.

'Thanks!' says Yumi. She wraps her arms round Ruth in a massive hug, then points a finger. 'Are the knitters down that way?' she asks.

'They are,' says Ruth, and Yumi strides off down to the back of the shop.

Ruth watches me through her blue-rimmed glasses. 'I'm glad you came tonight,' she says, and I manage a smile.

'Thanks, Ruth,' I say. 'For everything.'

She puts a hand on my shoulder and I rest mine briefly on top of it. She doesn't mention the day in the hospital, and neither do I, but there's something different in the air between us now. An understanding.

Yumi's already set up at the back of the shop by the time we get there, plonking herself between Diane and Frank. Like she knows that's where the fireworks will happen. Min is on the other side of Frank, and Sofia is across the table next to Alistair. Everyone waves hello except Susan, knitting steadily alone down one end of the table. Alistair beams, then shuffles over to make room for me to sink gratefully down beside him.

'How have you been?' he asks softly. 'I heard your gran had a fall; I've been meaning to get up to the hospital to visit.'

'They just transferred her back to Glenhaven today.'

Across the table Yumi pulls out – I kid you not – five balls of wool, and starts bartering trades with Frank.

'And Ruth mentioned that you were on tour with that young whippersnapper who was in here last time?' says Alistair, picking up his six rows of stitching.

The thought of Declan has me swallowing a lump in my throat, and I'm working out how to answer Alistair's question when there's a knock at the door.

My entire body goes numb.

It's no one important, I tell myself, trying not to count the people in the room, to notice that everyone is already here. *It's probably just someone who couldn't make it last month.*

But my heart doesn't give a damn. It pounds against my chest, and I'm vaguely aware of Alistair looking curiously at me, but I can't keep my eyes away from the back of the bookshelf, waiting to see who Ruth will bring round the corner.

Still, nothing prepares me for the jolt that snaps through me at the sight of his messy black hair and the green eyes that scan the group as though they're looking for someone.

They stop when they catch on me, and it's not even been a week since I've seen him, but every part of my body is aching to run towards him, to press my face into his chest and to tell him that I'm sorry. That I loved his book. That I don't care that he used to date Tessa, or that he didn't tell me because he's private, and I know that. That I don't even care that he didn't tell me he was moving. That I don't like it, but I understand. That I think maybe we could make things work, if we really wanted to.

But I don't do any of those things, because, apparently, I'm frozen in my chair.

'It's Clarrie's fellow!' says Sofia in a voice I think is meant to be a whisper.

'Declan freaking Archer!' says Yumi with delight. Then, 'Knit, Stitch and Yarn is just as good as I thought it would be.'

Declan's eyes don't leave mine, and he takes a step forward. My heart skips, and I finally manage to unfreeze, but just as I'm about to push to my feet, someone else beats me to it.

Susan marches out from her place at the end of the table, and it is the first time that I've ever seen her upright. What she lacks in height, she makes up for in strength and enthusiasm, and Declan doesn't get a chance to do much more than blink as she begins shepherding him towards the seat beside hers.

Then she reaches up and pushes on his shoulder until he sits. She pulls out her piece of string and starts measuring his head, as though she is totally unaware of the tense silence that's descended over the group.

Declan's eyes are fixed straight ahead, but I can't take mine off him. I can feel everyone watching us, waiting to see what happens. I want to go to him, but I don't know how he'll react. And I don't want to make him uncomfortable in a group of almost-strangers.

'You're staring a little bit,' Alistair whispers to me out of the corner of his mouth, and I manage to yank my attention back to him. Then, more loudly, he says across the table. 'Yumi, did you say it was?'

Yumi grins at him, her eyes bright.

'Yumi, I wonder, do you have any red wool to—'

'I don't pity you.' Declan's hoarse voice cuts through Alistair's query, and the entire group snaps quiet again.

He turns to look at me, ignoring Susan's tugs on his head until she finally gives up and starts measuring him where he is.

'What?' I whisper, but it's so silent in the shop that he hears me anyway.

'You said that you don't want my pity,' he says. 'And I don't. But I don't want us to be a pause from reality, either.'

Even Susan has stopped what she's doing now, and out of the corner of my eye I'm aware that everyone is looking back and forth between the two of us, but I can only see him. His green eyes, bright on mine.

'I want to talk to you and kiss you and argue with you and drive with you and I want us to build whatever we're doing together. I want to date you, Clarrie.'

'I thought he didn't date,' whispers Diane.

'Sounds like a bit more than dating,' grumbles Fred, and I choke on a laugh.

'Fine,' says Declan mildly, like he's not bothered that this is all happening in a room full of people. 'I want to more than date you, Clarence Brooks.'

It feels like we're on the edge of a moment. Like what happens next might somehow determine the rest of my life. And I don't know nearly as much as I'd like about Declan Archer, but I know that, somehow, we can make this work.

'I spoke to Tessa,' I say.

Declan's eyes spark, and I swallow the lump in my throat, then stand.

'I'm sorry for accusing you of telling her about the shop. I'm sorry that I wouldn't listen.'

'They never listen,' mutters Frank.

'Stop ruining the moment, Frank,' whispers Diane.

'I'm not ruining anything,' says Frank.

'Shut up, both of you,' says Alistair.

'This is so fun,' whispers Yumi.

Declan gently moves Susan's hands away from measuring his head, then he stands as well.

'I'm sorry I didn't tell you about Mayfield,' he says softly, his eyes still on mine. 'I was confused about how I felt about it, and I was trying to avoid thinking about it. But it was selfish, and it was unfair, especially when you shared so much of yourself.'

I walk round the side of the table, and he meets me halfway. And then he's there, standing in front of me, the scent and the warmth of him all around me.

'You didn't write back to my message,' I whisper.

'I was a little busy,' says Declan. 'Organising to not move.'

My heart kicks in my chest, flares automatically with hope. 'What?'

Declan exhales. 'See, that's the thing. I thought I needed to be there to write the book about Dad. But then I kept thinking about one of the last things that Dad told me, the thing that made me want to write the book in the first place. We were at the carols, and he said, "Sometimes you don't even notice the light until it fades." I thought that Mayfield was the light.'

'Mayfield is not the light?'

Declan reaches up to brush a hair from my cheek. 'Maybe it was Dad's light. But it's not my light. I want to honour him, but I don't need to be there to write something that does that. Besides, my workplace is pretty flexible. I can go up for weekend trips.'

'That's really beautiful,' calls Diane, and Declan's lips twitch.

'My light is here,' says Declan. 'It's brownies from the Garden, and being close enough to my mum to be embarrassed by her, and it's the idea of more-than-dating my second favourite bookseller.'

'Seriously?'

'It would take a lot to top Margaret,' says Declan. He sways closer, until his forehead is resting against mine.

'I spoke to my mum,' I whisper, warmth and hope flooding my chest.

'Speak louder!' calls Min.

'Is everything okay?' says Declan, ignoring the onlookers, his eyes fixed completely on me.

'It's good,' I tell him with a small smile. 'I think it's all going to be okay.'

'Good,' says Declan. 'I'm so pleased, Clarrie.'

I'll tell him all of it, later. And the hope that we might have a later means that I hesitate for only a fraction of a second before I reach out, and when I rest my hand against his cheek, Declan closes his eyes and exhales.

'I don't want to pause, either,' I say. I swallow, and I make myself say the next part. 'I really, really like you, Declan Archer.'

When Declan opens his eyes again, there's a light in them – relief and maybe something else. 'Good,' he whispers. 'Because I'm planning to be around for a while.'

He leans forward, like there's not a table full of people over seventy, plus Yumi, watching on.

'Yes!' calls someone – maybe Min? – 'Kiss her!'

Declan doesn't retreat into himself. He doesn't even flinch. He just smiles his lightning smile, his eyes fixed on me.

'I very much intend to,' he says, before doing just that.

Only to pull back a few seconds later.

'You read the book?' he whispers.

'I read the book.'

'And?'

'I have some notes,' I tell him, before pressing my lips to his again while Gran's friends cheer.

Chapter Thirty-six

When Annabel Stone comes into the bookshop two days later, it's to Yumi rolling her eyes at me for the 'stupid grin' she tells me that I need to work on moderating.

But honestly? I can't help it. Declan is picking me up for lunch in an hour, and the thought of seeing him, of knowing that I can kiss him and slip my fingers through his without it being temporary makes me smile. This afternoon I'm going to take him to Glenhaven to visit Gran. And this weekend we're going spotlighting with Jed just out of the city. Bri is flying in to come with us – she tells me spotlighting is the perfect romantic setting for finally wooing him.

'I'm just going to get something to eat,' calls Yumi. 'Nice to see you, Ms Stone.'

'Likewise, Yumi,' says Annabel with what I think might actually be a little warmth in her voice.

The bell above the door rings as Yumi leaves with a sly grin, and Annabel turns to face me.

'Hello, Clarence,' says Annabel, and I smile brightly back at her, because today I am feeling confident that I can find every last one of her difficult-to-find books.

But she doesn't ask me to attend to her immediately, or drop a list of authors that I've never heard of. She just starts walking around the bookshelves, looking at the books.

'I've come to talk to you about your romance selection,' she says finally, and my mouth actually drops open a little before I can stop it.

Annabel pauses when she reaches the section where Yumi's housed our modest romance collection – surprisingly, it's never been a huge seller for us apart from big-name authors.

'I normally buy my romances online,' says Annabel, running a finger along the spines. 'But I have been thinking that your collection could use work. I am here to offer my assistance.'

'What?' I say, before I can stop myself. 'Why?'

Annabel stops her perusal, and looks up at me, and in that instant, *I know.*

'My son has come to care very deeply for a woman that I both like and admire,' says Annabel, her bright green eyes holding mine. 'And now that my son is staying in town I intend to do everything I can to ensure their happiness. Even if, occasionally, I slip up and tell his ex-girlfriend incorrect information.'

Shut. Up.

'You're his mother,' I breathe, and Annabel half smiles.

I finally manage to gather a modicum of my crap together – at least enough to narrow my eyes at her. 'You told Tessa about the sale?'

'I was here when your mother came in,' says Annabel.

'I overheard the conversation with the estate agent, and I wanted to help you, if I could.'

'You made it worse.' *Annabel Stone is Declan Archer's freaking mother.*

'I am sorry,' says Annabel.

'I know about the dedication too.'

'Of course you do,' says Annabel imperiously. She straightens and looks me in the eye and *how did I never notice how similar her eyes are to Declan's?* 'But do you know who leaked that you were the bookseller to the press?' And, oh my goodness, she actually, legitimately winks, and I find that I don't even have it in me to be mad at her.

A laugh bubbles up in my chest, and I can't stop the snort that comes out.

'So you don't want the latest Francis Coates, then?' I ask her.

'God no,' she says. 'Dreadful, boring stuff. I was only buying things for Declan because he wanted to support the store, but was too embarrassed to come in himself.' She shrugs one shoulder. 'I found a better way.'

'Thank you,' I tell her. Because even though she apparently played a part in an apple core being thrown at my head, and in what happened between Declan and I, she's also legitimately responsible for some of my current happiness. Not to mention all the obscure books she and Declan have bought from the shop over the years.

'You are most welcome,' says Annabel.

Then she starts marching around the bookshop, telling me about her ideas for an in-person romance book club.

Epilogue

Declan's third book comes out to massive hype and critical acclaim.

It's even better than *Talking to Trees*, but it's possible I just think that because I got to watch him write it.

I know which parts made his brow crease when he couldn't think of the right word. I know the section he thought of during the middle of dinner with my family, the one that was originally scribbled on one of my mother's napkins when he was in their bathroom. I know that in a particularly difficult chapter he let me convince him to lie on the floor with me and recite poetry loudly, even though he thought I was insane. I know that he drove up to Mayfield the day it was finished, to sit on the hill and look at the Christmas tree. To remember his dad. I know that his mother didn't write this dedication.

At least, I don't think she did. I haven't actually seen it yet.

It's a cold, wet morning when our copies of the book arrive in store. I flick on the lights and the kettle, and I text Declan to let him know it's here. Then I text my mother and tell her I'm going to postpone my visit to Gran until later, if she still wants to come. She texts back almost immediately to tell me she'll meet me at the bookshop, and that I should keep one of Declan's new books aside for her. Because of course she somehow already knows they're in.

Yumi's out planning a science-fiction festival with Alistair, and I spend the next hour drinking coffee and trying not to give in to the temptation to open the box before Declan arrives. Luckily, business is steady enough to keep me distracted, but not so busy that I'm run off my feet the way it is some days now that Annabel Stone has taken over the shop's marketing.

Then, finally, the bell above the door tinkles, and Declan is there, taking off his beanie and shaking his curls out. He ignores my protests that his coat is making the floor wet and plants a hot kiss on my lips. He tastes like snake lollies and mint, and for a second I forget about the books.

'You already opened them, didn't you?' he murmurs against my lips. I pull back to meet his eyes, which are gleaming.

'I promise you I did not,' I say, and he kisses me again.

'Have you spoken to Bri?' I ask when he finally pulls back.

Declan nods. 'She said this tour is going to put the last tour to shame,' he says. 'And apparently Jed has made slideshows of all the rare birds mentioned in the book.'

The thought of Jed and Bri together in the same space again is enough to make me grin. They still aren't officially together, but Bri has taken up what can only be called competitive birding. Last week she took a picture of a bird Jed's wanted to see for years.

Declan follows me out the back to where the ten boxes of

books are ready and waiting; one of them already has a rip in it. He raises one eyebrow at me.

'I didn't *open* it,' I tell him, raising both of mine back at him. 'Just took a tiny peek.'

Declan's eyes scan the boxes. 'It does feel a little excessive not to let a bookseller open their stock when it arrives,' he says apologetically, and I slip my fingers through his.

'You can make it up to me by signing all of them,' I say.

'All of them?' says Declan, sighing when I nod. 'Will you at least kiss me between each book?'

'You know there are about three hundred copies here?'

'I do,' Declan says solemnly. 'We will both be working very hard.'

I lean over to press my lips to his, and it's a few minutes before we finally get to the first box.

I nudge it along the wooden table towards him, and he picks up the Stanley knife to finish opening it.

He reaches in to take one of the books out.

'You ordered more copies of *Flight Risk*?' he says when he sees the cover, his eyes laughing when they meet mine.

'I thought they'd sell well with the new one out,' I tell him. 'Plus, it's better than I remember.'

'High praise,' says Declan. 'You want me to sign these too?'

'Please,' I tell him, and he kisses me quickly again. Then he cuts open one of the other boxes and passes me a copy of his new book, *After the Light*.

I run my hand along the black jacket and shimmers of gold wink in the light. I can feel him watching me.

'I love you,' he tells me softly.

'Are you just preparing me for the dedication?' I ask him, keeping my eyes on the book. It really does look great.

'Maybe,' he says. He touches a hand to my cheek, his eyes warm, and I lean into his palm.

'I love you too,' I say.

'I know,' Declan grins.

I roll my eyes at him, then open the book.

For my favourite bookseller.
And for her granddaughter, Clarrie,
Who shines even when there's no light.

Acknowledgements

This book started as a sneaky passion project while I was on another deadline. Writing the first draft was a source of joy and warmth, a place I could escape to in snatches of time between the work I *had* to finish. It never stopped being that, even after I met the other deadline.

Rereading my first draft, on the other hand, was . . . less joyful. Massive thanks to Marisa Pintado, who read it, and saw the joy in it, and whose feedback helped me dive back in, and to Zanni Louise, Zoe Gaetjens and Lisa Stokes, who all encouraged me (and who always encourage me!) to keep going. Thanks also to Taylor Norman, for eating cookies with me and chatting about Clarrie and Brooks' Books when they were just an idea, and to Christine Ricketts, Heather Thomas, Edwina Wyatt, Rhiannon Williams and Sally Gardner for reading early drafts.

Huge thanks to everyone at Headline who shaped the book into what it is today, especially to my amazing editor Bea Grabowska, and to Kashmini Shah, Sherise Hobbs and designer Alice Clark. Thanks to Debs Lim for the gorgeous cover illustration, and to copyeditor Jill Cole for your incredible (and insightful!) eye for detail.

To my agent, Sophie Hicks, and to Morag and Sarah – thank you for all you do! I'm so grateful that we get to work together.

This is a story about family, and I am so lucky to have the best. Special thank you to my grandparents – Nan, Pop, Grandy and Billie – who has a garden wherever she goes, and whose love of people is infectious.

To (wildlife warriors) Lachie Hall and Sabrina Velasco, for bird and spotlighting tips (any errors and/or creative licence about methods are very much my own!), and to Mum, Dad and Jade, for everything.

And to Luke, Eli, Eva and Mae, always. I love you guys.